Underground

Underground

Mark Chadbourn

PIATKUS

For my Mother and Father, for instilling the writing urge, and for Elizabeth, for inspiration

Dedicated to the memory of Cecil Eames, a hardy miner and a good Grandfather

"Up from Earth's Centre through the Seventh Gate
I rose, and on the Throne of Saturn sate,
And many a Knot unravell'd by the Road;
But not the Master-knot of Human Fate."

From *The Rubaiyat of Omar Khayyam*

Chapter One

The worm was bloated and desperate to emerge. It had fed on bitter fruit for months; years; and now it had grown too big to be contained.

His anger, that red blaze, was imbued with such power that it had become a living thing, wriggling in his gut: the worm was rage. Michael Leary had recognized it a long time ago, but he had never expected it to grow so large. Or so fast.

Hunched over the wheel, he peered blindly through the streaked windscreen. He could not control himself enough to slow down. The last corner had been the worst; he had actually felt the rear nearside wheel skid on the grass verge. If Hannah had been there she would have been screaming at him to slow down, to take it easy, but without her influence there was nothing to restrain the self-destructive fever that often consumed him.

Four hours ago he had been in his London office, quietly contemplating the journey home and a restful evening in front of the TV with his wife and son. Then Whicker had walked in with the old, familiar expression on his face, the one that said, "Guess what? You've had it." And now here he was, a hundred and forty miles away, at night, in the middle of the worst storm he had known for years and en route to a place that no one in their right mind would want to visit. He doubted it was even on the map. Yes, he was bitter. He had every right to be.

His fist hammered on the resilient plastic of the steering wheel, once hard, three times soft, beating out the rhythm to some forgotten song. The rain was streaming down in sheets,

1

corpulent drops that exploded on the glass. The windscreen wipers were not powerful enough; he might as well have been blind. Visibility was down to ten yards and the darkness closed in on him on both sides, thick hedgerows and skeletal, thrashing trees obscuring any twinkling light that might have signified some life in the area. A rational person would have slowed to a crawl; Mike gunned the accelerator and watched the speedometer leap to sixty-five.

The turbo kicked in smoothly, propelling his car forward with another near-fateful skid, and then down a sharp incline that curved sharply to the left at the bottom. Mike took it on the wrong side of the road. If anything had been coming in the other direction he would have been dead, but all his rational faculties were swamped beneath a seething hatred for his boss and his job.

Lightning crackled briefly on the horizon, throwing the rolling clouds into stark relief before the deep drum-roll of the thunder broke through the roar of the engine. Not even dogs would be out on a night like this, Mike thought sourly, as Whicker's face, replete with smug grin, hovered in front of his mind's eye. Sometimes he wanted to punch him. Just once. A solid right to the jaw. Lay him out over his desk and then everyone else in the office would applaud and cheer before Mike picked up his coat and walked out for good.

A village passed by so quickly that it was just a sodium-orange blur; a handful of houses huddling together in the face of the storm. For a second he thought he had seen a patrol car parked in a lay-by, but then it was gone, in a haze of spray, and he was once more alone in the blank, disquieting darkness of the countryside.

"*One man missing*", the hastily-sent telex had said.

How could that be? Weren't those hicks numerate? A whole night shift had been counted in as they went down the mine. A whole shift minus one had been counted back up. For five hours they searched for him before the colliery manager had admitted defeat and set the wheels in motion that had ruined Mike's weekend. Somehow they had managed to lose a miner along tunnels that were as regularly used as a city centre shopping precinct – an achievement so impossible, so farcical, that he at first thought Whicker was playing a

2

typically nasty-minded trick on him. But then he had seen the file, the long list of accidents, injuries, sicknesses, that suggested this particular pit was one of a kind; the most incompetently, or criminally, run colliery in Britain.

"You'd better check it out," Whicker had said, tossing the dog-eared file on to Mike's desk.

"Can't it wait till Monday, Richard? I promised Hannah . . ."

"No, it can't wait till Monday!" he had snapped back, deliberately aiming to embarrass Mike in front of his colleagues. "This pit has been on the agenda for months. Something has got to be done. We just want you to make some preliminary enquiries and then we're going to send a full team up there. Take your time. Let us know when you've got some results."

Yeah, take your time, Mike. Stay up there as long as you want. Don't come back – *because we don't need you here*.

Rounding the corner, for once on the correct side of the road, he frantically stamped on the brakes, his reactions triggered by a sudden movement in his field of vision.

The rear end of the car danced and weaved, threatening to flip off the greasy road in a stylish and potentially fatal pirouette, but it righted itself more out of luck than judgement, before coming to a juddering halt. His heart pounding madly, Mike peered over the wheel, trying to see what had caught his eye. A small child? A fox? A bird?

All he could perceive was a strange motion in the watery arc of his headlights. It was an undulation, a ripple of darkness in the glare. For a moment he looked at it, uncomprehending, straining his eyes to draw any details out of the gloom, before realization dawned with a sense of gnawing disgust.

Rats!

A thick, brown wave of them, pouring across the road like lemmings on a helter-skelter ride to oblivion. Big fat ones, skinny, wiry ones, packed so tightly side-by-side that they seemed one mass. He had never seen so many. Leaning over to one side to follow the flow, he saw their sinuous bodies scrambling out of a gaping hole at the side of the road; some of the hedge had collapsed into it. Mike could only surmise

3

that the torrential rain had washed away part of a sewer, although he could not imagine anyone building one so far from a town. And even that could not account for the vast numbers of the creatures; hundreds of them, perhaps thousands, heading from the hole to the field across the road.

Shaking his head as if it would dispel the image, he slipped the car into first and pressed the horn three times in the futile hope that it would clear them out of his path. In the end he could do nothing but creep forward, listening to the faint "pok-pok-pok" as numerous bodies burst beneath the wheels.

The curious nature of the rats' exodus had one reward; Whicker had been momentarily forgotten. Mike's temper quietly subsided, at least enough for him to reach his destination without going above thirty.

There seemed little hope of the storm abating that night. The gutters were becoming swollen with water, eddying and swirling to cover most of the road on some of the lanes. The storm had not seemed a particular hardship along the M1 and even the A50, but there, on those quiet back lanes where he rarely encountered another vehicle, its full, primal force was evident. The wind channelled between the hedgerows in sudden, violent gusts, tugging the car dangerously towards the verges, and in one hollow the road was so flooded he feared the water would splash up onto the spark plugs and bring the car to a halt.

Mike recognised the lights of the pit from five miles away. The white luminescence of the lofty lumps in the yard and the intermittent red of the warning bulbs that lined the drift's enclosed conveyor belt were almost welcoming in the storm. Although the sky was an impenetrable black, the main body of the mine seemed somehow blacker against it, rising up high above the rolling fields. It slipped from view when Mike entered the bright lights of the village which clustered close by and when it reappeared Mike had no time to pick out the details of the buildings before he was upon it, his headlamps briefly flaring on the coaldust-streaked sign: *Colthorpe Colliery, British Coal, South Midlands Division*. The main road bisected the site completely with a complex of buildings on either side, linked by a small railway line. The red lights on the raised crossing barriers blinked pitifully through the rain.

4

Mike swung off to the left through the main entrance and carefully negotiated the speed bumps before bringing the car to a halt next to the largest office block. Further on, at the pit head, he could make out a frantic disturbance as people scurried around beneath hastily rigged-up emergency lights. For a few moments he sat watching them, listening to the unrelenting splatter of the rain and the intermittent howling of the wind; wishing he had another job, wishing he was at home with Hannah and Jack. Before there was time for his temper to rise again, he pulled on the mac he had hastily flung into the passenger seat and stepped out into the storm.

He had almost reached the surging crowd, his head bowed into the rain beneath a rapidly disintegrating newspaper, when a strident voice called out to him. "Oi! Where do you think you're going?"

A short, fat man with a balding head and a thick black moustache marched over, his face as thundery as the weather. A young policeman dogged his every step. "I said, where do you think you're going?" he repeated, in a voice spoiling for a fight.

"I'm probably coming to see you," Mike replied coldly. "I'm Mike Leary, the . . ."

"Oh yes. Leary. They said you were coming," the fat man said with a hint of bitterness. "Those bastards in London don't trust us to sort out our own business." Mike shrugged, refusing to be drawn. The fat man continued, "I'm Tom Bulmer. This is my pit." He stuck out a stubby hand and wrung Mike's until his knuckles hurt. It was a brief, territorial warning.

"So what's the state of play?" Mike asked, turning his face away from the rain.

"He's still missing. Been twelve hours now."

"How?" Mike said, unable to control his exasperation. "How could you *lose* someone?"

It was Bulmer's turn to shrug. "Ay, well, that's your problem now, isn't it?" he replied with a faint sneer.

Mike ignored him and looked towards the crowd. There were miners, faces still grimed with black dust that not even the rain would shift, a couple of ambulancemen and a handful of policemen, sheltering uncomfortably in plastic capes. To

Mike, the miners seemed to have stepped from a period painting; the very structure of their faces belonged to another time. Their bones were hardier somehow, their cheeks ruddier, their eyes, though bright, shrouded heavy brows. Even their clothes, their filthy overalls and dusty, scuffed boots, looked like museum exhibits. Their gaze was fixed on the entrance to the lift building and the few that talked did so in concealed whispers. There was an expression on their faces that was not concern alone; it seemed to say, *it could have been me, it could still be me*. Fear: that was there too, though it was well-hidden. They knew as well as Mike that it would take an extraordinary state of affairs for a man to go missing underground.

A white-faced woman was sobbing hysterically, her cries and words plucked from her mouth by the howling wind so that she seemed to have stepped from a flickering, silent movie. Two miners attempted to comfort her, their movements awkward and embarrassed.

"Sorry I yelled at you back there." Bulmer was at his elbow, watching the same scene. "I thought you were the press. We've had some local reporters snooping around and I didn't want any of this getting out."

"Too right," Mike added. "Bad publicity would only make things worse."

"It's not looking too good for us, is it, with . . ." he carefully chose his words ". . . with everything that's happened before?"

"You haven't got a particularly good track record, if that's what you mean. I haven't had a chance to read the file properly yet. I'll start on that tomorrow."

"Go easy on us. We've got special problems up here." Bulmer's voice was dejected and beaten. Mike wanted to ask him what kind of "special problems" he was facing, but there was a sudden disturbance at the door of the lift building.

"They've found him!" someone yelled. "They've just radioed up!" The crowd surged forward with a jubilant cheer, the miners yelling and chattering with repressed relief.

"We better get in there," Bulmer said hastily. "They might have found him, but that's no guarantee he'll be all in one piece."

6

Bulmer barged his way through the crowd with Mike and the policeman close behind and when he made it through to the other side he turned and raised his hands. The men stopped in their tracks. "Go back now, lads. I know how you feel," he said, in a commanding bass voice that even rose above the wind, "but Alec might need some help."

There was a general muttering and nodding of heads among the crowd and then they dropped back to allow an ambulance to come forward at Bulmer's summons, its blue light flashing. Bulmer turned to Mike. "They'll keep back now. Let's get inside and have a look."

When they stepped into the lift building, the faces of the two operators told them all they needed to know. "They reckon he's dead," one of them said, his face mournful.

Bulmer shook his head. "Poor bastard." Mike got the impression that it was only what he expected. "What happened?"

"They didn't say. Just said he'd snuffed it." His voice was a hoarse whisper and the noisy trundling of the lift mechanism almost drowned it out. Within seconds it had stopped, the cage of the lift clicking snugly into place, followed immediately by the sound of the men inside pulling the sliding doors back. There were five of them carrying a stretcher with a blanket over it. What struck Mike instantly were the men's faces; they seemed uniformly drained of blood, their eyes glassy as if they had died and been brought back to life.

"Get him over here quickly," Bulmer said, with a note of panic in his voice.

The men laid the stretcher gently at his feet and then drew well back, shifting uncomfortable. "Jesus," one of them muttered.

"What happened to him?" Bulmer asked. Mike could tell he did not want to pull the blanket back to see for himself.

The men were shaking their heads, refusing to speak. Mike leaned forward impatiently and tugged at the top of the blanket. The miners turned away as one and Bulmer clapped one chubby hand to his mouth, transfixed by what he saw. Mike fought back instant nausea.

The corpse had no eyes.

Where eyes had been there were only black sockets,

rimmed with encrusted blood, which also stained the cheeks like purple tears. Beneath those gaping holes the mouth was contorted into an expression of such abject horror that Mike shuddered involuntarily. The corpse appeared to be screaming for help, or in crippling agony, the blackened lips pulled back so far from the teeth that pink gums were revealed.

"Jesus Christ! What the fuckin' hell's happened to him!" Bulmer yelled, his own eyes bulging like a frog's.

The men, pale beneath the grime, remained silent, until one of them said, hesitantly, "An accident?"

"An accident? What kind of bloody accident!" Bulmer was raging, as much in fear as anger.

"With the . . . with the cutting machine."

"That's right." Another took up the story. "It could have busted. Thrown something out. Taken his eye out."

"What? Both of them?"

"We'll check it tomorrow. First thing. We'll get right down to it, boss."

Bulmer shook his head incredulously. "Jesus Christ. Well, cover him up then! We can't have them out there seeing him like this! What the fuck am I going to tell his wife?"

"There's no need for all this to come out straight away," Mike said. "We've got to examine all the evidence first. Just tell his wife he died in an accident. You don't have to go into the gory details."

"She might want to see the body."

"Talk her out of it." He turned to the men, shouldering the authority as best he could. "I don't want you talking about this to anyone. Right? We're the only ones who know the full details. If I find it's leaked out you'll be looking for work." The miners nodded hastily, responding instantly to his suit and tie despite having no idea of his identity. He turned to Bulmer and whispered, "It'll be all around the site in a few days. We'll have to take steps to minimize the consequences."

"I'll have to make a report," the young policeman interjected, his face a chalky pallor.

"Slow down a minute, son." Bulmer had regained his composure, his expression serious. "I'll have a word with your Super. We go back a long way." The policeman nodded, happy to be relieved of his burden.

Outside the gathered miners were drenched to the skin, but they still waited. After the policeman had taken the dead man's wife to one side, Bulmer made a short speech, telling them that there had been an accident, calling for their support and promising to set up a memorial fund on the following day. Mike was impressed by his consummate professionalism in controlling the situation, sizing up the men's emotions and responses and forcing them down the avenue he wanted them to travel. Eventually they dispersed, saddened and dispirited, but not as horrified as they would have been if they had begun to suspect the truth.

Mike hurried across the yard in Bulmer's footsteps and followed him into his cluttered office where they dried out in front of a small electric fire. Although the pit manager's demeanour was brusque, Mike was impressed by him. Bulmer was efficient and level-headed, with an obvious compassion for his employees. Mike estimated that he was in his fifties, and though his appearance seemed uncompromising, there was a gleam in his eye that suggested a lighter side.

After a few minutes of forced small talk, Bulmer tucked himself behind his desk. "So, are you going to do me out of a job?"

His question was so direct that Mike almost flinched. Bulmer was looking at him with an unwavering stare which showed the extent of his concern and hinted at exactly what Mike would have to overcome if he wanted to "do him out of a job".

Hesitantly, he replied. "I don't think there's any need for that." He ended his comment there, but Bulmer's stare told him to continue. "I just want to clear up exactly what's wrong here. The company's pretty concerned about some of the things that have happened over the last few months. I only glanced at that report, but I saw lists of missing machinery, above-average breakdowns, accidents – foolish accidents. You know, you're lucky you haven't had a death on your hands before this."

"They're going to close the pit, you know."

"It won't go that far. It . . ."

"I'm telling you, pal. They're going to close the pit." Bulmer's labourer's hands bunched into fists of repressed anger

9

and frustration. "They're just looking for a reason. I've seen it happen in other places and the rumours going round say we're next on the list."

Mike started to protest and then slumped back into his chair. "I'll be honest with you: I just don't know. That could be the case. All I'm saying is that I haven't heard anything. I certainly don't want to see your pit shut down and I'm not going to give them any unnecessary information."

Bulmer continued to stare, sizing him up as if they were two dogs in a pit. "That may be, but it doesn't get away from the fact that we're up to our necks in it. I don't know what the answer is. I don't know why we've had all these accidents. If I did I'd have put them right by now. They're good men here. Bloody good. They work hard. They don't want some jumped-up yuppie telling them they're a bunch of good-for-nothings."

Mike smarted at this insult. "I've got no intention of doing that. I just want to find out what's wrong. I'll stay here as long as necessary, file my report, then hopefully we'll be able to put everything right."

"Aye, and pigs might fly."

"If you're going to take that attitude . . ."

"Look, lad, I've got nothing against you personally. It's just that we've got a lot of problems here which everybody concerned is aware of. We're not shirking our responsibilities. If you're going to work with us, then fine, but if you're agin us then the men will give you a rough ride."

"I can't ask for more than that." He stifled a yawn, suddenly realizing how tired he was. "Now, if you don't mind, I'm going to get some shut-eye."

"Have you got somewhere to stay? I could get the missus to . . ."

"Thanks a lot, but the office has found me a guest house nearby. Have you got a room here I can use as an office?"

"We can find you one."

As he rose from his chair Mike asked, "You mentioned some special problems earlier. What were you talking about?"

Bulmer smiled tightly, giving nothing away. "You'll find out soon enough, lad."

The guest house was homely enough, and after a plain meal prepared by the chirpy owner, Mike borrowed the phone and dialled home.

"Hello?"

"Hannah, honey! It's me."

"Mike! How's it going? You got there okay? I was really worried after I heard all the reports about the storms. The news said there'd been a lot of accidents."

"No, no, I'm fine. You wouldn't exactly describe my digs as a palace, but it'll do."

"How long are you going to be up there?"

The line crackled, and suddenly Hannah seemed thousands of miles away. Loneliness crept up on him and he realized how desperately he wanted to be with her. "I don't know. As long as it takes. I just wish I could believe I'm here for a good reason, not just because Whicker would do anything to get me out of the office."

"Don't worry about it, Mike. Things will pick up. You know they will."

"Sure." He caught himself before he lapsed into another of his famous monologues about how sick and tired he was of his job; God knows, Hannah had heard the same lines so many times she could probably recite them with him. "So how's Jack?"

"He was wearing me out tonight. Questions, questions; juggling acts with his Transformers; Garfield went swimming accidentally in his bath. I had to fetch the tranquiliser gun!"

"I told you not to use that." He laughed.

"Only half a dose, honest. Anyway, he's asleep now, the little dear. I think he was hyper because you weren't coming home."

"I know how he feels. And how about the other little one?"

"No problems, but I'm completely wiped out carrying this great lump around. I just want to lie back and make whale noises."

"Only two more months."

"Only! Easy for you to say. This one'll be bigger than Jack, you wait and see."

"Oh no! I fathered a monster."

"Like father, like son, I say."

11

They laughed together and after he replaced the receiver Mike found himself wondering why they ever fought. These days the arguments were getting worse and he realized, deep down, that he was the cause of most of them. It was as if he had some sick impulse to damage the thing he valued most. There was something squirming around deep inside him, something sour and twisted that wanted to destroy the happiness that they had built together. He lay awake thinking about it for an hour or more, until the rhythmic patter of the rain lulled him into a dream of shafts and dark tunnels with, at the end of each a screaming, hollow-eyed miner.

Chapter Two

She picked up the pen, put it down, picked it up, scribbled on a pad, put it down, walked over to inspect the word processor and then wandered into the kitchen to make a cup of coffee. The article was not going well. Hannah had long ago mastered the skill of applying herself to her work with intense concentration, even when Jack was frantically running from room to room, raising hell. She had been working from home ever since he was born, four years in which she had mastered the new rules of her trade, but since Mike had phoned the previous evening her mind had been on anything except her work.

Perhaps with another child on the way she should just give up for a while and take it easy. She nestled her bump lovingly. There was something about being pregnant that she really enjoyed; she felt graceful somehow, despite the awkwardness of her shape: more relaxed, less anxious. In a way it helped her to cope with Mike during his more extreme moments, those times when he was fraught or just plain angry, coping badly with the pressure of his job. Perhaps his own calmness would come after the birth.

For once Jack was quiet, although that was just as disturbing; it normally indicated he was involved in some mischief. Still, it was a rare moment of peace and she abandoned herself to it. Taking the coffee and a couple of biscuits she sauntered through to the lounge and leaned against the window, looking out on to the still street. The morning sun was powerful and had wiped out all traces of the previous night's rain, adding a fresh lustre to the last fading blooms of the summer in the front garden.

Looking at the expensive, well-tended houses around them, Hannah felt a faint twinge of anxiety about the financial nightmare that was beginning to dog them daily. They could not really afford their home, but Mike had insisted they buy it and she, against her better judgment, had reluctantly agreed. He thought that a small townhouse in trendy Clapham would be a better image to present to his bosses than a large flat in some suburb with no claim to being upwardly-mobile. But they had still passed him over for promotion, as they had twice since; even his "investment" in a couple of expensive suits from South Molton Street and a sporty, turbo-charged car had not helped, although Hannah had never for a moment thought it would.

When she was still editing the magazine, her salary had been more than enough to keep them going, but with her decision to go freelance after Jack's birth, the cash flow had taken a natural dip. They still paid her over the odds; she was good, she knew that. But it was still not enough. And with another one on the way . . . well, it wasn't worth thinking about. But as Mike had pointed out, a lack of cash for luxuries was no reason to deprive the world of a child.

Tenderly she picked up the framed photograph from the coffee table, a window on a much simpler time. There was Mike, handsome with his jet-black hair and those little curls just above his ears that she loved, his dark, warm eyes and that Kirk Douglas dimple in his chin. He was smiling. And there she was, a little plump in parts, but she wasn't bad, and her hair was long, the way Mike liked it. She was smiling too.

She couldn't exactly understand the nature of Mike's problem at work. He wasn't bad at his job, she was certain of that, but for some reason he seemed to have progressed within the company as far as he could. Maybe they realized how he really felt: that he wished he was in a more exciting, more demanding career. Whatever the reason, his failure to keep climbing the ladder had affected him badly. At university he had been such a success; the student Most Likely To. His old room mate always spoke about "Mike's great potential". Now he had suddenly realized that the time for potential had passed, that he should have converted it into achievement. He hadn't. And what would happen to them if he never did?

At the soft sound of padding feet, she turned and smiled. Jack had mastered the ragamuffin style with ease; however much she plastered down his mop of brown hair it still seemed to be standing out at right angles from his head five minutes later, and he had a great ability to ensure his tee-shirt never remained tucked into his shorts for long.

"Mummy, I want a dog."

"I want gets nothing. Now what do we say?"

"Please may I have a dog?"

"We'll have to ask your father. Why do you want one?"

He wrinkled his brow in thought, in that instant looking so much like his father that Hannah felt a sweeping, almost tearful, surge of emotion. Perhaps this was what Mike was like as a child: sensitive, intelligent, amusing.

Free from rage.

"Because," he continued carefully, "Garfield should have a friend."

"But he's got a friend. You're his friend."

"He needs another friend. In the comic, Odie is his friend. I'm like John, but he needs Odie."

Hannah stifled a laugh. She really didn't know what he was talking about, but then she blamed Mike for spending all that time reading comic strips to him. Especially when Jack asked her a life-or-death question about Garfield or Calvin and Hobbes. "We'll see, then. Wait till Daddy gets back."

Jack grinned, pleased with any response that was not an instant dismissal. Hannah carefully replaced the photograph on the table. A dog. That was all they needed: more expense. Of course, Mike would probably agree to it; when it came to Jack's wishes he found it almost impossible to say no. He doted on him. If there was one thing that could save the world from collapsing around them, it would be Jack.

He clambered up on to her knee and rested against her belly, suddenly tired. His warmth against her unexpectedly freed Hannah from an oppressive feeling of apprehension which had been hanging in the air since Mike had called to say he would be spending some time in the Midlands. That morning, just after she awakened, a clammy wave of claustrophobia came over her. It was so strong at one point that she felt she was suffocating, but then, just as quickly as it came, it had disappeared. It had, however, left behind a feeling of unease that was much more difficult to dispel.

The regularity of Jack's breathing suddenly altered and his eyes flickered open. "Mummy, Daddy's all right, isn't he?"

She stroked his head, baffled by his strange question. "Of course he's all right, darling."

His eyes closed again and Hannah pulled him tight, as much to comfort herself as to reassure him. "Of course Daddy's all right," she whispered.

Chapter Three

Early the next morning, Mike set off from the guest house on foot. He was determined to be on site before any of the management team, a show of efficiency and determination that he hoped would give him some authority. He was extremely aware that he was an unwanted outsider in a volatile situation. Subtlety and skill would be necessary to keep everything under control.

It was seven am, and there were few signs of life in the surrounding countryside. The sky at that early hour was pale yellow, tinged with mauve on the horizon. Wan sunlight broke through at irregular intervals, doing little to dispel the crisp chill in the air that signified the onset of autumn. Grey clouds, flat as stones, were still backed up over his head, holding the threat of more rain. The storm had blown itself out during the night after shrieking and howling into the wee hours, and there were pools of water the size of small lakes in many of the lower lying fields. Subsidence from decades of mining had left basins in most of the flat land which made building an impossibility. Ideal for the green belt campaigners, Mike thought. A sprawling estate of Barratt Homes would never suddenly materialize on your doorstep in this area. Of course, that self-same doorstep might be slowly sinking into the mire itself – but that was another story.

As Mike walked steadily out of the village, shivering slightly despite his overcoat, he saw the mine in detail for the first time, looming up ahead of him as if it were an ancient temple and he the solitary supplicant. There were no steeples, minarets or spires, but its architecture still radiated an air of

17

reverential mystery, spanning generations in style and construction. As he drew closer, it appeared as if it had been thrown up from the earth, as timeless and natural as the ground on which it stood.

The main road which ploughed neatly through the centre of the site also served to carve a line between two eras. On the right, as Mike strolled up the incline towards the entrance, were lofty, brown-brick buildings resembling Victorian workhouses, their grime-encrusted windows the length of three men. What lay within was unclear, not even the chequerboard of smashed and unreplaced panes giving any clue. There was a brooding, heavy atmosphere seeping out of those crumbling walls, a thick seam of anger and despair, of toil for little reward. No attempt had been made to tidy the yards that lay around them. Scrubby yellow weeds poked up through the thick layer of coaldust that covered the whole site, while piles of rocky coal and slag were heaped at irregular intervals, as if a giant mole were loose in the area. Nothing moved; the only sound was the faint clank of a chain blown by the wind against the side of a lone train truck.

In stark contrast, the buildings on the other side of the road were a fading remnant of the dated modernism of the sixties; prefabricated concrete, flat, squat buildings with blue and black panelling and shiny-leaved rhododendron bushes lining the drive. It was here, in the lighter and marginally less oppressive compound, that the canteen, showerblocks and offices had been sited after the colliery was redesigned in its heyday.

The door to the deserted office block swung open silently, the only sound the soft click of Mike's leather soles on the lino. As the sunlight glinted through the glass entrance door in a mottled explosion of bright patches on the walls and floor, he felt more at peace than he had done in a long time. There was no heavy rumble of London traffic outside, no constant reverberating drone. The ringing silence was broken only by the excited cries of birds swooping over the fields. Even the air had a crystal clarity, as far removed from London's fume-laden atmosphere as sparkling spa water was from the chemical-doused liquid that passed through decaying Victorian sewers to gush from the capital's taps.

The purity of the moment dimmed briefly the thoughts that had been troubling him: the worries about his career, the tension at work, the growing paranoia that Whicker was about to wreck any chance he had of success. He walked along the corridor, past the closed door of Bulmer's office, and into the room that had been designated for his use. It was stark, with only a utility desk and chair for furniture, a phone, and a black and white map of the mine and surrounding area on the wall. A large window looked out over the yard to the fields.

It was not until Mike had settled himself in his seat, enjoying the heat of the sun on the back of his neck, that he noticed the writing on the floor.

It was tucked into one corner, a jumbled mass scrawled in what looked like either charcoal or coaldust. His curiosity piqued, he bent down to inspect it. It seemed to have been written by several hands, but much of it was gibberish, a jumble of half-formed words and odd symbols, over-written and tiny. Making a mental note to tell the cleaner about the strange graffiti, Mike started to return to his desk when one group of words caught his eye.

WHATS HIS NAME. MICHAEL. CAN HE SEE. HE SEES. MICHAEL. LEAVE, LEAVE NOW.

Mike dropped to his knees to examine in detail the tiny scrawl around the boldy stated central words. A chill ran through him as he distinguished, or thought he did, the words HANNAH and JACK. Nervously he moved closer, his nose only inches from the lino. Eventually he decided it was just a trick of the confusing mix of letters, like the shadow faces on rocks and trees. No one in the area knew the names of his wife and child. He marvelled at how small some of the words had been written, as if they had been scratched with a compass point, but there seemed to be no rhyme or reason to them.

"LEAVE NOW." For some indefinable reason, those words brought a shiver to his spine. It could be construed as a warning, he supposed. He tried to ignore it, but it had already triggered a feeling of uneasiness.

As the sun crawled up the sky and the dark clouds scudded away on the back of a strong wind, his thoughts returned to the task which faced him. What irked Mike more than anything was the thought that Whicker may have foreseen the problems ahead and was secretly gloating over a mission that could keep him out of the office, and away from protecting his back, for weeks. That would give Whicker enough time to twist the blade a few more times with his superiors, ruining whatever fading hopes he had of progressing within the company. The flip side of that was, of course, that if he succeeded in clearing up Colthorpe's problems in record time he would be lauded on his return. He would have the last laugh on Whicker then, a prize almost worth more than promotion.

At nine am, Bulmer knocked and shuffled in. His face seemed even ruddier in the light of day: a permanent flare that could have come from too much alcohol or too many days in the chill Leicestershire wind.

"Eh up, lad. You must have been up with the larks." He appeared to have slept little; his eyes were puffy and red-rimmed and he moved wearily.

Mike nodded. "I told you I wanted to get an early start." As he swivelled round in his chair, the forgotten writing on the floor caught his eye. "When I arrived I found that." He pointed at the scrawl.

Bulmer stood over it, fingering his chin uneasily as he read. There was something in his demeanour which suggested to Mike that the writing came as no surprise, but when he looked up, a slight smile playing on his lips, there was no indication of it in his face.

"Funny, isn't it?"

"Funny?"

"Oh, you don't want to take it serious, lad. It's a joke. The men just wanted to welcome you with a joke."

"'Leave now', it says. Is that a joke?"

"You bloody southerners," Bulmer laughed, "you've got no sense of humour." He put one foot on the patch of writing and dragged it firmly backwards, smudging it until it was unreadable. "It was just a joke, lad. Just a joke. Now come on and I'll take you on a tour of my pit. You can meet some of the men. You'll have to get to know them if you're going to be around for a while."

Bulmer's voice was amicable enough, but there was steel in his eyes which suggested he would brook no dissent. Mike eventually broke his gaze and looked down at the black smudge on the floor, feeling strangely dissatisfied.

"Mr Bulmer?" A sturdy blonde appeared behind Bulmer's shoulder in a state of mild agitation. "Mr Bulmer, that Richmond man is here again."

"Oh, bloody hell. That's all we need."

"What's wrong?" Mike asked curiously.

"A reporter from the local rag. He's been on my back for the last few months now. Reckons there's some kind of big story here that we're covering up." Mike smiled sardonically, but Bulmer ignored him. "Bastard! Well, I don't want to talk to him. Get rid of him, Julie."

"Wait."

"What?"

"Let me talk to him. If we send him on his way it'll reinforce any idea he's got about this place. He'll think we're covering something up."

"Well, we are, aren't we?"

"Yes," Mike snapped exasperatedly, "but he doesn't have to know it."

Bulmer shrugged. "Your funeral. I'll take you for your little tour after you've sent him packing. You know where to find me."

Three minutes later Richmond knocked and entered. He was older than Mike had imagined, probably in his mid forties, and he seemed retiring to the point of shyness. "Mr . . . ?" he said in a whispery voice.

"Leary. Michael Leary." Mike motioned to the chair he had just brought in from Bulmer's office, but Richmond ignored it for a second and leant over the desk to shake hands firmly.

"I'm Terry Richmond, the *Mail*. I presume Mr Bulmer told you about me?"

Mike nodded. Richmond slumped into the low chair as if he was lounging in front of his TV, his bulging belly hanging precipitously over his belt. He looked, Mike noted, a mess. His black hair gleamed with too much grease, strung haphazardly across his head in a futile attempt to hide the encroaching bald patch. His striped shirt was as creased as if he had slept in it and there was an unsightly brown stain on the breast.

21

"Well, Mr Leary," he began, pushing his glasses awkwardly back on to the bridge of his nose as he fumbled with a dog-eared notebook, "I'd like you to tell me about the sudden death here at Colthorpe last night." He paused, watching Mike like an owl through his thick lenses. "If that's at all possible?"

Mike licked his lips, choosing his words carefully. He opened the file he had hastily snatched from Bulmer and, careful to appear as helpful and conciliatory as possible, replied, "Alec Jakes. He was forty-eight. But I expect you know that."

Richmond grunted. "The police told me this morning."

"What else did they tell you?"

He shrugged. "Not much. They said you were still looking into it."

Mike held up his hands in agreement, as if to say "What more is there?", but Richmond ignored the inference. "Can you tell me any more?" He sounded almost apologetic.

"I can't, I'm sorry. I don't want to prejudice the results of our investigation." Mike was worried that his sincere smile was rapidly becoming fixed.

But Richmond, in his unassuming way, refused to be deterred. "I heard it was quite . . . horrible. Something about his eyes?"

Mike felt the false smile slip slowly from his lips.

"In fact, I'd heard that he'd lost both of them. That's quite odd, isn't it?" Richmond continued.

Behind his glasses, Richmond was blinking innocently although Mike thought he could see a note of triumph reflected somewhere in his face.

"Okay," Mike began, unable to hide the irritation in his voice. "You obviously know more than you're saying so there's no point in trying to gloss over the details. Yes, Jakes did die in a particularly horrific manner, but we're not trying to cover that up. We just don't know what caused it yet. We've got an experienced team of accident investigators underground at the moment and we expect to have a full picture pretty soon. I know I can't expect to stop you writing whatever you want, but I can try to appeal to your better nature. Mrs Jakes is as much in the dark as we are at the moment and I don't think it would do for her to find out the bloody details of her husband's death from your rag."

Richmond chewed on the end of a splintered biro in thought. Eventually he replied: "So what are you doing here?"

"What do you mean?"

"You're not local. I was told British Coal sent you up here to check on Colthorpe's record. A pretty appalling record, I hear."

Mike shook his head in resignation. "That's quite a contact you've got there."

Richmond laughed shyly. "I just know people." He doodled almost absent-mindedly on his pad. "Tell you what, I'll hold off on the full details of the Jakes story if you give me the guff on what's wrong here at Colthorpe when you're ready to make your report."

"How do you know you can trust me?"

"Oh, you seem like a decent chappie. Bit of a short temper, but that probably comes from living in the Smoke."

"All right," Mike said. "Nothing about Jakes now and I'll tip you off when I make my report."

"Can't say fairer than that."

Richmond stood up abruptly and shook Mike's hand. His shirt had pulled out of his trousers and he was revealing a wide expanse of curly-haired belly. "Whitehouse, my news editor – he's a good fellow, but he likes to see results. Your report will put me in good with him. Probably keep his migraines at bay for a while as well! Tell you what, I'll be doing a little background research on Colthorpe and if I come up with anything that might help you, well . . . I'll let you know."

Mike nodded in resignation.

"Oh, one other thing," Richmond added as he reached the door. "I like to study local history. Bit of a buff, really. I remember reading about a similar accident back in the . . . eighteenth century? Seventeenth century?"

"Really."

"It was in a book by a local historian. Professor Eric Williams. Good fellow. Very keen on preserving our local heritage. But I digress. He wrote about a miner who had both his eyes put out while he was underground. His partner who

23

was down there with him at the time was hung for murder, but right up to his death he protested his innocence. Blamed the death on the Tunnellers."

"Tunnellers?"

"Some kind of spirits that haunt old mines. Probably the ghosts of miners or something. That's part of our local folk-lore. You find these mining communities are very supersti-tious. It's always been a dangerous job and when death's just around the corner people start to believe in those kind of things. A bit of superstition, a good luck charm, it gives you that extra bit of protection."

"Yes, very interesting." Richmond's dull, droning voice had set Mike's mind wandering and he suddenly found himself picturing the blood-stained, eyeless face of Jakes. He shivered.

"Well . . . I'll be seeing you." Richmond brought him back to the here and now as he closed the door behind him, but the image stayed with him. Eyeless, in a dark place.

With the heat of the late summer sun he began to feel uncomfortable and irritable; he had enough difficulty con-trolling his temper at the best of times. It hadn't always been a problem. His school reports had described him as good-natured and he had been fine at university, when he met Hannah, even when he started at British Coal as the thrusting young blade tipped to ride straight to the top. But somewhere along the line something had gone wrong. It had probably started when his career stalled, bubbling up from deep within like a spring that had been backed up until the pressure grew too much. Looking at the size of the file on his desk and knowing the amount of time it would take him to conduct an adequate investigation, the weeks his work would keep him apart from Hannah and Jack, he could feel the fire rising within him again.

Something, he thought as he bit his lower lip, would have to be done.

"So what did he say?" Bulmer halted in the middle of the yard and glanced curiously at Mike.

"He said, fine. I still can't believe it. Or maybe I can. When I said it looked like I would be up here for a while and I wanted Hannah and Jack to come to stay with me, he said the company would pay for it."

"So what's wrong with that?"

"He's not doing it out of the goodness of his heart. Whicker doesn't *have* any kindness in his heart. He only agreed because he was happy to hear that it was unlikely I'd be wrapping the job up in the near future."

"Oh, stop your worrying." Bulmer clapped a hand on his shoulder and pushed him until he started walking again. "Make the most of it. I know just the place you can all stay. There's a bungalow down on Canal Lane, belongs to British Coal. It was used as offices for the lorry park for a while, but the powers that be decided it was surplus to requirements so they've had it converted back to living quarters ready for a quick sale. What do you reckon?"

"Sounds good to me."

"I'll make the necessary arrangements."

Whicker was still hovering at the back of Mike's mind like a ghost, but the knowledge that he would not be separated from Hannah and Jack for as long as he had expected made it almost inconsequential. With his family around him he felt so much stronger – the pressure at work which seemed to have been grinding him down for so many years became an easier burden to bear.

Bulmer led Mike around the colliery as if it were a tour of a national monument. The sights were pointed out with a *spiel* that would have done a tour guide proud, placing their importance in a rich historical context: there was the storehouse where the great fire of '68 started, and over there was the office building where Bulmer had opened the window to hear Arthur Scargill's emotional plea to the working miners during the divisive strike of '84. There was a billowing pride in his voice when he spoke and it was obvious to Mike that the mine meant more to him than a simple workplace.

The long, sunlit canteen was a crowded hubbub of hungry miners and shrieking kitchen staff, the air pungent with the aroma of frying bacon and eggs and thick with bellowed expletives and hoarse laughter. Although his passage between the polished tables with Bulmer went unnoticed by most, he could still feel some eyes locked on him in mistrust and suspicion, if not downright hatred. The men knew why he was there; it was futile to try to fight their natural reaction. He kept his eyes down and continued the journey, trying to attract as little attention as he could.

They passed through the old lamp room and another string of offices quickly, arriving at the shower block where a few straggling miners scrubbed the thick grime from their bodies. Steam clouded the air, catching at the back of Mike's throat.

One miner poked his head out of the white-tiled shower area, his face flushed and dripping, and yelled at Mike, "Don't forget to give your bollocks a good soaking, lad!"

"This is your last stop on the grand tour," Bulmer said. "Any questions?"

Mike had no time to reply before a broad, bear-like man with a face like a shovel walked up, his eyes glinting darkly.

"Hello, Bob." Bulmer registered no emotion, but his attitude signalled that the new arrival was important.

"Mr Bulmer," he nodded, without taking his eyes off Mike. His arms were a gallery of blue tattoos stretched thinly across muscles steeled by the hardest labour.

"And this is Mr Leary."

"Aye, the bloke from London."

"Bob here's our union representative," Bulmer continued, trying to disperse the tension in the air.

"That's right," his voice grated. "Bob Packard, UDM." His heavy-lidded eyes were like an animal's, cunning and vicious. "You'll be hearing a lot from me. I know what you're doing up here and all the prying that'll be going on. And I want you to know now that I'm not going to let you bully any of my men."

"I'm not here to bully anyone," Mike replied.

"That's not the way I see it. We know they want this pit closed and that'll happen over my dead body. We'll fight you all the way if we have to." Packard's eyes had narrowed until they were two dark slits in his puffy face, the veins standing out starkly on his forehead.

"At risk of repeating myself," Mike said, straining to control his voice, "I am not here to pick on you or your members or to precipitate the closure of this mine. I'm merely looking into the safety and efficiency record . . ."

26

"That's just words, pal, and you know it. We won't be fooled by management jargon. Just bear me in mind when you come to write your report."

"That's not a threat, is it?" Mike's teeth were clenched.

"I don't need to make threats. I control all the men on this site and if we so decide we can 'precipitate' a situation that you won't like. Despite all your mechanization and computerization, you still need good workers." He stared into Mike's eyes fleetingly, sizing him up and giving a warning. Then, before the tension of the situation erupted, he nodded to Bulmer and walked off.

"Don't mind him," Bulmer said, putting a calming hand on Mike's shoulder. "Some of these men think they're fighting for their working lives. Tempers are bound to get a bit frayed. There are just too many rumours going round about closures and cutbacks. It's a bad time for the mining industry."

"You don't have to tell me, Tom. I know just how bad things are." Mike wondered if the tempers were getting frayed enough to actually kill. He thought about Jakes, blind in the dark and now blind in the light, and then he thought about the cruel brutality that was etched into Packard's face. "I don't like him," he said softly.

"Who? Bob? Don't be fooled by that. He might be acting tough with you, but that's because it's expected of him. He'd do anything for the men. Anything. He's dedicated." He glanced at his watch. "I've got to get back for a meeting. You take your time and I'll see you back at the office later on. All right?"

Bulmer walked away briskly, leaving Mike to amble slowly back through the quiet buildings. He had no plans to begin his investigations that day. The interviews he felt would be necessary to discover what had happened to Jakes and to do a full report on the previous flaws in the record would take a while to set up; there was no point in rushing.

As he wound his way back into the old lamp room, enthusiastically mulling over how he would break the news to Hannah that she and Jack could spend some time with him, he heard a faint sound on the edge of his hearing. He stopped and listened.

Silence.

27

The room was deserted and the only noise was that of a shovel scraping against tarmac on the other side of the yard. Still listening intently, he glanced around the room. The sole sign of the room's former use was row upon row of brass hooks where the miners would have hung their Davey lamps at the end of a shift in more dangerous times. Now it was barely used. Across the yard, the worker had stopped his shovelling and was yelling angrily to a colleague.

Then he heard it again.

Faintly, but perceptibly, he could hear a soft scratching coming from somewhere beneath the room's thick concrete floor. It continued for a few seconds and then stopped abruptly, pausing for a couple of minutes before restarting. It was like the scrabbling of a small animal's claws, although at times it seemed much louder.

Before Mike could locate exactly the source of the scratching, a tall, hollow-cheeked miner entered. "Can you hear that noise?" Mike asked, motioning him to remain still.

The miner looked around, puzzled. "Can't hear anything. What kind of noise?"

"Like a scratching of some kind. From beneath the floor." The miner's face, for some inexplicable reason, paled. "I think you've got rats," Mike continued. "I bet that's quite a problem here."

"It's not rats." Mike's musing was halted by the conviction in the miner's voice. He was staring at Mike askance.

"It must be," Mike disagreed. "I heard this scratching, like something digging. It was coming from about there."

The miner stepped nimbly aside from where Mike was pointing. "Rats," he said eventually, "that's right. It's a big problem. We'll have to get another load of poison soon. Kill 'em stone dead." He looked at Mike warily, then walked through the room and out of the far door.

Mike remained for five more minutes, still listening, but the scratching did not return. The more he thought about the noise, playing it back in his mind, the more he decided that it didn't sound like an animal.

In fact, he thought, it sounded more like the noise fingernails made when they were clawing at brick or rock.

A sudden chill washed over him, he walked outside, happy

to feel the midday warmth of the sun on his face. The sky was now powder-blue, with no trace of storm clouds, and the wind had died down so that the heat steamed off the yard. He raised his hand to shield his eyes and looked out over the rolling peaceful countryside. As he did so a huge cloud of crows rose suddenly from a nearby field, their black wings beating frantically like thunder as they rose into the sky. Swooping high they became one mass, obscuring the sun for a second, their cries like those of frightened children.

Chapter Four

As she replaced the phone in the cradle, Hannah felt a slight buzz of excitement at the prospect of joining Mike in the Midlands. Since she had decided to work from home she seized on every opportunity to get out and about in an attempt to keep the encroaching boredom at arm's length. Although she enjoyed her work, the moment each article was finished the walls of the house began to close in on her. Her only escape was a long walk on the common. A short stay in a tranquil, semi-rural retreat would do wonders for her relaxation in the weeks up to the birth.

Jack would enjoy it too. She had never wanted him to grow up in the city, but Mike's job prevented them moving out to the country and his salary precluded them escaping to one of the leafier suburbs. It would be a good holiday for all of them, even though Mike was working; the first family holiday they had taken in years.

"Jack," she called. There was a muffled reply. "Jack, come here." The sound of scampering feet came down the stairs and then her son bustled into the lounge in a whirlwind of overactive limbs.

"Yes, Mummy."

"How would you like to go on a holiday?"

He frowned and then asked quietly, "What, without Daddy?"

Hannah laughed. "No, *with* Daddy! We're going to stay with him."

"Yay! When are we going? Tomorrow?"

"No, not tomorrow. Soon. As soon as Daddy has found us somewhere to stay and you a nice big bed to sleep in."

"Is there a beach?"

"No, but there'll be plenty of trees for you to climb and cows and sheep and things."

"Wow! Animals! Live animals! Like the zoo!"

"Yes, like the zoo."

"Can I take my Transformers?"

"Yes, you can take your Transformers," Hannah said with mock weariness. "And Garfield and Batman and every single toy you've got tucked away upstairs."

She poked him in the stomach and he crumpled up giggling, protecting his sides from one of her spontaneous tickling attacks. "Now you'd better go and get yourself ready for bed, or you'll be so tired you'll sleep through your holiday."

"I don't want to go to bed now."

"Look at the time! It's way past your normal bedtime."

"But I'm not tired!"

"Don't argue with me," she said sharply. "Bed." Although Mike wasn't the strictest father in the world he always seemed to be able to get Jack to do whatever he wanted. Jack dutifully obeyed even the quietest order, but it was different whenever Mike was not around. She wagged a finger at him and Jack sulked briefly before jumping up and down on the spot a few times and running out of the room. "And don't run! You'll do yourself an injury."

Smiling softly to herself, she lounged back in the armchair and stroked her belly for comfort. It was big now, even bigger than when she had had Jack. The best thing about the holiday was that Mike could do some of the running around for her. She relished the thought of taking the weight off her feet for a while. Mike was always good like that. He had worked tirelessly throughout her first pregnancy, pampering her every minute of the day. Regretfully, she imagined what their life would be like if he never let his frustration and temper get the better of him. At least in the Midlands he would be away from Whicker and that damned office, she thought; he was always better when it was too far removed to be an influence.

She had, however, been disturbed by Mike's graphic account of the death of the miner. The image of the eyeless body being brought up from the bowels of the earth had stayed with her since he had described it, haunting her waking hours as much as her dreams. It was one of those abiding images which, once pictured by the mind, was difficult to shake off. There was something about the mysteriousness of the death which did not bode well. The other night she had dreamed of Mike suddenly being dragged into a hole in the ground, like Alice having the tables turned on her by a predatory white rabbit. She could still picture it: the expression of horror on his face as his fingers clawed in a last futile gesture at the grass and the soil before he disappeared over the lip and into the depths.

Absent-mindedly she fumbled down the side of the cushion and plucked out the remote control to switch on the TV. As it hummed into life, the first image she saw was a bloody childbirth scene on some BBC medical documentary. Her muscles clenched involuntarily at the sight of the mother's pain, but then the picture switched to a dowdy-looking expert who spoke in a dull monotone about infant mortality rates and the possibility of complications during pregnancy.

"Obstetricians are as confused about the correct method of childbirth now as they were fifty years ago," the voice droned. "Although one baby in twenty was born by caesarean section in 1970, the figure is now closer to one in eight and rising. The reason, many obstetricians claim, is that because of the threat of being sued they are under considerable pressure to avoid complicated vaginal deliveries which may endanger babies."

The picture switched, revealing a concerned-looking man with a pale, moon face and piercing grey eyes. Beneath him were the words *Gareth Holborrow, Obstetrician*. "Babies are now being forced out of the womb rather than welcomed into the world," he said haltingly. "Babies are very susceptible to outside influences while they are in the womb. For instance, oxytocin, the drug administered by drip, reduces the blood flow to the baby. That means vigorous contractions could starve the child of oxygen and increase the likelihood that it will become distressed."

"That's all I need," she muttered, pressing a button to flick to another channel. She rubbed her belly and dreamed of a labour free of pain.

Chapter Five

"What happened to Alec Jakes?" Mike doodled on the pad in front of him. After seven dreary interviews he no longer expected any meaningful response. He couldn't even remember the name of the miner before him; it really didn't seem to matter any more. Seven interviews, all of them exactly the same. Mike could predict the answers to his questions down to the exact wording, whether he was asking the engineer who checked and double checked the underground machinery or the last person to see Jakes alive. *I don't know. It certainly wasn't . . . the cutting machine/a flying stone/anyone who held a grudge.* Fill in the blanks yourself.

"I don't know." The face of the miner opposite him bore the history of years underground, a thousand lines, scars and cuts that told of a lifetime of hard labour. It made him seem twenty years older than he actually was. Two fingers were missing on one hand and his skin had a blue sheen from the coal dust ground into his pores after a tunnel collapse. "I knew Alec better'n anyone else. Fifteen years we'd worked together. No one had a grudge against him. No one. He was popular, always a laugh and a joke. He could have been the next Bernard Manning if he'd gone on the stage."

Really, Mike thought sourly. What a tragic waste of talent.

"It must have been an accident. No other explanation for it."

"The experts don't think that," Mike said automatically, staring at the blank wall behind the miner's shoulder and wishing he was a continent away. "No machinery had malfunctioned and none could have caused the kind of injuries he sustained, I'm told. So where does that leave us?"

33

The miner's rheumy eyes blazed with a cold hatred that took Mike by surprise. "Who are you accusing? His own workmates? We were like brothers to him."

Mike continued, undeterred by the level of emotion he had aroused. "Something killed him. What do you think it was?"

His smile was tight. "Don't ask me, pal. That's your job."

Mike sighed. "Okay, that's all. You can go." He had a headache thumping behind his temples and his limbs were suffused with an aching weariness. Every attempt he had made to discover something, anything, about what had happened to Jakes, was stonewalled. He had expected a certain amount of surliness. After all, he was an outsider brought in because they obviously couldn't keep a tight ship themselves, but he had still thought that they would comply with an investigation which was so obviously in their best interests. Instead they were treating him like a sworn enemy. Someone to be feared and reviled at the same time. Someone who could not be helped under any circumstances.

Furiously he snapped his biro in two and flung it at the far wall.

"Problems?" Bulmer leaned against the door jamb, a faint expression of amusement on his face.

"Why the *fuck* . . . !" Mike took a deep breath ". . . can't I get any help from these . . ." He sighed and shook his head.

"They probably don't know anything. Have you thought of that?" Bulmer slumped into the chair opposite, his smile becoming a little more sympathetic.

"They know more than they're saying. I'd stake my salary on it. For some reason they just won't tell me!"

"I didn't think you'd have an easy ride. You know what they all think."

"What?"

"That you're just some lackey from the Company sent up here to stab them in the back and whip the rug out from under their feet."

"For Christ's sake, I just want to make sure it's safe for them down there!"

Bulmer shrugged. "It's as safe as it ever was."

"And that's not saying much. Your safety record was one of the reasons I was sent up here." Mike picked up the thick file

34

and let it drop heavily to the desk to emphasize its weight. "In the last five years, one of your men has lost an arm, two have lost fingers, there've been injuries requiring almost three thousand stitches and the damage to machinery and British Coal property is five hundred per cent higher than the national average. What the hell do they think about that?"

"They think there's a bit of a jinx." Bulmer was unruffled by Mike's anger.

"A bit of a jinx!" Mike closed his eyes and rubbed his forehead, trying to ease the pressure that was building up. "Can't you see it's different this time? Someone has died! You can't just put it down to human error, to a mishap with machinery. There are a lot of questions to be answered. What are you going to tell the police? The Health and Safety Executive?"

"The police are satisfied it was an accident and I saw the Health and Safety bloke this morning. Jakes fell on the cutting machine and took his eyes out on the machinery."

Mike shook his head in disbelief. "Jakes wasn't anywhere near the cutting machine!"

Bulmer shrugged again, nonchalant. "That's what they say. Who am I to argue?"

"Did you tell them that?"

"They made a few enquiries."

"But don't you care that it's a blatant lie?"

"All I care about is that a bloody unpleasant episode has been put behind us and now we can get back to the job of running this pit properly." There was a note of finality in his voice.

"I'm still going to have to look into all the other episodes," Mike added.

Bulmer walked over to the window and looked out into the grey afternoon. "That's your job."

"You're not making it any easier."

"I'm not making it any more difficult. Look, you're a decent sort, but, to be honest, we didn't invite you up here. In my view, in *everybody's* view, there's nothing to look into."

"But what about all the accidents, the damage?"

"I told you. A jinx."

"You don't honestly believe that!"

"I do honestly believe it. You flash bastards from London might not have any superstition in you, but we have different beliefs up here. Sometimes a place gets a run of bad luck for no reason and there's nothing you can do but sit it out. Colthorpe is jinxed at the moment. The men know it too, but it'll sort itself out."

As far as Mike was concerned, Bulmer's outlook was rooted in medieval times, but his voice was so adamant he didn't want to mock. He remembered Richmond's comments about the superstitions of miners brought on by their constant proximity to danger. Then something else the reporter said came to mind. "Did you ever work underground?" he asked.

"Oh, aye," Bulmer replied proudly, resting against the window ledge. "When I was a lad. I'm not one of this new breed who's got no idea what it's like to work down there."

Mike nodded. "Did you ever hear talk of an old folk tale about . . . what were they called now? . . . Tunnellers? That's right. Tunnellers."

There was a flicker of recognition across Bulmer's face and his eyes narrowed suspiciously. "Vaguely."

"Richmond told me about them. Some kind of ghosts or something. Do the men still believe in that kind of thing?"

Bulmer turned back to look out of the window, his voice sounding strangely flat and disembodied when he spoke. "Aye. Probably. But you won't get any of 'em to admit it in the cold light of day."

Mike laughed. "Weird, isn't it? Thinking about those things in this day and age."

"It's easy to say that when you're up here, lad." Bulmer's voice was barely more than a whisper now. "But it's a different world when you're down there in the dark. It's a damned sight easier to believe in a lot of things."

"What, even the Tunnellers?" Mike laughed again, but there was no humour in Bulmer's response.

"Even the Tunnellers."

It was a fitting day for a funeral; a little grey, a little dismal, with the faintest hint of drizzle in the wind adding to the sense of loss. Mike stood apart from the growing crowd of mourners at the graveside, wanting to be seen to be paying his last

36

respects but not wishing to be intrusive. After all, he thought bitterly, no one would want the management nark to be standing in the front row.

He had found a spot beneath a gnarled yew tree on the perimeter where he could watch the proceedings. Off to his left was the church, dour and stoic like the people who worshipped there, its steeple jutting dark against the slate sky. The main expanse of the graveyard lay before him, tightly packed with headstones dating back hundreds of years. There was barely room for Alec Jakes' own little plot. They had managed to squeeze him into the area bordering the section where the oldest gravestones were situated, their mildewed stone slouching and slipping in the clipped grass.

Another sharp blast of wind brought the first few leaves of autumn tumbling across in front of him, prompting Mike to pull up the collar of his overcoat even though it offered little protection. He shivered slightly, but he was warmed inside by the prospect of Hannah and Jack's arrival on the following day. Efficient as ever, she had made the necessary arrangements in record time. All her articles had been completed by working deep into the night and she was on schedule for a noon arrival. Mike had already reconnoitred the bungalow and although he had had to arrange for a bed and a few items of furniture to be brought in at the company's expense, he was sure it would suit their needs during their brief stay.

Mike caught sight of Bulmer when the line of mourners wending their way down from the short service in the church slowed to a trickle. He nodded discreetly as he took up position on the fringe of the crowd with Bob Packard at his side. The union rep was barely recognizable from their earlier confrontation; his hair had been slicked back smartly and he was wearing a double-breasted charcoal suit and a pair of shiny leather shoes.

A minute later the sound of anguished sobbing broke through the intermittent howling of the wind. Mike recognized Jakes' wife, her tearful eyes rimmed with red, as she leant on the arms of two teenagers, obviously her children. The boy was pale-faced and staring blankly as if he had suddenly become privy to some terrible secret. His sister was crying furiously, her lank, mousey hair falling across her face.

They took up positions at the graveside, followed closely by the vicar in his pristine robes, his sparse hair lashed across his head by the wind.

Eventually the bearers began their interminable journey down the sloping sandy path from the church door to the grave. The six bulky miners, some of whom Mike recognized, carried the gleaming coffin as if it was made of balsa wood, barely straining under the weight of Jakes' body. They effortlessly lowered it on to the supports over the hole and then the vicar coughed and began to say a few words in a rich, sonorous voice. His message passed Mike by. All he could think about was Jakes, about to make his last journey underground where he had spent most of his working life.

There was something about that image that chilled him. In one way it was fitting, but in another it was as if purgatory lay seething only a few yards beneath his feet. Darkness pervaded both life and death in the mining community; there was no easy line drawn between the two.

A couple of umbrellas sprouted at the back of the crowd as a few heavy drops of rain fell, but the threat of a downpour was swiftly blown away by the wind. When the vicar had finished and the sobbing had reached a crescendo, two men stepped forward and removed the struts while another pair lowered the coffin into the ground.

And that was when all hell broke loose.

In retrospect, the beginning was almost comical. Like a novice surfer on his first big wave, the vicar suddenly shot his arms out horizontally to steady himself as the earth crumbled beneath his feet. The side of the grave sheared off in a single landfall and for one single moment the vicar hovered on the brink, an expression of total horror on his face and a silent prayer on his lips. Then his kicking heels followed the grass and stones and mud into the gaping hole.

If the tableau had been frozen at that moment it would have been a terrible experience, but one soon forgotten. It was, however, as if God had decided to unleash a flood of bad luck in one moment, relentlessly piling indignity upon indignity.

Looking back, Mike could only focus on what had happened as individual moments, single snapshots in the mind. The vicar disappearing beneath the coffin, his hands clutching at air. Two miners vainly struggling to keep the box horizontal while the earth continued to fall in, then finally releasing the ropes to save themselves. Other bearers gaping in shock as the coffin flipped up on end. Mrs Jakes clapping a hand over her mouth in disbelief, viewing a scene that would haunt her until her dying day, before she disappeared into the grave herself in a sudden clownish fall. Three mourners pitching into the rapidly widening hole like drunken revellers at a party leaping into the swimming pool. Screams. Shouts. The sounds of panic as the women ran back, the men ran forward. A frantic stampede.

The grave finally stopped expanding when it was big enough to take a car. There was no sign of the vicar, Mrs Jakes, the coffin or any of the others; they had been swallowed up like Jonah in the whale's mouth. The miners were milling around uselessly, partly uncomprehending, wholly shocked, when Mike finally reached the graveside. He dug his heels in and teetered forward, surprised to see that the bottom of the grave now lay a further ten feet below its original level.

"Don't get near the edge! Bulmer yelled. His face was scarlet with concern. "It's still slipping!"

The men pulled back nervously, but Mike snatched off his coat, threw it on the ground and lay on it, inching forward to get a better view. When his eyes finally adjusted to the darkness at the bottom of the hole he saw a sight which sickened him.

The coffin was almost vertical, lodged against the grave wall, but it had burst open on impact and the corpse of Alec Jakes lolled out drunkenly like a marionette with its strings cut. The undertaker had stuffed the eyes, but he had been forced to sew the lids tightly shut, creating an expression of sudden surprise. Mrs Jakes had been knocked unconscious by the fall, her skirt up around her waist, and she now lay against her husband's corpse, their cheeks touching in a parody of romance. Mike watched as her eyes flickered open, struggled to pierce the darkness, then focused on the thing next to her. Horror crept slowly on to her pale face as she gradually realized her situation; the first glimmer of hysteria slipped into her eyes soon after. Then she opened her mouth and screamed.

And screamed.

And screamed.

The vicar, his virginal robes filthy with mud, scrambled out from beneath the coffin and dirt and tried to comfort her. She thrashed out at him like an animal and then curled up into a foetal position at her husband's feet.

Her agonized cries shocked a few of the mourners into life and they leapt into the grave regardless of their own safety, lifting her up like a child and passing her from hand to hand and shoulder to shoulder until she was safely back in the light, where a gaggle of chirping women struggled to console her as they led her back to the church.

The rest of the men were brought out with the ropes which had been used for lowering the coffin. Mike gave a helping hand to the ashen-faced vicar, pulling him over the brink and to one side where he flopped down on a gravestone.

"Dear Lord," he muttered, shaking uncontrollably.

"What in heaven's name happened?' Mike sat down next to him, placing his mud-smeared overcoat around his shoulders.

"Subsidence," he gasped.

"Mining subsidence doesn't happen that quickly," Mike replied incredulously. "It's a gradual process."

"No, no. There was a tunnel down there. I saw it for a second. Nothing to do with the mine. It stretched off under the graveyard towards the church."

"Well, you can't see it now." Bulmer had walked up to them while they were talking. "If there was a tunnel down there, the landslip's filled it in."

"Where did it come from?" Mike asked.

Bulmer shook his head. "I don't know. There's been min-ing in this area for as long as people have lived here. It could be centuries old."

"But underneath the churchyard? Don't you think we should dig down and find out?"

Bulmer shook his head firmly. "We're not digging under the churchyard. It wouldn't be right."

"We've got to find out. Aren't you curious?"

Bulmer pondered for a second and then shook his head.

"Poor Mrs Jakes." The vicar, still shaking, put his hand over his eyes briefly. Then he rose and wearily headed back to the church.

40

Mike retrieved his coat from the gravestone. "I wonder if British Coal will pay the dry cleaning bill."

Bulmer grunted. "You're joking. It's an unnecessary expense . . . same as most of their pits."

"The least they can do is pay for a new funeral."

"Did you see Mrs Jakes face? I don't think she could cope with another one."

"Maybe you're right. Disasters seem to happen quite regularly round here, don't they?"

"That's not very funny," Bulmer growled.

Around the grave, clods of earth broke away from the topsoil and dropped into the abyss silently. There were minute cracks in ground which had not moved in generations, radiating out from the hole like a spiderweb. In the distance, Mike heard the echoing sound of sobbing.

It was soon lost in the wind.

Chapter Six

"What a wonderful place!" Hannah looked out of the kitchen window over the rolling fields and searched for some sign of civilization. From her vantage point all was green – fields, hedges, trees. They might have been living in the middle ages. If she squinted she could just make out the line of hedges where the road ran, but that was all. The mine could only be seen from the front of the house. "It's nothing like you described it."

"It's difficult for me to be objective. I'm here under duress, away from my wonderful, supportive family with a pitful of belligerent miners between me and the solution to the task at hand. It's hard for me to appreciate the joys of a few green fields."

Hannah smiled mockingly and kissed him on the cheek. She would have preferred a little more in the home comfort stakes, but for a brief break it was more than adequate. Waltzing through to the sparsely furnished lounge, she shouted out, "And what do you think, Mr Leary Junior?"

Jack rocked morosely backwards and forwards on the sofa, his knees tucked beneath his chin. "There's no video."

"Yes, and there's no jacuzzi or swimming pool either. How will we ever cope? You'll survive without a video."

He stuck his bottom lip out sulkily, unconvinced.

"Look at all those fields you can play in," Mike said, prodding a finger in his son's ribs until he squealed with laughter. "You can't do that in London. And all those trees. I bet you've never climbed a tree!"

"Mike, don't encourage him to do anything dangerous."

42

"Climbing trees isn't dangerous. All kids climb trees. It's not as if he's going to scale a mighty Californian redwood."

"You know what I mean." Hannah flashed him a cool, hard look before the corner of her mouth flickered. She was happy to be with him; a dull ache of loneliness grew in her even when they were apart for a few days.

"Will you climb trees with me, Daddy?"

"Well, I'll give you a leg up. Now you run outside and explore. Your mother and I want to have a chat."

"Okay." Jack slipped down from the sofa and scampered through to the kitchen. The door banged and his shrill whoops faded slowly as he ran down the garden towards the fields.

"Well, you really messed up this time, didn't you?" Hannah was scowling.

"What do you mean?"

"No video. I mean how are we expected to live . . . ?" Mike grabbed her before she had time to continue and dragged her down on to the sofa. "Not fair! You only caught me because I'm carrying all this extra weight."

"Indeed. And how is the forthcoming addition to our family unit?"

"Seems fine, touch wood. I'm sure he – or she – will love all this fresh air."

"Well, he or she can thank me personally in a couple of months' time. In the meantime I think you owe me a huge backlog of these." He planted his mouth firmly on hers and gave her a sloppy, mock-passionate kiss before her pliant mouth converted it into something deeper and more erotic. Mike felt the familiar twinge in his groin and pulled himself away hastily. "Christ, any more of that and I'll explode. Why don't we bind and gag our son and have the rest of the day to ourselves?"

Hannah's reply was a slanting, suggestive half-smile. "Don't worry," she said softly, "we can finish this off tonight when he's tucked up in bed."

"I can't wait that long."

"Well, unfortunately you'll have to," she laughed, dumping him on to the floor. "Right now I've got some unpacking to do."

43

Mike reclined against the sofa and watched her wander into the bedroom. The tension of the previous few days seeped gently from his limbs like oil; for once he felt totally relaxed. Hannah often had that effect on him. It was only when the pressures of work reached a crescendo that she had no hope of controlling his frustration and fury, and that was when the real problems began.

"Mike?" Hannah's voice from the bedroom sounded perplexed and a little worried.

"What is it?"

"Can you come here a minute?"

Sighing, Mike struggled to his feet and obediently went through to Hannah. She was standing near the window staring into space, with her head cocked on one side. "What is . . ."

"Ssssh! No, it's gone now." She turned and looked at him, her forehead wrinkled. "They're not digging under here, are they?"

"What, the mine you mean? I shouldn't think so. Why?"

"I thought I heard something just beneath the floor, like digging. Not with a spade or anything. It sounded like someone scrabbling with their hands. You know, like when you're moving a pile of rocks."

Mike laughed. "They may be a bit behind the times round here, but I don't think they dig with their bare hands!"

Hannah laughed too, but she sounded unconvinced. "Yes, I know it's stupid. Who'd be digging under here? The fresh air must be making me hallucinate!" She turned back to the open suitcase on the bed and continued her careful unpacking. For some inexplicable reason, she felt disturbed, uneasy.

Had she heard something?

Chapter Seven

Mike felt the slightest twinge of apprehension as the heavy metal doors clanged together. The atmosphere within the cage grew more oppressive, and as he inhaled the taste of dank, cold depths clung to the back of his throat. A thin line of sweat broke out on his forehead where the fabric restrainer held the hard hat snug to his head.

Bulmer stood to his right, his hands clasped behind his back. "Down we go," he muttered.

There was a sudden jolt and the powerful gears ground into life, causing the lift cage to lurch before beginning its downward journey. Mike subconsciously clung to the wire mesh of the walls.

For some inexplicable reason, he had tried to delay his inevitable journey beneath ground. He knew it was necessary to see for himself the place where Jakes' body had been found, and to lodge the layout of the system firmly in his mind's eye, so that when he came to write his report it was all clear. But when Bulmer had suggested it to him he had felt something turn in his stomach. He had managed to dissuade Bulmer for a day, but eventually his excuses were sounding increasingly pitiful, even to his own ears.

The journey down seemed to last forever, although it was probably only three or four minutes. There was another grinding jolt when the lift cage reached basement level and then the doors rattled open, revealing a long tunnel lit by the cold glare of strip lights. The craggy walls gleamed slick with moisture and there was a chill in the air which penetrated even the thick cloth of his boiler suit.

"Well, here it is," Bulmer said. His voice had lost its normal resonance and was barely more than a growl, almost deferential. Mike understood why. The sheer weight of the earth above their heads, hundreds of feet marking the passage of millions of years, was humbling. It made even the hardiest man seem insignificant. They were just ants scurrying along minute tunnels that could be crushed in a second, flattened into dust by ton upon ton of unyielding rock and soil. Mike could almost feel it pressing down in a claustrophobic wave that would engulf him if he let it. He subconsciously slid a finger next to his neck to loosen his collar.

"Been a while since you've been underground?" Bulmer asked.

"A few years," Mike replied.

"I always reckon it's like being a sailor. You know, having to find your sea legs. It takes a while to feel really natural down here."

Bulmer led the way along the tunnel, walking permanently half-bowed. Mike failed to take his lead and cracked his head on a supporting girder which ran horizontally across the passageway. The helmet protected him from any serious harm, but it still left a ringing in his ears. "You'll get used to that," Bulmer noted. "The more time you spend down here the more you start walking with a stoop."

Mike wanted to tell him that he intended spending as little time as possible beneath ground.

A short walk along the tunnel brought them to the underground railway. Bulmer nodded to the dusty miner who was manning the controls and clambered in. "Get settled in, lad," he said. "It's only a short hop."

To Mike the train was a rusty metal roller coaster, an archaic piece of machinery that should have been junked long ago. When it jerked into life and smoothly slid into the dark tunnel he found himself gripping tightly on to the seat in front, as if it were about to loop the loop in a terrifying funfair ride.

They trundled along shakily, the claustrophobic atmosphere growing stronger, almost palpable. There was little space around them and it was easy to imagine becoming trapped, the oxygen slowly dwindling until he was gasping and clawing at his throat. Mike found himself vividly recalling dreams he had had as a child, after reading *Lord of the Rings*. Like Frodo, he had scurried in his nightmares through the tunnels and cathedral-like chambers of the dark, underground land of Moria pursued by goblins and a host of other evil, slithering creatures. During his dark childhood nights he had woken each time the dream recurred, terrified by the thought that there was no way out, and that the things behind were getting closer and closer.

And then the train slowed down as the tunnel opened up into a wider dropping-off point. The light was much brighter, although it was still the sickly glow of the strip lights. In one corner two miners sat chewing on thick sandwiches from plastic boxes, eyes white in black dust faces.

"Here we are," Bulmer said, leaping out almost lithely. "How's it going, Stan?"

The older of the two miners swallowed loudly. "All right, Mr Bulmer. We've just stopped for a snap break."

Bulmer laughed. "That's all right, Stan. I didn't think you were skiving. I'm just showing Mr Leary here the sights."

"Taking him on the scenic route?"

"Something like that." Bulmer's relationship with his employees was easy and relaxed, their positions well-mapped and unchallenged. There was none of the crippling tension, the back-stabbing and snide comments, that Mike experienced every working day. His thoughts must have reflected in his face, for Bulmer looked at him quizzically and asked, "Something the matter, lad?"

Mike shook his head. "Just thinking about Jakes," he lied. "I can't work it out at all."

"Well, don't give yourself a brainstorm thinking about it. This is a different world down here. Sometimes accidents just happen – you can't always explain them."

He walked on ahead, leading the way down the deserted tunnel. Somewhere in the distance Mike could faintly hear a miner singing "Hound Dog" in a poor imitation of Elvis. It could have been just around the next bend or hundreds of yards away. He knew how the bizarre acoustics of the underground tunnels distorted perspective, carrying sounds clearly over a great distance while muffling those close at hand.

"That's not good enough for me," he continued. "I want to know the truth. I'm not trying to cause trouble, Tom, but I'm not going to be fobbed off with whatever half-baked explanation you gave the police and the Health and Safety Executive."

Bulmer might not have heard him for all the response he showed. His broad back bobbed along in front of Mike, obscuring the way ahead as he strode onward. Eventually he said: "We're nearly there."

Two more turns and they arrived at a wide area where a piece of rust-brown and grey machinery lay dormant against a partly worked seam. Lumps of coal were discarded around and the conveyor belt was motionless, signalling the sudden halt of work. Nearby there was a section which had been hurriedly cordoned off; metal spikes had been hammered into the ground, linked by bright orange cord.

"That's where we found him," Bulmer pointed.

Mike knew he was lying. "Is it really, Tom," he said with an edge of sarcasm. "He was working the cutting machine on his own when he died, was he? That's not very good practice, is it?"

"If Jakes chose to ignore the rules . . ."

"So you're going to tell his wife that he died because he was an incompetent who fucked up?" Bulmer remained silent. "Just for a cover-up?"

"It's not a cover-up." The words were heavy with warning.

Mike shook his head in annoyance and turned away. A second later, a howl of pain, loud and piercing, reverberated along the tunnels.

"Jesus!" Mike shouted. "What the hell was that?"

Bulmer's eyes were wide and staring and there was a look of growing terror on his face. It was an expression that seemed completely alien to him and somehow it was a little too stricken to be a simple response to that fading cry.

Mike started to run in the direction of the scream – or at least in the direction from which he thought it had come – but before he had travelled three paces Bulmer roughly grabbed his sleeve. "Don't run off," he growled, "you'll get yourself lost."

He had cleared his face of all emotion and now it was as

48

impassive as stone. Only his eyes showed any sign of what was going on within and they glowered hotly beneath his bristling brows. "Come on. Follow me." He strode off as powerfully as a man half his age, with Mike close at his heels.

"How do you know where it came from?" Mike asked.

"I don't. These tunnels carry sound in a strange way. But I do know where the men are working nearby."

Five minutes later they came upon a group of seven miners huddled in a tight circle. From what Mike could make out through the crowd, they seemed to be inspecting the back of a man in the centre of the group.

"What the bloody hell's going on here?" Bulmer yelled, his easy camaraderie brutally discarded.

The men, who had not heard his approach, jerked round, startled. One seemed about to speak, until he saw Mike behind Bulmer. His flickering eyes betrayed the lie before it came. "Nothing. It was just . . ."

Mike, fired by sudden, senseless anger, pushed past Bulmer and thrust his way through the miners to the man at the centre. A bulky, ruddy-faced man of about fifty started to turn, but Mike caught his arm and held him in position. The back of his overalls, and shirt beneath, were ripped apart, so that the pale flesh was easily visible. Four long red lines ran from his right shoulder blade to near the left-hand base of his ribcage, the skin ripped as if it had been raked by the claws of a tiger.

"How did that happen?" Mike said darkly, no longer able to subdue the feeling of uneasiness within him.

The miner remained silent, his gaze firmly fixed on a spot on the tunnel wall.

"Are you all right, Gordon?" Bulmer nudged his way through, pushing Mike aside as he passed.

The miner eyed Mike furtively, then spoke directly to Bulmer. "Aye, it's just a scratch."

"What happened?"

He shook his head. There was a quick flash of panic in his eyes, as if he were fighting to deny what he had seen.

"Christ, something's ripped your back open and you don't know what happened!" Mike said incredulously. Bulmer held his hand up to silence him, but Mike ignored the gesture.

49

"That was no accident. Somebody attacked you. Didn't they?"

The miner continued to ignore him. The others shifted nervously.

"*Tell me what happened*!" Mike yelled. He felt the adrenalin surging through his arteries. "What is fucking wrong with this place? What are you all trying to hide?" He looked from one face to another, but no one, not even Bulmer, would meet his gaze. "There's something very, very wrong here," he said quietly but with suppressed emotion, "and I'm going to find out what it is."

He was interrupted by a sound echoing along the tunnel. Scratching. Scratching like he had heard through the floor of the mine buildings, only louder. And closer.

"What's that?" No one answered. "I'm going to see." He started to move when four pairs of hands suddenly grabbed out to hold him back.

"I wouldn't do that," one miner said.

"Wouldn't be right," another added.

"You'd get lost. These tunnels, they all look the same."

"It's a maze if you don't know them."

By the time he had shook them off, the scratching had faded away. Mike considered going in search of the culprit anyway, but the heavy, claustrophobic atmosphere beneath ground was starting to disturb him and he did not want to spend any longer out of the fresh air than he had to. Reluctantly, he turned to Bulmer and said, "Get me out of here."

They journeyed back to the surface in silence. Mike's thoughts whirled in an attempt to make some sense of what was happening in Colthorpe, Bulmer watching him constantly out of the corner of his eye.

Outside the lift building, the sunlight seemed as bright as a halogen lamp and the warmth on Mike's face was comforting. They had not walked far into the dusty yard when they were confronted by Packard and a cadre of three miners. They appeared uncomfortable and out of joint in their cheap, dated suits, white shirts buttoned tightly at their throats, but Packard was more at ease; his suit was expensive and he wore it naturally. There was a faint smile on his face, but Mike recognized a hardness in his eyes which belied his welcome.

"Tom," he nodded in greeting. His glance slipped over Mike without registering his presence.

"What can I do for you, Bob?" Bulmer's irritation at this latest annoyance was barely concealed.

"I'm calling a meeting, Tom."

"What's the problem?"

"I've just been on the phone to John Smart in the union office." He paused, watching Bulmer's face intently for any flicker of insight. "He reckons he's got proof, documented proof, that Colthorpe is up for closure. A report from the Company, leaked out yesterday."

Bulmer shook his head. "Don't know anything about it, Bob."

Packard was not about to be placated. His eyes narrowed and thunder grew on his face. "You've always been straight with me, Tom, so I believe you. But not *him*." He jabbed a finger at Mike without removing his gaze from Bulmer's face. "It's too much of a coincidence that he's here now. They've sent him up here to sneak and spy on us and you're being taken in by him. Wake up, Tom, before it's too late! We're not going to take this lying down. There's going to be a fight and it's going to be soon, you mark my words." His mouth paused, half-open, as if he was about to say more, but then he closed it slowly, clearing the emotion from his face with a purging shrug. "I'll see you after the meeting Tom." He marched across the dusty yard to the canteen with his surly and silent entourage behind him.

After a thoughtful second, Bulmer turned to Mike. "Is he right?"

"About what?"

"About you. Am I being taken in by you?"

"Don't be stupid, Tom. I'm not that good a liar."

"No, I didn't think so."

"There's another angle." Mike felt the first kindling of his anger spring to life. "What if Whicker knew about this? What if he sent me up here because he knew what was planned at Colthorpe? It's just the kind of thing he'd do. He sent me up here because he knew I'd be at the centre of this hotbed, with every finger pointing at me as one of the instigators!"

"Surely not."

51

"You don't know him. He'd do anything to make my life hell. Anything." He halted, staring into the hazy middle distance. The early afternoon heat was heavy beneath the clear blue sky and the atmosphere over the mine yard was thick with dust, arid, prickling the back of his throat. "That bastard's trying to break me," he muttered.

"Why do you keep doing this job if you hate it so much?"

"Why?" He snapped around as if Bulmer had slapped him in the face. "Why? Well . . ."

"No point doing a job if you're not happy."

Mike stared at Bulmer incredulously and sighed. "I couldn't expect you to understand. It's my career. That's all."

Bulmer laughed. "You London yuppies! Bloody job's be-all and end-all! What about quality of life?"

Mike merely grunted in reply. "I'm going to call Whicker now," he announced adamantly. "I'm going to have it out with him. I want to know the truth."

The determination in his eyes impressed Bulmer. He watched Mike stride across the yard to the office buildings. Then he tucked his thumbs into his belt and smiled in admiration.

Mike kicked the office door shut and angrily punched out the number on the phone. He recognized Whicker's harsh tones instantly.

"It's Mike Leary."

"Mike! How are you doing?" The insincerity in his voice was obvious.

Mike tried to keep his voice level, but his anger made the words clipped. "I'm not too sure. I've got this gut feeling that you've not been entirely straight with me."

"What do you mean?" Whicker replied hesitantly.

"I've just seen the union rep here. He's got some leaked documents. From British Coal. Apparently they say the mine's going to be closed."

Whicker laughed. He seemed to think it was all a joke – instead of a subject which threatened the livelihood of thousands. Mike's fingers closed around the phone until the knuckles cracked and turned white. "Sorry, Mike. I can't comment on that. Classified information!"

"This isn't a joke, Whicker," he hissed, unable to control his anger any longer.

The sneer in Whicker's voice rose to the surface triumphantly. "Whatever the problem is up there, Mike, I'm sure you're more than well-equipped to deal with it."

"You knew this was going to happen when you sent me up here. All that shit about accident records . . . it was just a smokescreen, wasn't it? You wanted me in the frying pan. You want to see me screw up when the shit hits the fan."

"I'm a bit busy at the moment, Mike. Could you call me when you've got something concrete on the accidents? That's . . ."

Mike slammed the receiver down. He hated Whicker at that moment more violently than he had hated anyone in his life. He hated him enough to kill him.

Chapter Eight

"You've got to get out of there," Hannah said, quietly but firmly, stroking the taut tendons on the back of his neck. The unfamiliar sound of wind rushing through the trees outside and the dull, background murmur of the TV was soothing, but Mike was as rigid and unyielding as stone. He was slumped forward on the sofa with his hands clasped tightly between his legs, his eyes focussed firmly on an inner horizon. She had seen him like this many times before. Anger and frustration surged violently within him, turbulent emotions that he did not have the capacity to release until they exploded out of him in one blinding burst of temper.

"Why don't you give up your job, Mike?" she continued, trying not to say anything which would aggravate his condition. "It's affecting your health. You're always so tense. And you worry too much. Give it up. We don't need your job do we? I earn enough to keep us going while you look for another one."

"We need it." His voice was cold and harsh; a warning.

Hannah chose to ignore it. "Mike you're banging your head against a brick wall. With Whicker there, you can't win. He'll block you every step of the way."

"I can win. I'm not going to let that bastard beat me."

"Don't just think of your job. Look what it's doing to us! We never used to argue like this. It's wearing us down."

His face was blank and she realized with resignation that it was another one of those occasions when she couldn't get through, when he had shut her out as forcefully as if she were a total stranger. Fighting back the sadness, she sighed and sat back to stare vacantly at the TV screen.

54

Mike could barely contain his fury. His foot tapped out a staccato rhythm on the floor and he noticed he had started chewing his thumb knuckle once more, bringing back the callous that had only just healed. It wasn't even just Whicker that was aggravating him. What was happening at the mine was preying on his mind, scrabbling at the back like a rat in a hole, and he couldn't make sense of it. Why were they trying to cover up Jakes' death? What had really happened there? And what had raked the miner's back that morning? All he knew was that there was some secret which the men of Colthorpe were intent on keeping at any cost.

In the hush of the living room, Hannah heard the muffled murmur of a voice seeping through the closed door of Jack's room. She glanced at Mike, but he was lost in thought. If only to escape the stifling atmosphere, she got up to investigate, pausing outside Jack's door. She listened intently, but although she could hear her son's voice, she couldn't make out any words. His tone and the rhythm of his speech, however, gave her the impression he was talking to someone. For one brief moment she thought she heard a reply and a quiver of fear clutched at her sharply. Slowly, she opened the door.

Jack sat contentedly on the floor in the centre of the room, his toys scattered around him. He was alone. He beamed when she entered. "Hello, Mummy."

Her eyes searched the stark room. There was little to see apart from the bed in the corner and a small table adjacent. "Hi," she replied cheerily, her voice echoing slightly. "Having fun?"

"Yes. Playing."

"Did I hear you talking to someone?"

Jack grinned and looked down at his Transformer shyly. "Yes."

"Who were you talking to?"

He considered her question with a curious expression on his face until Hannah thought he had decided not to answer. Then he replied simply, "Elves."

"Elves?" Hannah felt strangely relieved.

"Yes, they came to talk to me."

"What did they say?"

"Lots of things."

55

"Really? Like what?"

"Just things." He had lost interest in the conversation and was concentrating on lining up two robots to fight each other. Hannah shook her head and closed the door; she had had an invisible friend herself when she was younger. Mr Jeebs. Her constant conversations with him during one hot summer had driven her parents to distraction, but then he had faded away almost overnight. Hannah knew it was not a problem unless it was allowed to get out of hand. Many children created a companion, particularly the intelligent, sensitive ones and the loners; it was a sign of a healthy imagination. Yes, she decided, it was a good omen. Elves! She laughed quietly.

Mike brooded until bedtime, but by the time they retired he had managed to shake off most of the black mood which had engulfed him. Hannah fell asleep almost instantly, muttering softly beneath her breath each time she stirred. By the time he leaned over to kiss her goodnight and to feel the warm swell of her belly, Whicker's office machinations were forgotten; only the strange events at the mine disturbed him, rumbling on the edge of his subconscious as he slid into dreams.

He awoke with a start much later. The bedside clock said it was three am. As he fought off shifting memories of a dream and clawed his way back into consciousness, he realized Hannah was thrashing about next to him, speaking so loudly in her sleep that she was almost shouting.

At first the words were lost to him, but then he understood that she was yelling, over and over again, "There's something in the cellar! There's something in the cellar!"

"Calm down," he said gently in her ear. He caressed her upper arm. "You're having a nightmare."

She lowered her voice slightly, her movements becoming less frantic, but there was still an air of panic in her tone. "There's . . . something . . . in the cellar!"

"Hannah!" Mike said louder. "Wake up!" He shook her, not roughly, but just enough to pull her out of her dream.

She stopped thrashing and stirred sleepily. "Whassit?"

"You were having a nightmare."

"Oh." Then she turned her head to one side and slipped easily back to sleep.

Something in the cellar? Mike considered with faint amusement. They didn't even have a cellar. He put his arm around her and within seconds he was asleep too. But his dreams didn't fade so easily; they were just buried deeper. Much deeper.

Chapter Nine

The next day was blustery and overcast, but still dry. There was an oppressive atmosphere, a heaviness in the air, which suggested more storms. Mike prepared for them by unearthing his raincoat from the depths of the wardrobe, even though it was too warm to wear it. He felt strangely tired, a level of exhaustion which normally came from a troubled sleep. He only recollected waking once after Hannah's nightmare, but the muscles in his arms and legs complained and his eyelids were heavy. He managed to muster a few words over the breakfast table and Hannah herself was similarly unresponsive and sluggish; only Jack seemed bright and lively.

Outside the house he inhaled deeply, savouring the clean, fresh air and wallowing in a feeling of instant relief. The walk to work acted as a further pick-me-up and by the time he reached the mine he felt in better humour.

His new-found verve slipped slightly when he saw the night shift pouring out of the lift building, blackened and exhausted but laughing and joking. Their mood changed, too, when they saw him, as he had expected: their faces suddenly sullen, their white eyes shifting.

Shielding his own eyes from the dust which the wind whipped up around the yard, Mike strode forcefully towards his office, feigning ignorance of their stares. Silence followed him, apart from a few muttered curses as the men filed into the shower block.

One of the miners at the rear of the queue stopped so suddenly it caught Mike's attention. He recollected seeing him wandering around the site, a youth in his late teens with an innocent bemused expression that was as out of place at Colthorpe as a troupe of ballet dancers.

The youth hung back until the rest of the men had passed through the door. Then he was alone, staring at Mike. Confident that there was no one else in the vicinity, he surreptitiously motioned to the miner to come over, then walked around the back of the office block to a place where they would not be disturbed.

When the youth arrived, he was glancing from side to side nervously, aware that he was breaking the unwritten rule of Colthorpe, of any work place: violating the boundary between "us and them". Though his face was engrained with coal dust, Mike could tell he was moderately good-looking. His bone structure was more refined than that of Colthorpe's other inhabitants and his large, hazel eyes blinked beneath a shock of brown hair. Thin lips and a straight nose gave him an almost aristocratic look; Mike would have taken him to be a bank clerk or an accountant rather than a miner.

When he spoke his words blurted out in a chaotic jumble before he managed to compose himself. "Mr Leary?" he began again.

"That's right."

"Can I talk to you? Now?" He looked around him again. "There's no one around and it's . . . difficult . . . at other times."

"Go ahead."

"Everyone says the Company's sent you up here to investigate." He looked at Mike as if he were expecting an answer.

"Yes. What's your name?"

"Charlie Robson." He brushed aside the introductions, more concerned with haste than politeness. "So you want to find out about old Alec?"

"That and other things."

He looked so troubled that he seemed about to burst into tears. "I don't like doing this, grassing on me mates. But somebody's got to say something. Otherwise it'll just keep on happening."

"What will?"

"What happened to Alec. I'm scared, Mr Leary." This time

there were definitely tears in the corners of his eyes. He shook his head and dragged a filthy sleeve across his face. "It ain't right what they're doing."

"Who?" Mike was becoming frustrated at trying to decipher the conversation.

"The rest of them. The men. They don't want anyone to find out. Most of them won't even admit it to themselves. They just blank it out of their minds and shut their eyes so they can go about their work everyday like nothin's happened. But Alec . . . he was a good bloke, Mr Leary. He didn't deserve that. His missus didn't deserve it. They reckon she's gone a bit funny in the 'ead." For a second there was a flash of fire in his honest face. "Something's got to be done."

Mike nodded sympathetically, but his curiosity was raging. Here, he felt, was the heart of the matter. And here was his weapon against Whicker. "Start at the beginning, Charlie. Let's go through this carefully. I need to know everything."

The youth shook his head. "I can't – not here, Mr Leary. We'll be seen. The men reckon you're closing the pit down, and if they see me talking to you I'm in the shit."

"Aren't *you* concerned that I might be closing the pit down?"

"I don't care any more, Mr Leary. It might be for the best anyway. I just want to get out. I know I could get a good pay-off if I stick it out to the end, but I'm not going to, I'm just going to get away. I'd rather be on the dole."

"Will you tell me all about it?"

Charlie bit his lip in thought. "I'll take you down there. Underground. You've got to see for yourself what's going on. But it's got to be when no one will see."

"Don't worry, I'll sort it out. Just tell me one thing before you go. Alec Jakes didn't die accidentally, did he? Someone killed him."

It seemed that Charlie wasn't going to answer; he stared at Mike with a score of different emotions racing across his face. Finally he said, "It weren't no *person*, Mr Leary. There's something else down there."

As the furrows crept across Mike's brow, Charlie turned and hurried away around the side of the office block. There was something in his tone which had unnerved Mike. It started a warning ticking in the back of his head.

As he turned to walk to the door of the office block, he glanced fleetingly out across the fields and stopped in his tracks. The surface of one field about half a mile from the mine appeared to be rippling like water – as if it had been hit by an earthquake which had not travelled beyond its boundaries. The short-cropped grass and patches of mud seemed to have no substance, shifting like a movie projected on a wall of smoke. But the bizarre effect – surely an optical illusion – ended almost as soon as he looked at it.

Puzzled, even more disturbed, he walked into his office. He felt he had made some progress, that he had discovered a tunnel through to the heart of the mystery. But what would he find? How bad was it if it had forced the Robson youth to break ranks from the tight-knit work community?

There were many kinds of mysteries, he thought. And this was rapidly becoming a different sort of mystery altogether from the one he had come to Colthorpe to investigate.

Chapter Ten

When the keys on her dirt-clogged, ink-stained portable type-writer jammed for the umpteenth time, Hannah decided enough was enough. It was time for that bane of all working writers – the coffee break. Easing herself out from behind the creaking, utility table that she had transformed into her desk, she breathed deeply, happy to forget the half-finished feature for a while. She had positioned her work station in front of a side window which looked out over the fields. It would give her inspiration, she thought: distil the mind so the words would flow more freely. Instead she found herself staring outside at regular intervals, transfixed by the verdancy; charmed by the way the birds swooped, cawing harshly, into the garden; just daydreaming, enveloped in the pure peace and quiet of it all. It was a long way from London.

A twinge of pain ran along her kidneys and up her back as she rested in the kitchen, waiting for the kettle to boil. She felt a mass of aches that morning; she wondered if she was sickening for the flu. Of course, she had not been sleeping well. Her dreams had been disturbing, waking her several times during the night. Somehow she could never seem to remember them by morning.

Mike had been the epitome of restraint. She woke him each time she stirred, but he always took the time to comfort her. Despite all his problems, he always put her and Jack first.

She made the coffee black and strong, hoping the sudden charge of caffeine would jolt her out of her reveries and focus her mind more clearly on the task at hand. She was working harder now than she had done in months. It was her ultimate aim to make so much money as a freelance that she could convince Mike to give up his job and take time off to find work that he really enjoyed. She was sure that that would be the solution to all their problems; he was always so much happier when they were on holiday. Then he was just like the man she had married.

Glancing absent-mindedly out of the window, she was suddenly entranced by something she was not quite sure if she was seeing or imagining. Clutching the hot mug between her palms, she blinked hard, wondering if it had been caused by a speck in her eye. By the time her eyes opened again it had stopped.

That field, the one where the grass had been cropped close by the cows that grazed there every afternoon, had shifted and shimmered like a road seen through the petrol haze of a hot summer's day. For the briefest moment it looked like water, a huge green lake rippling gently in the breeze that drifted down from the mine. Hannah imagined she could have leapt from the boundary fence and disappeared beneath the turf and scrub, swimming gently into the earth with slow, languorous strokes.

Hannah laughed out loud at how easily she had been taken in by an optical illusion caused by the wind in the grass. But hadn't the ripple effect been too much, too deep, to have been caused by that?

Walking back into the lounge, her thoughts, naturally, turned to Jack. During the last couple of days he had been uncommonly calm and restrained, barely straying from his room where he played for hours with his toys, talking to himself. That was what was worrying her the most. Every time she stood outside his bedroom door he was mumbling quietly to himself, or "talking to the elves", as he called it. She was starting to think it was unnatural and had made a mental note to mention it to Mike if it continued. If she was honest to herself, she would admit that in the daytime quiet of the bungalow it unnerved her to hear the constant mumble of a voice conversing with someone – something – she could not see.

Sipping her coffee, she walked slowly over to Jack's door. There it was again; his voice, quiet, at times almost imperceptible, interspersed with giggles and louder shrieks of joy. He was certainly playing his part well. She strained her ears to pick up any of his comments, slowly catching the rhythm of his words.

"You don't!"

A pause, long enough for a reply.

"Really? Really, truly?"

Another pause.

"Where's that?"

Silence.

"Below where? Tell me, tell me, tell me!"

Silence.

"Can I come? Soon?"

The exchange agitated Hannah in a way she could not comprehend; it sounded too real. As if there was someone there; someone she could not see or hear, but who had inveigled his way into her son's confidences.

Half-expecting to confront a stranger hunched over in the corner of the bedroom, she eased open the door gently, hoping not to disturb Jack mid-flow. But the moment there was enough space for her to peer round the door, she saw Jack, there waiting for her, only a couple of feet away.

"How did you know I was there, honey?" she asked, feeling the nerves tingle along her spine.

"The elves told me."

"They told you I was outside?"

"They said you were coming in so they had to go away."

Hannah laughed, but she was not even convincing herself. There was something about Jack's conviction that was almost eerie. She crouched down next to him, tugging at the bottom of his tee-shirt. "Honey, it's okay to play games, but you've got to know when to stop."

Jack looked at her quizzically, a comical expression that suggested he had no idea what she was talking about.

"What I mean is," she continued haltingly, "it's okay to make-believe as long as you *know* it's make-believe. You know the elves aren't really there, don't you, Jacky?"

This time his expression was one of shock. "They are!"

"No, they're not, Jack. It's make-believe." There was a sharpness in her voice that she regretted, but could not control.

"Mummy . . ."

"Shush! I don't want to hear another word." She wagged a finger in his face and his mouth gulped twice like a fish. She thought he was going to cry and her heart sank, but then he bit on his bottom lip and nodded silently. "Good. That's right. Now, why don't you go out and play . . ."

"I don't want to."

"Go on. It'll do you good." She herded him out of the room before he had time to argue and then closed the bedroom door firmly. As she did, she heard, or thought she did, the faint sound of scratching coming from somewhere beneath the bedroom floor.

She ignored it, blanking it out of her mind completely. She returned to her desk, but for the rest of that day the words would not come.

Chapter Eleven

"Give me a pint of that . . . what do you call that local ale?"

"Pedigree."

"Yeah, that. That'll do." Mike leaned on the end of the bar at the Colthorpe Arms and surreptitiously surveyed the room. The pub on the corner of the village crossroads was well off the beaten track for anyone searching for a sophisticated night's drinking, but it provided everything the thirsty mining community could want. Furnishings were sparse, perfunctory. Benches lined the wall, the soft seating material worn and split, and the stools were the squat, tough type with the plastic seat that was handy in a fight. The tables were polished, but rickety and carved with the names of a generation of drinkers. The floor was mere linoleum, dirty yellow and scuffed. A pub for people dedicated to the art of drinking.

Although it had only just opened for the evening, there were already a handful of miners within. Three of them played darts with an archer's dedication. The rest gathered in twos and threes around the fruit machine, at the bar or in the corner near the toilet.

"Busy tonight," Mike said to the ruddy-faced barman, his tattoos rippling as he cleaned the glasses with muscle-flexing gusto.

He shrugged. "Same as usual. I always get a few in at this time. They get a couple of beers in before they go on the night shift. T'others like to have a pint before they go home to the missus."

Mike nodded.

"Who're you then?" The barman pulled up a stool on the other side of the bar. Although he was in his fifties, he had a carefully sculptured quiff that would have done Elvis proud.

"Mike Leary. British Coal sent me up . . ."

"Oh yeah, I know. The lads mentioned you."

"All bad, I hope."

"You don't get much worse. You're up here to close down the pit then?"

Mike shook his head wearily. "I can see me saying this until I'm blue in the face. It's just not true. I know as much about pit closures as the next man."

"Folk are a bit worried . . ."

"They're bound to be worried. I'd be worried. But I don't know anything. There's no point in me lying about it. The truth is that I was sent up here to look into the accident record and to do a report on the death of a miner underground. Nothing more, nothing less."

"Oh, that. That was a rum do."

Mike drained a good quarter of his glass; his hard day had not only made him thirsty, it had also made him desire the simple joys of getting drunk. With the stress and pressure building up around him it was a much-needed release. "Did you know him?"

The barman shook his head. "Who, Alec? Oh, aye, he liked a drink. Not too much, just a social pint."

"Was he popular?"

"Seemed to be. They talked about him a lot in here, after it happened. In mourning, you know. He was a good bloke. Used to come in here regular as clockwork on a Friday night. No one seemed to know how it happened. They just kept saying it were an accident." He looked at Mike slyly. "What did happen?"

"An accident," Mike replied, ignoring the request for enlightenment. He felt annoyance that he probably knew as much as the barman. "It was pretty horrible. Enough to give people nightmares."

"Don't mention nightmares around here."

"What do you mean?"

"Don't tell me you haven't heard. Everyone's talking about it! When I went down to Mrs Mossop's shop there must have

67

been half a dozen of them in there having a good chinwag about it."

"About what?"

"Nightmares."

Mike shook his head. "You've lost me."

"Listen up, then. It started a couple of weeks ago. Pat, was it? Yes, Pat Wilson, he runs the post office, came in here one night and started talking about this dream he had. Not once, you know, but six or seven bloody times. I remember telling him he'd gone off his rocker. Not natural, you know."

"What was the dream?" Mike asked, suddenly intrigued.

"Hang on, I'm getting there." He paused with the drama and timing of a veteran storyteller. "He reckoned he kept waking up in the early hours terrified there was something, a giant rat or something, digging its way up into his house. He always woke up just as it was coming through the floorboards. Every few nights, he'd get it the same – a big bloody rat."

Mike laughed, although the image had started to niggle at the back of his mind, inciting other thoughts, other memories.

"Sounds funny, don't it? But it didn't stop there. When he mentioned it to Mrs Carter she told him she'd been having exactly the same dream. Only she said it wasn't a big rat, it was a mole."

"A mole. Right."

"I'm just telling you how it was told to me." He walked to the other end of the bar to pull six pints for the increasingly raucous crowd near the toilets. Their faces were flushed with the first stages of inebriation and their braying laughter was growing louder and louder.

When he returned, Mike ordered another pint and then said, "So two people with a similar dream. I suppose that's quite unusual."

"Not two, pal. More. Probably about seven or eight. A couple of kids. Educated folk . . . one of the local teachers and a solicitor. A few women."

"Exactly the same dream?"

"Well, not exactly," the barman added haltingly as if this admission would suddenly dispel the wonder of the story. "But almost the same. They're all dreaming about something

68

under their house. Animals, men, summat that digs its way up and into their bedroom. Like a bleedin' Hammer Horror, ain't it?" He smiled, happy that Mike was still intrigued by the tale he had woven. "So what do you think of that?"

Mike shrugged. "Bizarre. Just collective paranoia, I suppose."

The landlord leaned heavily on the bar, an amusing expression of bafflement on his face. "You what?"

"Well, it's obvious they're having these nightmares because they're worried about the pit closing and the effect it will have on the village." The barman did not look convinced by Mike's amateur psychology. "It's just been lurking in their subconscious and it comes out when they're asleep."

The barman grunted and looked at Mike as if he was an idiot. "I don't see how that can explain them all having the same dream."

Then Mike remembered Hannah's dream from a few nights ago. What did she say again? *"There's something in the cellar"*? The memory made him feel uneasy; that was something he could not explain. Hannah had no emotional investment in Colthorpe, so it was unlikely she would be so concerned about the pit's closure that it would affect her sleep.

"What's the problem?" the barman asked as he pulled Mike another pint.

"Nothing. Well . . . I think my wife might have experienced something similar."

"Hah!" the barman laughed triumphantly. "See, you can't bloody explain everything."

"There must be a logical explanation."

"There might be. There might not. Maybe it all means summat."

"What, like precognition? Seeing the future? You think some bloody big mole's going to dig its way out of the earth and eat Mrs Carter?"

"I wish something would. She don't half go on."

They laughed together at the absurdity of the image. Dreams of rats and moles: Kenneth Graham had a lot to answer for.

As the evening drew on, the barman became busier and Mike was left to his own thoughts, drifting through the alcohol haze between a mild reflection on the mystery of Jakes' death and curious observation of the others around him. The darts match continued unabated, though it was now watched by a growing crowd. More women had entered the pub as the night drew on and they seemed to be matching the men in both drinking and raucousness. The group near the toilets had grown even more drunk. In between bouts of laughter, they were trying to entice three young women who sat in the corner, chatting quietly. The women smiled mockingly each time one of the men beckoned.

"Come on, love," said one miner. His blonde hair was cropped close to his skull, contrasting sharply with the redness of his face. "You never know, you might like it."

"Do I look daft?" a brunette with overly red lips replied tartly.

"I can't tell from over here. Come a bit closer so I can get a better look."

"A better fuck, more like," his friend said, howling with laughter.

The blonde crop told him to be quiet and then turned back to the women, his eyes sly and shifting above an insincere smile. "Don't listen to him. I just want us to be friends."

"Oh yeah," the brunette replied, bored by words she heard every week just before closing time. "With friends like you, I wouldn't need enemies, would I?"

"Don't be like that, love. I'll buy you a drink."

"I don't come that cheap, you know."

"How cheap are you then?" blonde crop said, losing interest as his advances failed. "Twenty quid?"

"Fuck off," the brunette replied masterfully, before huddling close with her friends.

The blonde crop, who was the most inebriated of the group, stared at them, blinking heavily, a look of dark annoyance on his face. Finally he shrugged and staggered to his feet for another drink. For one second his eyes caught Mike's, then the expression slowly changed to one of recognition.

"Hey, lads," he said loudly. "That management bastard is here."

Mike froze, his drunkenness sloughing off at the sudden

onset of potential danger. He avoided the swaying miner's gaze, but the large muscular man was already sizing up for a confrontation.

"Come to close our pit, have you?" he sneered as he moved slowly along the bar towards Mike. "Come to put us out of bloody work?"

"I don't want any trouble here, Ray," the barman snapped. "Go back to your seat."

The miner whirled, his eyes blazing. "Shut up! It's not *your* fucking job on the line!" Then he turned back to Mike. "Come on, then. Be a man. Tell me to my face you're going to send me to the dole queue."

"Listen to him." Mike jabbed a thumb at the barman, his anger muffling the knowledge that in any fight he would be beaten to a pulp. In the background he could see the brunette dash worriedly over to the group near the dartboard to plead with one of the spectators. "Go back to your seat and I won't call the police," Mike continued. "And I won't get you the sack tomorrow."

The moment the words left his lips he realized it had been the wrong thing to say. The miner lurched forwards in fury, his fists bunching automatically. Mike almost fell off his stool as he avoided the blow that had been levelled at him, but before he had time to retaliate or flee, the miner had been grabbed by another burly man from the darts crowd. The situation surged out of control immediately. Blonde crop swung his fist at Mike's rescuer, a bearded man with a huge, wobbling beer belly, catching him full in the face. Mike watched in horror as the nose exploded beneath the ham-like fists, showering blood over his stretched white tee-shirt.

The bearded man howled in agony, but as he raised his head, scarlet streaming down his face, there were hate and vengeance in his eyes. His first punch caught the snarling blonde miner in the right eye. His head snapped back, and as he righted himself another blow powered into his jaw.

Mike stepped back to the periphery of the scene as the brawl continued in earnest. He was amazed, and horrified, by the sheer savagery of the fight. Within moments their fists and faces were sheets of red. Blows rained down like pistons, pounding, turning flesh and gristle to pulp. "They're going to

71

kill each other," he thought, but he could not take his eyes off the violent episode, fascinated by the bestial rage and how quickly the humanity had been stripped from the two protagonists.

After what seemed like an hour, but was probably only five minutes, the rest of the men in the pub moved in and dragged the fighters apart. It was obvious to Mike that they would need hospital treatment; they could hardly stand.

As they were hauled outside, Mike returned to the bar to finish his pint, carefully avoiding the puddle of blood that was slowly congealing on the floor. "I didn't think much of the floorshow," he said icily to the barman.

"I don't believe those bloody idiots," he said. "What the fucking hell's come over them?"

"What do you mean?"

"That's about the fourth fight we've had in here in the last month. We never used to have any trouble at all. They were always high-spirited, but they never used to let it get out of hand. Now they're acting like . . . bloody animals. Animals!"

Mike finished his drink and left quickly, before he tempted another confrontation. There was an icy chill in the late September night. It was colder than London; autumn had already arrived, loosing summer's hold on the land and heralding bleaker times. Though drunk, Mike was amazed that he could see the stars glittering in the windswept, black sky. There were hundreds of them, thousands, random pinpricks of light scattered across the heavens. In the city they were forever obscured by the haze of the street lights. Just staring at them ignited a sense of wonder he had not felt since he was a child.

There was something about the night and its peacefulness, rarely disturbed by the rumble of traffic or the distant roar of a plane, that served to exacerbate his anger at how his work was denying him a similar peace in his own life. When he thought of the wearisome days he spent week-in, week-out at the office, ignoring Whicker's jibes, doing his best but never quite doing well enough in Whicker's eyes, it brought the frustration within him to such a boiling point that he felt a hot tear well up in the corner of his eye.

By the time he reached the bungalow his fury was like a

storm, raging from pillar to post without direction or intent. Hannah was making herself a milky drink in the kitchen when he arrived, but although she smiled at him he brushed past her coldly and went straight to the lounge.

"Mike, what's the matter?" she asked, concern clear on her face.

"Nothing," he snapped.

She sat down on the sofa next to him and attempted to caress his neck, but he flinched at her touch. Hurt, she slowly withdrew her hand. She wanted to ask again what the problem was, but deep down she knew; it was the same as it always was.

"What the hell am I doing here?" he said loudly. "Whicker's making me waste my life."

"Keep your voice down, Mike. You'll wake Jack."

He turned on her, his face blazing. "What about me?" he hissed. "Think about me for a change!"

She knew he would not listen to reason in this mood and the alcohol in him only made the matter worse. There was something within that was eating away at him, something that wouldn't die, something that slept and then roused hungrily whenever she thought their problems had been overcome. He was staring at her coldly and she was distressed to see there was no love in his eyes.

Fighting back the tears of despair, she wanted to plead with him, to say, "Michael, fight this thing. Kill it quickly, because for Christ's sake it's killing us. I can't take much more."

But she didn't even say that, because she knew that if she so much as opened her mouth he would rant and rage like a man possessed until he verbally battered her into submission with his fury and sent her to bed sobbing.

So she turned and left him to cope with his anger alone. In the loneliness of the bed, she lay on her back and thought about the future, hoping and praying, but not seeing an end to the dark tunnel.

Chapter Twelve

Hannah was still sleeping when Mike arose. Her night had been disturbed more than usual by violent dreams and although the alcohol had caused him to sleep heavily, Mike had woken several times to calm her. He dressed quickly in the twilight of the bedroom and left the house before she stirred.

It was seven am and the razor chill of the pale morning quickly dispelled his lingering hangover. But there was little it could do to eradicate the guilt he felt. He looked back on the previous night like he was watching the actions of a different person. Why did he lose his temper so suddenly? Why did he always turn it on the things he cherished the most instead of directing it at the real root of the problem? Hannah coped well under the circumstances, but it was wearing her down. He could see that plainly, yet he was impotent to do anything about it.

He had decided to take the luxury of going into work late. He needed to be alone with his thoughts and in London an early morning walk always helped, although he had to rise at five am to beat the traffic and the joggers. He wandered down to Colthorpe village, a tiny collection of houses nestling close around little more than a general goods store, a sub-post office and the Colthorpe Arms pub. It was an old place. Some of the houses dated back to before the Industrial Revolution. The effects of the coal boom were evident in the row of tiny terraced homes which had housed the mining families in the days when the industry was a grim, harrowing affair. In recent times, attempts had been made to modernize and brighten them. Colourful doors and window boxes drew the attention away from their cramped design, and well-tended gardens added a flourish of colour at the rear. Yet an atmosphere of toil and suffering still hovered around them.

Mike stood at the crossroads and looked along each street, past the larger, opulent houses on the outskirts, over to the rolling fields that surrounded Colthorpe like a sea of green. A milk float trundled past, the bottles and crates rattling loudly in the still morning. Behind the wheel the milkman smiled cheerily and nodded. There was no one else around to disturb the day.

Pulling his coat tightly around him, Mike strode out towards the fields. He wanted to lose himself in them, to hide in acres of verdant peace and forget his job and all the strains and pressures it placed on the rest of his life. He could lie in the grass and pull the turf over his body. It would be a grand escape.

As he reached the end of the street his attention focused on the last house, a rundown cottage separated from the nearest home by almost two hundred yards. Although small – only two-up two-down – he was surprised an enterprising businessman had not converted it into a bijou residence for some upwardly mobile young couple who commuted to work in the city. On closer inspection, he realized it would have cost a small fortune to make it habitable.

It had obviously been deserted for years. The windows were broken – target practice for school children – and the frames rotten, while the peeling brown front door sagged inward on a shattered hinge. The tiny front garden was waist-high with dry, yellow grass and willow herb, and untended ivy trailed up over the windows and guttering to the badly-holed roof where it turned back and flapped in the breeze. Mike leaned on the splintered gate post next to the disintegrated fence and looked over the decaying building, surveying its crumbling, orange brick, salted with age and pitted by the elements.

He paused for a moment, listening to the soft moan of the wind as it blew in the rafters: a peaceful, though mournful, sound. Then, as he turned to move down the road, he heard another noise.

There was a scrabbling sound, soft, almost inaudible, emanating from somewhere within. It was a curious noise, intriguingly difficult to define. Mike looked around to ensure no one was observing his trespass, then stepped nimbly over the remains of the fence. The front door offered little resistance to his shoulder, its one remaining hinge squealing in protest as it juddered open. His nose wrinkled at the smell as soon as he stepped over the threshold. The clammy atmosphere was filled with the odour of decay and decomposition – and something else, the stale redolence of long-sealed air suddenly released. It was carried on a cold breeze that brought forth memories of the mine's winding tunnels far underground.

The large front room was bare. The floor was thick with dust and crinkled brown leaves piled high in the corners where they had blown through the broken windows. The remnants of an ancient fire lay in the grate, but there was nothing else to signify anyone had occupied the place for years.

The scrabbling noise was louder now, backed by a muffled high-pitched sound, rising and falling in the rear room which was sealed by a sturdy door. Cautiously he moved towards it and listened. The sound grew quieter. Whatever was behind the door knew he was there.

There was a voice in the back of his head saying, "Don't do it, don't do it, *don't do it*." He wilfully disregarded it, almost daring the consequences to be bad.

His hand closed around the metal latch and he tugged.

In the half-light that filtered through the dusty front windows, Mike stared at hundreds of tiny pin-pricks of light. Then a few of them blinked.

The first rat moved forward.

Mike stumbled backwards in shock as the high-pitched sound became squeals of delight and freedom. He hit the floor as a dead weight. There was only time to raise his hands in futile protection and then the rats were on him, swarming thickly to the half-open front door.

He yelled out loud, rolled desperately from side to side, but there were too many to avoid. They swarmed straight over him, tiny claws scratching his arms and face. He felt feet and fur in his mouth, on his eyes, his nose, hundreds of stinking, lithe, furry bodies surging over his body on their way to the light, a tidal wave of scurrying creatures that threatened to drown him. He could not breathe. He could not move. He wanted to scream and vomit at the same time. And it seemed to be going on forever. Wet fur slithered across his face, tails lashed his skin.

Then it was over.

The final pattering of feet disappeared past his head and out of the door. When the last one had gone, he lay on his back for two more minutes, not daring to open his eyes, amazed that he hadn't been bitten or attacked. He was shaking uncontrollably from head to foot. The experience had been nauseating, horrifying. He couldn't help but imagine what it would have been like if it had happened in the confines of a tunnel far underground; it would have been too much for his mind to bear. The feeling of revulsion threatened to overwhelm him, but he managed to fight it.

Weill's Disease. Hepatitis. A catalogue of diseases flashed through his mind. Frantically, he checked his body. Although he ached from a myriad tiny scratches, the skin did not seem to have been broken. Even so, he would not delay a medical check-up.

His breathing, and his composure, slowly returned to normal. The experience had been bizarre, unnatural. Why had there been so many rats? And how had they come to be shut in the back room? They could not have been there for long. If they had been starving, they would have torn him to shreds as soon as he opened the door. Their number and their single-minded purpose reminded him of the first night he had arrived in Colthorpe when the seemingly unending stream of rats emerged from the hole in the roadside.

Still trembling, he looked through the open door into the kitchen. It was as black as night within. The rear windows had been boarded up, but as his eyes adjusted to the dark, he made out a blacker shape in the centre of the floor. On closer inspection he saw it was a huge hole. The edges were jagged and crumbling and there was the smell of fresh earth, signifying a recent cave-in.

Mike inched carefully around the edge of the kitchen, fearing a further earthfall. Finally he could grip on to the filthy, chipped porcelain sink and rip the boards away from the windows. Reassuring light streamed in. Nervously, he leaned precariously over the lip and peered into the depths of the hole.

He had expected to see a short drop to a cellar, or at least an opening into a sewer which would have allowed the rats access to the room. Instead the floor had collapsed into what looked like a tunnel.

With great care, he lay on his stomach and edged forward to the rim. Had the rats at the roadside escaped from a similar tunnel? If that was the case, the network would stretch for miles.

As he lay, half over the edge, he suddenly choked on a foul blast of air. Coughing and spluttering, Mike quickly pulled himself back from the brink. The stench was rich, florid, like decomposing meat mingled with over-ripe fruit; it was the smell of something rotting, borne along on the channels of air which moved through the underground corridors.

Clutching his handkerchief to his face, he ventured over the lip again. This time he could *hear* something, deep within the bowels of the tunnel network. It was distant, but growing closer. *Scratching*! The same sound he had heard before beneath the colliery buildings. He knew then that it was not made by rats.

His heart began to beat faster and his breath clutched in his throat as he listened intently to the digging drawing closer.

Suddenly it stopped. Mike had the impression that whatever was down there had broken through into a clear tunnel. In the stark silence of the deserted cottage, other sounds became clear; scraping noises, like a man dragging himself slowly but surely along a tunnel. And was that breathing he could hear? Harsh, laboured breathing?

Unexpectedly Mike was filled with a feeling of dread. His instincts long-suppressed, fired into life; he did not want to confront whatever was moving along the tunnel towards the hole. Frighteningly, he found he could not move. He was rigid on the floor, his fingers hooked over the edge, digging into the soft earth beneath the broken tiles. He could hear it clearly. It was close, very close.

Just as his eyes caught the first glimpse of movement at the foot of the shaft, he was freed from his inactivity. He leapt to his feet and bolted out of the door before he could distinguish the shape in the tunnel.

The sunlight and fresh air was comforting and he gulped huge draughts into his lungs as he ran as fast as he could along the road. He rested only when he had reached the crossroads.

He had never been so scared in his life; and even there, in the daylight, that unexplained fear did not seem ridiculous. There was no logical reason for his feeling, but a primal warning had been triggered deep within him. In that small, childlike element at the core of everyone, he could not escape the impression that he had had a close brush with the unknown.

He stood at the crossroads staring towards the deserted cottage for ten minutes. Nothing emerged. Eventually he turned and walked up the road to the mine, trying to dismiss the first glimmer in his mind that whatever was happening at Colthorpe was beyond his comprehension.

Hannah had not worked all morning. The only thing on her mind was Mike, and the cold, loveless expression on his face the previous evening. That look was haunting her; when she closed her eyes, when she looked in the mirror, when she daydreamed at the window.

She lay on the sofa, softly stroking her swollen belly, as the fingers of the clock passed midday, suddenly aware that tears of sadness and frustration were running down her cheeks. She had spent the past few years hoping the problem at the heart of their marriage would magically disappear, but it was obvious to her then that, not only was it there to stay, it was quickly getting worse. She was convinced that if Mike gave up his job he would return to normal. It was that constant, bitter battle – which he could never win – that had changed him. Somehow the despair brought on by the realization that his dreams within the company would never be achieved, had generated something bad inside him. Instead of seeking another route to what he wanted, he continued to act like some dumb animal, battering his head against a brick wall until he was bloody. It had now become such a conditioned response to the problems that faced him that he could not see another option.

If only she knew what to do.

The constant bursts of scratching from somewhere beneath the house did not help her thought processes. It had been going on all morning: a short burst followed by half an hour of silence, and then a renewed outbreak. She was sure it was not caused by rats. It certainly didn't sound like rats, unless they nurtured very strange rodents in the Midlands. She still clung on to the idea that it was merely vibrations travelling through the ground from the digging going on beneath them, but Mike had already dismissed that, and if she was honest she had to admit to herself it was a pretty feeble explanation.

It had already started to irritate her. With each new period of activity she found her stress level rising and she would angrily pace the rooms to locate the exact spot where it originated. It always ceased before she found it. If it was going to continue every day in the same manner she would ask Mike if they could move somewhere else, even if it meant him driving in to work each day.

That wasn't the only thing that was concerning her. There was also Jack. He was spending more and more time in his bedroom, even when the sun was shining and the fields looked so inviting she wanted to run and tumble in them herself. She would cajole and tease him; she would beg with him. She would even physically lead him outside, but a few minutes later she would find him sitting glumly on the doorstep and she would relent and allow him back inside. Then he would skip happily back into his bedroom and within minutes she would hear the dull murmur of his voice as he struck up another conversation with his imaginary friends. She wished Mike didn't have so much on his mind; she was sure he would know what to do.

After the latest bout of scratching, which again had stopped when she was agonizingly close to pinpointing it, she found herself outside Jack's room. The familiar sound of his voice echoed monotonously through the door, running through another unnervingly one-sided chat. She could never stop herself from eavesdropping; she was fascinated by everything her son did and said. But this time his voice sounded livelier, more excited.

"When are you coming?" he shrieked, his voice trailing off into a series of giggles. His laughter raised Hannah's spirits.

There was a pause, followed by, "Will you meet my Mummy and Daddy?"

Another pause.

"Will you come today?"

Pause.

"Will you come tomorrow?"

Pause.

"When are you coming?

Pause.

"Tell me!"

Pause.

"Tell me!"

Pause.

"Tell me!"

"*Soon*."

She heard it. A voice. Rasping. Harsh.

A cold hand clutched at her heart. Her body was rigid, unmoving. *There was someone in the room with him.*

With a shriek, she swung open the door. She expected to see some pervert, hands grasping hungrily for her son. She expected to see a dirty old man in a stained brown mac. She expected to see the bogeyman.

Nothing.

She looked to the left, to the right, all around the room. She ran to the window, her heart beating madly. Frantically she scanned the garden.

Nothing.

Just Jack, sitting in the centre of the room with his toys scattered around him, staring at her in astonishment.

"Who was in here, Jack?" she said sternly, her voice starting to break with the panic. "*Jack*! Answer me."

"I was playing."

"Who was *in* here?" Her voice rose sharply. Jack gaped like a goldfish in reply.

Eventually he said, quietly, "I was just talking to the elves, Mummy."

Hannah stormed into the lounge, her initial fear mutating into frustration and doubt. Had she really heard a voice? Or had it been in her mind, filling in the gaps in Jack's imaginary conversation? No, she hadn't imagined it. She hadn't.

81

Had she?

The stress was becoming too much for her. She wanted to scream and shout and yell. Instead she meekly wandered into the kitchen, the tears welling up in her eyes. Blankly, she put the kettle on. She *had* heard a voice, she repeated over and over again, as if it were a mantra that would dispel all her worries. A horrible voice. Croaking. Somehow evil. But there was certainly no one in the room, so what did that mean? Her mug slipped from her fingers and shattered on the floor. It was the final straw that summoned the tears in force.

She crawled into a corner where she sat hugging her knees, sobbing and sobbing till her eyes stung, wishing she was a million miles away.

Chapter Thirteen

For the rest of the day, Mike could not stop his thoughts drifting back to what had happened in the cottage that morning. The metallic taste of fear in his mouth would not go away; a feeling made somehow more powerful by the fact that he had no idea what had scared him.

Whenever he closed his eyes to rest them, he was back in that dark kitchen with the rats. He could smell the foul odour drifting up from the hole as strongly as if he was still there. And he could still hear something shuffling along in the darkness beneath him. His mind kept asking what it was down there in the tunnel. He was unable even to contemplate the answer.

The day had been an annoying repetition of so many others. He had half-heartedly continued his interviews with more of Alec Jakes' co-workers, but they had given him no insight. It had merely served to reinforce his belief that if he was to make any progress it would only come from an under-cover investigation, or tips from insiders like the Robson youth. A brief swell of relief had come over him when he had discovered a scrawled, unsigned note left for him in a sealed envelope at reception. It indicated that Charlie was prepared to reveal his secrets the following day. "TRAVEL DOWN WITH THE AFTERNOON SHIFT TOMORROW", it said in faltering, blocked writing. "I WILL WAIT FOR YOU AT THE FOOT OF THE SHAFT."

He screwed it up and flicked it into the waste paper bin, trying to damp down his feelings of success at a possible breakthrough. Before he had the chance to reflect on what he hoped to achieve, a knock came at the door and Bulmer walked in with a face like thunder.

"What's the matter, Tom?" Mike asked.

"Bloody unions," he fumed. "Bloody unions! We've got enough problems up here at the moment. Why are they doing it?"

"Doing what?"

"I've just had a meeting with Packard. He reckons they'll all be out next week. They're playing right into the company's hands!"

"You've got to expect them to fight, Tom. It is their livelihood."

"Oh, right. Well, tell me why they didn't fight back in '85 when Scargill told them this pit would be closed within ten years. Tell me why they all scabbed and left the NUM. Bloody fools! If they'd had a bit of solidarity, then they wouldn't be reduced to making futile gestures now."

Mike laughed. "You're management now, Tom. You're not supposed to be talking like that."

"I might be management now," he replied, letting the anger slip from his face for a second, "but it doesn't mean I've gone stupid. I could've told them how it would all turn out. Old Scargill might be a bit of a leftie, but everything he said has come true. It's too late for them to fight now – they haven't got the power. They're just prolonging the agony and making things bloody difficult from me. I just want a nice payoff that'll see me through to retirement."

"You'll still get it."

"Not without a bloody fight with Packard and his boys." He grunted. "Sorry for running off at the mouth. I had to get it off my chest. Fancy a quick pint before you head off home?"

Mike shook his head. "Thanks, but I had too much last night. I'd better get back to Hannah. Make up for being such an obnoxious, drunken boor."

"Get down on your knees and grovel," Bulmer said despondently. "See you tomorrow, lad."

Two hours later, Mike was still sitting behind his desk staring blankly at the far wall. The sun had slowly set, turning the sky behind him to red, then bruised purple, then black. He had risen once, to switch on the office light, and then he had morosely returned to his seat. During that time he had thought of a thousand things to say to Hannah, but no words seemed to capture the depth of his emotions: his fear that things were falling apart beyond his sphere of control.

Doth Job open his mouth in vain? he thought. He could see it going the way of so many other apologies. A few mumbled words, a strained atmosphere until bedtime, with frantic, apologetic love-making the last rites over a problem buried deep: a problem still alive and kicking. He could not do that again. It would all come back to haunt him.

In two hours he had not advanced at all, and with each passing moment the timer on his anger clicked a little closer to zero. Frustration was a powerful fuel. He knew he couldn't put it off any longer; he had to grasp the nettle. Be honest, speak his mind – if only he could.

If only he could.

He stood up with determination, knowing that if he paused he would quickly slide back into vacillation. In the distance, a lorry honked jarringly, disturbing the peace of the evening. When the noise faded away, Mike became aware of a strange sound, a trilling or faint ringing like tinnitus, that hung in the air, a ghost of the lorry's horn. It was almost subsonic and he wondered if it had been there before and he had not noticed it.

He shrugged it off, focusing once more on the task that lay ahead of him. Hannah would be cooking the evening meal now. They would eat and then she would put Jack to bed. Then they could talk. That was the best time. Not straight away. Later.

His coat hung from the back of the door. Hannah had chosen it for him; he was a failure when it came to fashion. He reached out to take it down and his hand jerked involuntarily. There was an unusual electrical charge in the room that made his fingertips tingle and the hairs on the back of his neck stand erect. He grasped the door handle and felt another sharp jolt of static.

The trilling grew slightly louder. There was the steely taste of ozone on his tongue. Curiously, he looked around the room, wondering if it was the result of bizarre atmospheric conditions that presaged a violent electrical storm. It was then that he noticed the floor.

It seemed to be swelling slightly, an odd optical illusion that made it appear to bulge in the centre of the room.

Only it was no illusion. He squinted, rubbing his tired eyes, with little effect. The concrete floor continued to swell upwards as if it were made of elastic. As he watched, it took on a strange, milky translucence, a pale light glowing through it from beneath.

Mike took a step forward, unable to believe his eyes, only to feel the floor spring up beneath his foot. Then the swelling reversed itself, sucking down into a hollow, before rising back up.

Horrified, Mike stepped back tight against the wall, clutching onto the door handle for support. Static crackled once more. The floor seemed to be breathing. In, out. In, out. Swelling up and down with unbelievable plasticity.

Then the faces appeared.

They surged up suddenly from beneath, pressing upward with their hands on each side of their head, pushing, pushing, trying to break through. Mike could see their features, distorted horribly. There seemed to be only a thin balloon-like layer of rubber between them instead of the unyielding concrete floor. Their mouths gaped in silent screams, of anger or agony he knew not, and their skin was stretched tight as they strained against the resilient floor. There were four of them – five – six – more and more each moment, and they all appeared desperate to reach him, fingers opening and closing in frustration beneath the membrane that looked in danger of snapping at any moment.

Mesmerized, like a mouse before a snake, Mike could not take his eyes from the sight, the fear spiralling within him. He could sense waves of black emotion swamping up from beneath his feet; hatred, despair, lust, jealousy – and anger, raging, blazing anger. They wanted him, he knew that. They wanted to break through, to clutch at his limbs with their bony white hands and drag him back down to the cold dark with them.

In, out, the floor swelled. In, out. Breaking point was near. Mike could take no more. When he thought he would finally crack under the pressure of standing on the edge, looking into the abyss of something that had no part in a rational, sane world, he suddenly snatched at the door handle and flung himself out into the corridor. The door slammed behind him violently, as if angry hands had vented their fury on it.

The whole experience had lasted only two minutes. He rested outside the office block wondering if he were going mad, if the stress of his job and the problems in his marriage were pushing him over the edge. But when he shut his eyes and massaged his temple, all he could see were those hideous faces, screaming for him.

And then, for the second time in one day, he ran wildly, like a frightened child on a dark night with visions of the unknown snapping at his heels. He did not care that he was a grown man. At that moment he was ten years old again and the world was a very frightening place to be.

Chapter Fourteen

In the cold, dim light of another grey morning, Mike gripped Hannah's hand and thought about love, hope and the warm security of the family. There was something of desperation in that grip, Hannah thought, and she was right. It was his final retreat: the only place left to go for someone who had looked life squarely in the face and realized it had descended into chaos.

He had not told Hannah anything of what he had seen in the office, even though she questioned him forcefully in the instinctive knowledge that something was preying on his mind. When he stepped through the door, slick with sweat from his headlong run, she was disturbed to see how pale and withdrawn he was. Later she watched, concerned, as he drifted off into reveries throughout the evening, turbulent emotions occasionally playing on his face.

Hannah could not guess what was troubling him. At first she thought it was Whicker, or someone at the office, but when she raised that idea, Mike dismissed it in the manner of someone whose work was the most insignificant thing in his life. It was something more. Something deeper.

She was more surprised when he spent the night with his arms wrapped around her, as he had when they had first started sleeping together. It was his turn for a disturbed night; his dreams were agonizing and on more than one occasion he cried out, although he did not wake. She held him tightly in return, tenderly stroking his head until the nightmares subsided. And then, that morning, he rose early and asked her to go for a walk with him. It was an unusual request. He always preferred to be alone in the early hours and she felt honoured, though slightly disturbed, that he wanted her at his side.

He seemed to be reaching out for some kind of support. She guessed that for some reason he did not want to be alone. Perhaps it was because he knew his mind would repeatedly stray back to his problem, whatever it was, forcing him to dwell upon it, turn it over and over in his head. God, she thought, he even held her hand when they stepped out of the bungalow into the crisp morning.

Mike led her down towards the village, but when they reached the crossroads he deliberately steered her away from the road that passed the deserted cottage. They continued straight ahead, walking for ten minutes in total silence. All round them was a cacophany of birds, an early morning babble of confused song, and when they breathed deeply they took in the soft aroma of wet grass, hedgerow and trees.

With the last house far behind them, Hannah squeezed Mike's hand tightly and said quietly, "Are you going to tell me?"

He stirred as if he had been dreaming, his eyes flickering back to the here and now. "Tell you what?"

"What's eating you. I've been around you long enough to know when you're bottling things up."

When he turned to look at her, his eyes were weary and there was a curious, almost baffled, expression on his face. "It's nothing."

"You shouldn't bury things inside you, Mike. It's not healthy. Do you remember when we were at university, just after we met? You suddenly wondered why I was being offhand with you, refusing to see you, talk to you." He nodded. "If you hadn't forced me to sit down and talk it through, you'd never have found out your ex-girlfriend had been spreading poisonous rumours to try to split us up. But you convinced me I should put my pride to one side. And if you hadn't we probably wouldn't be here today."

"I know what you're saying, Hannah – but it's nothing, really. Just the job and everything getting on top of me. I'll get over it soon."

She knew he was lying, but there was nothing else she could do; he would come round in his own time.

As she inhaled the clean, fresh air, she realized they had lost sight of Colthorpe behind them. It stirred faint worries about Jack, who would soon be waking, and she wanted to be back at the bungalow before he discovered they had gone. Mike, however, seemed as if he could walk for miles. His pace was relentless, his eyes firmly focused on the road ahead, oblivious to the scenery or the post-dawn peace.

But before she could ask him to turn back, he stopped sharply in his tracks, peering into a field to their left. "Do you see that?" he said.

"What?"

"There. A girl."

Following the line of his arm, Hannah located the frail form of a young woman clambering awkwardly over a fence, clutching a bundle to her chest with her right arm. "I suppose she's making the most of the morning too."

"Maybe." Mike was pleased to have something to occupy his mind. He leaned against the mildewed wood of a gate and watched her slow progress across the field, struggling with her burden as she tripped over sods and furrows, avoiding clumps of thistles but keeping her head well down, her chin occasionally brushing her bundle. Briefly she raised her face into the morning sun, revealing cheeks and eyes that were as stinging pink as ham, visible even at half a field's distance.

"She's crying," Mike said. "I wonder why?"

"Boyfriend troubles, I expect," Hannah replied, tugging gently at his arm. She wanted to go back. Thoughts of strange voices had entered her mind and she had become acutely aware of Jack's isolation.

"I don't think so. Look at the way she's walking. She's distraught."

"Come on Mike. I want to get back to Jack. We shouldn't leave him alone for too long." She had considered telling him about the voice, then decided against it. If she wasn't convinced she had heard it, what would Mike think?

"Okay. In a minute. I just want to watch . . ."

The girl's destination appeared to be a large pool in the corner of the field. Ringed by waist-high, yellowing grass and a few rushes, its water was dark and stagnant, a thick green scum floating heavily on the still surface. At one time, a farmer had tried to seal it off with a barbed-wire fence, but that was now rusty and broken, the fence posts lolling drunkenly. Oblivious to Hannah's increasingly insistent tugs, Mike watched intently as the girl approached the pool. Her pace slowed as she neared it, raising her head to stare at the muddy water. Finally she pushed her way through the grass and the rushes to stand on the edge only a hundred yards away from where Hannah and Mike were watching; she was so intent on her purpose she had not noticed them.

"Why is she standing there?" Jack was briefly forgotten as Hannah became intrigued by the girl's mysterious actions.

"She looks like she's praying."

There was an air of unbearable sadness about the girl and although she had stopped sobbing, her shoulders were bowed. She paused there for a moment, then solemnly raised the bundle, kissing it once with tenderness, before releasing it. It hit the water with a faint splash, floated for a second, suspended by the scum, then sank slowly in a gulp of thick, viscous bubbles.

For several minutes she remained, unmoving, until it had completely disappeared, and then she turned on her heels and ran back the way she had come in a frenzied headlong rush, powered by emotion.

"What do you make of that?" Hannah asked.

"I don't know. Let's go and have a look in the pool."

"Don't do that." The voice was stern, with a hint of desperation. Behind them was an old woman, her wrinkled face etched with concern. She was short, little more than five feet tall, with snowy white hair set smartly above her lined forehead. From one hand dangled an empty shopping bag, the other nervously clutching a brown leather purse to her stomach. "I'm sorry I startled you," she said anxiously, "but you mustn't go. Leave well alone. For the poor girl's sake."

"Is it your daughter?" Hannah asked.

The woman shook her head. "I don't know her at all. I've seen her around the village a few times. But I know all I need to know."

"Well . . ."

She silenced Mike in mid-sentence. "Hush now. Go back to your walk and forget what you saw. This is a secret that the poor girl needs to keep locked in her heart forever. Let it be."

Hannah smiled and prepared to move on, but Mike held her back. "I need to know," he said. There were so many mysteries in his life, he could not accept another. "If you won't tell me, then I'll have to find out for myself."

For a second he thought the woman was about to burst into tears. She shifted from foot to foot, smoothing the ruffles on her Sunday-best coat, before finally looking him in the eye and saying with restrained emotion, "You're a hard man and you'll regret asking when you hear what I have to say, but if it means you'll stop your prying then I'll speak." Mike nodded. "What you've just seen . . . this isn't the first time it has happened. Over the years it's taken place many times. It was common knowledge among the womenfolk in the time when my grandmother was a child. Maybe the men knew about it, maybe they didn't. They never spoke about it. They didn't *want* to know. It was something that was never voiced, a secret shared by women. And it lay like a stone in the hearts of some of us."

Mike listened closely as she spoke, her words so soft they were almost carried away by the breeze. At times, she kept her eyes closed, either remembering long-forgotten things or fighting to keep something within.

"Women hereabouts have always been blessed," she continued. "The Lord has seen fit to make us as fertile as the land. But not all the little ones that come our way are as welcome as others. Do you get my drift?"

Hannah's eyes widened in realization at what they had seen. "That's right, my dear." She looked down at Hannah's large stomach admiringly. "You're close to having a child yourself, so you should understand what I'm saying."

Mike broke in. "That was a *baby*? She dropped a baby into that pool?" He felt chilled to the bone and nauseated at the same time.

"Don't you judge!" the woman snapped. "What do you know about the pressures a woman faces? And it isn't what you're thinking. It was dead."

"So what?" Mike said. "Alive it would be a grotesque murder. Dead – it's still a crime."

The woman looked at him with contempt. "I don't know that lass' story and I don't need to. It's the same as it always

92

has been. Sometimes a young one will have a child and it will bring shame on the family to keep it. Sometimes the father won't have anything to do with it and the mother and her family can't afford to bring it up. Sometimes it's not natural – deformed – and it wouldn't be right to let it live."

"So you get some backstreet abortionist to terminate it? The village doctor does it on the quiet, does he? Or is it knitting needles and vodka in the bath?" Hannah gripped Mike's forearm tightly.

"It's not something we do lightly," she said with tears in her eyes. "A woman can't kill her own child without paying a terrible price. But sometimes it has to be done. Sometimes the price you pay if it lives is even greater."

"What's to stop me going to the police?"

"*She* will stop you." The woman pointed at Hannah. "She'll understand. We do things our own way round here, same as we've always done. We don't go to the police or the doctors, because it's our secret and our cross that we have to bear. They would just ask questions. They never see the cost, the human cost." She was almost begging now. "And if it'll help put your mind at rest, it's not something that's done often. Once every ten years, perhaps even longer." Mike could see she was shaking now as she stretched out one frail hand and rested it on Hannah's arm. "Think what that poor girl had to go through. Think what forced her to do it . . . how much she's suffered already. Don't make her suffer any more. Don't tell, love," she whispered. "Keep the secret."

She turned from them and walked slowly towards the bus stop further down the road.

Mike put his arm protectively around Hannah's shoulders as they set off in the opposite direction. "Should we tell?" he asked her.

She shook her head. "It's nothing to do with us." Her own heart felt heavy as she considered the old woman's words. "It was a real effort for her to tell us that. If she hadn't been so concerned about the girl suffering more . . . She's been through it herself," she added.

"How do you know?"

"I can tell. A secret like that leaves a scar."

93

Mike sighed. "It's horrifying. Knowing what lies at the bottom of that pool . . ."

"It's not horrifying; it's sad. Think of all the emotions that have been buried under the water. Love, hate, despair."

"I'm just amazed that that kind of thing could happen here – that a tradition like that – a ritual, even – could carry on down the years."

"Amazed? Why?"

"Well . . . it just seems incongruous. I mean this is the twentieth century, for Christ's sake, not the Dark Ages."

Hannah slipped her arm through his and moved close to him. "It's the same wherever you go, Mike. The twentieth century on the surface and the Dark Ages underneath. You just never see it most of the time, but that doesn't mean it isn't there."

The sun on their faces was warm as they meandered back to the village and up the incline to the bungalow. As Mike prepared himself for work, Hannah crept into Jack's bedroom and was relieved to find him still asleep. She stood at the side of his bed, watching him intently for more than a minute, before rousing him gently.

"Time to get up," she whispered. The smile that surfaced gradually through the sleep daze as he stirred, was enough to make her think that after all, everything was going to work out fine.

Chapter Fifteen

The claustrophobia was even stronger the second time around. A suffocating blanket wrapped itself tightly around his head. More than anything he wanted to run, scramble his way out of the rattling lift and into the light, but he fought it, as he knew he had to, hoping no one could see his hands clutching at the wire mesh behind his back as the cage began its trundling journey down the shaft. He had nothing to fear at the surface, where the miners around him acted as though he did not exist. They chatted to each other, laughed, joked, swore. No glance ever strayed his way. No overt indication was given that the enemy was in their midst. When the lift moved below ground level, it was different. On their home ground, their resentment was tangible.

His uneasiness the last time he was underground had seemed unfounded. Now he wondered if his instincts had been right. The panic this time came from real, concrete fears: of faces in the floor and clutching hands, of fingers scratching beneath the surface, of long tunnels that had no end. Of whatever walked along them.

His mouth was dry. *Fear of the unknown*. It had swamped all his other fears and problems, which now seemed trivial in comparison. The only thing that drove him forward was his desperate urge to *know*. To uncover the truth.

The cage hit the bottom with a jolt. For one brief moment there was complete silence, then the doors rattled back and the men filed noisily out towards their assigned tasks. Mike was the last to step into the tunnel. Charlie Robson was waiting to one side, pretending to adjust the strap on a heavy tool bag while the crowd of workers slowly dissipated. Soon there was just the two of them.

"Mr Leary." Charlie nodded in greeting, his shifting eyes revealing his nervousness.

"Hello Charlie," Mike replied. "I appreciate what you're doing. I know it's quite a risk for you to meet me like this."

"I had to do it." There was a flinty insistence to his words. "I didn't want it on my conscience." He shrugged with false casualness. "It'll be all right. If we're careful, we won't get caught out – and if someone does see us together we'll just talk our way out of it."

"It's nice to be so popular!"

Charlie gave a fleeting smile which only served to emphasize the fear in his eyes. Then he slung the tool bag over his shoulder and set off along the tunnels. "This way," he said with a wave of his hand. "If we follow the route carefully, we should be okay. All we need to do is steer clear of the train and all the main work areas."

"Is is far?" Mike strode out behind him.

"A fair ways. We're going down tunnels that haven't been worked in a long time."

An involuntary shiver ran down Mike's spine. "I don't mean to be pushy, Charlie, but isn't it about time you explained what's happening? My head is starting to ache from your cryptic comments."

Charlie struggled to find the right words. "I don't want you laughing at me. I'm not an idiot and I don't want anyone treating me like one."

"I'm not going to laugh at you. I just want to know what you have to say."

"It's not the men."

"What's not?"

"All the things that have been happening down here. It wasn't the men that caused them. All those accidents. Machine breakdowns." He paused. "Alec Jakes – it wasn't the men."

"Who was it?"

Charlie ignored his question. "You work in an office down in London. Wear nice suits. Drive a flashy car. You can't be expected to believe what happens down here. Shit, even the people up top wouldn't believe what happens down here. It's a different world. A different, fucking world." There was bitterness mingled in with something that could have been helplessness. There seemed to be a tinge of desperation there too. "There's things said down here . . . things that happen down here . . . they never make it to the surface. Are you a mason?"

Mike was wrongfooted by the suddenness of the question. "No. Why?"

"I saw a programme on them masons on TV. If they speak out of turn, or reveal any secrets, they get their stomach cut open and the bits thrown over their shoulder."

Mike smiled to himself. Ahead of him, Charlie's head was bowed, the light from his helmet lamp bobbing along the stony wall. "The rituals might say that, but I don't think they actually do it."

"I saw it on the box. It's like that down here. There's some things you can't talk about. Oh, nothin's said, like. But you know if you do open your mouth in the wrong places, then things'll happen to you."

"Is that what happened to Alec Jakes?"

"No, no. I told you – it wasn't the men. They don't have to do anything, because everybody turns a blind eye and a deaf ear to what's going on."

Mike waited for Charlie to enlighten him further, but he seemed to have had enough of talking for the moment. He adjusted the holdall on his shoulder and speeded up his step, leaving Mike struggling to keep up with him.

The tunnels they had moved into were noticeably older, the props and supports aged and worn like the bones of a feeble old man. There was a clinging odour of mustiness, more florid than the dank air of the new tunnels. It reminded Mike of castle dungeons. He found that at several points he had to stoop to avoid jutting rocks in the roof, and on one occasion he failed to see an overhang in time. The resulting blow knocked him off his feet.

"They made the tunnels lower in them days," Charlie said as he helped him up. "People were shorter. You can always tell the old tunnels because they're the lowest."

"Thank God they weren't dwarfs." Mike lifted the front of his hard hat to rub his forehead.

97

"If you don't like this, you're not going to like what's coming up," Charlie added ominously.

They rounded a corner and within ten feet were brought up against a dead end. For one frightening moment, Mike wondered if he had been lured to some out-of-the-way spot so he could be done away with like Alec Jakes. Then Charlie pointed to the base of the wall and said, "Down there."

There was a small hole, barely two feet from floor to roof. In the shadows of the tunnel, Mike had not noticed the tiny black square, which appeared to allow room for nothing bigger than a spaniel.

He felt cold sweat spring like needles from his skin. "Surely you don't expect me to go in there!"

"You're not afraid of a tight squeeze, are you? And you working for the coal board an' all! Well, you can't back out now. If you want to see what I've got to show you, this is the only way."

It was all Mike could do to drag his gaze away from the square of darkness. The tunnel was so small he would have difficulty even crawling on all fours. Very small. Coffin-sized, in fact. "How far does it run?"

"Not far. Hundred yards – maybe more."

A hundred yards. He tried to envisage how far that was. It seemed very far indeed. Before he came to Colthorpe he would not have baulked at the thought, but now it filled him with dread.

"There are quite a few tunnels like this," Charlie continued. "They're just boreholes really, but they're good short-cuts. Saves digging too many full-size tunnels, know what I mean? No point making unnecessary work. In this day and age, drill and a cutter sorts it out in no time. Back in the old days, they used to do it by hand, I suppose. Better tighten your pads."

"What?"

Charlie pointed to the square-shaped pads that were buckled around Mike's knees. "Tighten your pads. It's fucking murder on the knees when you're crawling for a long time."

Mike pulled the straps and felt the buckles bite into the flesh near the tendons. When he looked up, Charlie was already scrambling into the tunnel, a white rabbit disappearing down a hole into Wonderland. Like Alice, he felt compelled to drop to all fours and follow suit.

Mere feet into the tunnel his heart was constricting so tightly he thought it would burst. The only light visible was a small patch on the dusty ground inches from his face, a pathetically small illumination from the lamp on his helmet. He could not tilt his head back enough to shine it more than a foot in front of him and there was certainly no way he could look around to see the opening to the tunnel behind him; if he looked even slightly to one side the brim of his helmet clattered against the wall. The sensation of his shoulders constantly brushing against the sides and the soft scrape of rock on his back kept the pressure building within him. Above him, to each side, below him, was rock. He was totally sealed in. Trapped in a rat hole. If the tunnel collapsed, no one would know they were there. He would die, slowly, choking for breath in that tiny space, his fingers scratching and scrabbling until they were bloody and raw. It was an effort to catch his breath and he knew that panic was only just beneath the surface; if he allowed himself to think about it for one moment he knew he would start gasping and screaming and frantically scrambling for air. But there was no quick way out. He could not turn around and back out and Charlie in front would prevent any swift progress forward. All that focused his mind was the ache in his knees and elbows and the rawness at the back of his legs where the buckles were biting deeper. With a powerful effort he closed his eyes in concentration making the pain a beacon in the darkness. He had no idea how far ahead of him Charlie was. He could sense him there, although he had not seen him since they entered the tunnel, and he could hear the faint sounds of his passage. At first, his panic had forced him to try desperately to keep apace, but Charlie's experience quickly showed and he had pulled away. How far had they crawled now? Numerous tiny agonies racked his body. His head crashed on the tunnel ceiling. His hip bones ground against the wall. Each breath was an effort, dragged from deep within him. He could not swallow. Occasionally he would lose control and his breathing would come in a machine-gun surge, colours flashing behind his eyelids in psychedelic explosions, his fingernails gripping into the dust on the hard floor. Counting backwards from ten, he inhaled deeply, drawing in the flat, dead air of the tunnel, smelling and tasting the clammy, musty odour of earth and stone and coal dust. And he crawled on and on and on . . .

And then there were hands helping him out and pulling him to his feet.

Relief swept over him. He felt like he had been plucked from a raging sea just as he was beginning to go down for the third time. He inhaled deeply once more, but this time the air came in rich, gulping lungfuls. Never had he been so relieved to take a breath.

When he had recovered he looked around. The tunnel they were in was obviously disused. There was no electric lamps at regular intervals, no long, rubber-insulated cables snaking down from the ceiling in loops. Long abandoned, it had been stripped bare of any hint of the twentieth century. There was only the light of their helmet lamps to guide them. It was much bigger than the bolthole they had dragged themselves along for fifteen agonizing minutes and that was sufficient comfort for Mike. Above his head there was at least two feet of dark space and the walls were easily ten feet apart.

"You don't get that many people down here," Charlie said. The sound of his voice took on a hollow resonance. When the echoes died down the silence was complete. In that ultimate quiet, the pulse of the blood in Mike's ears created strange sounds: buzzes, swishes and murmurings.

"How long has this section of the mine been out of use?" Mike found himself whispering. The hush inspired the reverence of a cathedral.

"Years. Before my time. Probably before the time of the oldest bloke down here. I reckon this is the oldest part of the pit. These tunnels stretch right out past Colthorpe towards Overedge and Netheredge. Most of the access routes to them have been sealed up, but there's still two or three of the little tunnels left open."

"Why weren't they sealed?"

"If you hold your horses I'll show you." Charlie turned on his heel and walked away.

"You won't forget our route out of here, will you?" Every

100

now and then an image flashed into Mike's mind of him wandering lost and alone in the dark. It terrified him, but it kept coming back like the unnatural urge to jump when faced by a precipitous drop.

"Don't worry. I know this place like the back of my hand."

As they walked, Charlie talked about himself, reluctantly at first, but then with increasing enthusiasm. His concentration on the minutiae of his day-to-day life seemed to help him forget their situation. With pride he told Mike of his girlfriend – a legal secretary he had met a year ago at a village hall dance – and discussed tentatively, and with a little embarrassment, their plans to marry. He was shy of asking questions, but Mike responded by telling him a little about Hannah and Jack. Charlie reiterated his desire to quit the mine as soon as possible. He was, he said, hoping to go to a technical college to study engineering. Mike became a little morose when he tried to explain his own views on work, a feeling that was compounded when his words were met with bemused incomprehension.

"Why do you go on doing it then, if you don't like it?" Charlie asked, puzzled. Mike could not answer him.

They had walked for almost fifteen minutes before Charlie stopped sharply and looked around. "We're almost there," he said quietly.

Once more Mike could sense an undertone of fear in the youth's movements. "You're sure there's not going to be anyone else around?" Mike asked.

"Not at this time. I know when they come down here. We're alone." He walked on a few more yards, then turned to his left into a slim tunnel which Mike would have missed had he been on his own. It was as high as the previous tunnel, but it was a tight squeeze to walk down it. In the end he was forced to turn sideways and shuffle along carefully. "It's down at the end of this one," Charlie said.

After five minutes the tunnel began to widen out slightly and then suddenly it ended in an area the size of a box room. Their helmet lights cast bizarre dancing shadows on the glistening walls. There was some sort of object in the room, near the opposite wall, but before Mike had a chance to investigate Charlie dropped to his knees and fumbled around on the floor. A bright light flared up, illuminating the entire area. Mike blinked uncontrollably, dazzled by the sudden brilliance after the all-encompassing darkness that had surrounded them for so long. When his eyes finally adjusted he saw Charlie had switched on a lamp wired up to a battered old car battery.

"It's better than relying on our lamps," he said.

In the light, Mike could make out a series of drawings and writings on the walls. Much of the graffiti was just lists of names and commonplace obscenities, but there were also streams of text in a scrawling script which had so many flourishes he deduced it must have dated back more than a hundred years. He tried to read it, but it was incomprehensible and he quickly lost interest. A few of the drawings were faded with age and some of the oldest had all the colours and intricacies of Stone Age cave paintings.

In one area there was a string of pictorials like a comic strip, which told an ongoing story of a group of men digging underground. He followed the pictures from one to the other, attempting to make sense of the tale. The men were digging deeper and deeper until white forms either men, or animals, he wasn't entirely sure which – broke out from beneath and dragged them down one by one. The final picture showed a huge underground chamber where the men were piled in front of a strangely-shaped white blob which seemed to have both eyes and a mouth, but resembled nothing that Mike had ever seen.

"What's this all about?" he asked Charlie.

"That? That's the story of the Tunnellers."

Mike remembered what the reporter, Richmond, had told him about the ghosts of dead miners who still haunted the tunnels of the pits. "Why is it here?"

Charlie shrugged. "It's always been there."

Mike dragged his attention away from the graffiti on the wall and surveyed the rest of the tiny room. The thing he had half-seen in the shadows was now revealed as a small wooden table covered by a dirty lace cloth. On closer inspection he saw the table was an ornate antique with delicately carved legs, but it was the objects laid out on top of it which really caught his eye. There was an array of personal items, from pen-knives, heavily rusted with age, to cigarette lighters and pipes, to belt buckles and shoelaces.

Mike turned to Charlie and said, "Is this what you brought me here to see?"

Charlie nodded sagely.

"I think it's time you explained things." Mike felt a growing irritation that he had been put through great discomfort for the sake of a subterranean jumble sale.

"I was brought down here for the first time a few weeks after I'd started work," Charlie said, squatting down in one corner and removing his helmet to wipe the sweat from his brow. "All new blokes are brought here eventually." He broke off and looked at Mike with surprising intensity. "Do you believe in God, Mr Leary?"

"God? Yes, I suppose so. You won't find me sitting in the pews every Sunday, but that doesn't mean I'm a heathen."

"All the men at Colthorpe believe in God too. They go to church. They're good people."

"You don't have to convince me, Charlie." Mike was floundering once more on the illogical twists and turns of Charlie's thought processes.

"But that's when they're above ground, Mr Leary. When they're down here, it's different. Do you reckon it's possible to worship God and something else as well?"

"I don't know. Like what?"

"This here's an altar," he said, motioning to the table. "But it's not for God. Leastways, not the Bible's God. When I was brought down here that first time I was told this had been here for as long as there'd been a mine at Colthorpe. It was, like, tradition that you had to leave a little offering so the . . ." he laughed in embarrassment ". . . so the ghosts didn't get you. It was just a bit of fun, you know what I mean? Anyway, I thought it was. They told me I had to go through a ceremony – a service – if I wanted to be accepted. Bit like the masons, only better. A gang, like – a secret gang. I had to swear I wouldn't tell anyone."

"So why are you telling me?"

"Because it's not just a bit of fun any more. They've started taking it too seriously. In the beginning it was like a super-sition: like actors don't whistle backstage. There's loads of little things you pick up when you've been working here a while. A lot of the old blokes used to really believe in spirits, or whatever you want to call them . . . things down here. You had to be real careful, they'd say."

"They made you go through some kind of ceremony?" Mike had heard of sailors doing something similar.

"That's right. I never thought anything about it. Every now and then, people would come down here and leave a bit of something, something personal, just for supersition's sake. It was just the done thing."

"Harmless, I suppose." Mike was thinking aloud. "Most trades have their superstitions. Sailors, soldiers, anybody who faces danger. What's wrong with that?"

Charlie's sigh echoed wearily and sorrowfully in the still air. "Ever since the rumours started about Colthorpe being up for closure, some of the men have been . . . it's not a joke any more. I've heard them down here, the ones that are really worried because they've got families to keep. They've been – praying. That's sick."

"Are you trying to tell me that these men killed Alec Jakes?"

Charlie shook his head; in the glint of the light Mike could see there were tears in his frightened eyes. "I told you – it's not the men. There's other things down here that are listening to them."

Mike's heart beat faster. He remembered the deserted cottage, the faces in the floor.

"You won't believe me . . ." Charlie whined, the tears running freely down his face now.

"I believe you," Mike said bluntly. "I know there's something happening here . . . something that I can't explain. I've tried to push it out of my mind, but that doesn't make it any less real."

"It's – the Tunnellers!" Charlie blurted the words out, as if to speak them would suddenly fill the room with the things he feared most. "What the old men said . . . it's true! I've heard them!"

"Calm down," Mike said, dropping down by his side. "Just speak slowly. Tell me everything you know."

Charlie stifled a sob and continued. "Sometimes you can

104

hear things through the walls. Scratching noises. Voices. Whispering. They've always been there, but I just thought they were echoes. You get strange noises down here all the time. Over the last few weeks it's been getting worse. It's the Tunnellers! They killed Jakes and they're going to kill more before this is all over!"

"Have you seen them?"

Charlie shook his head. "You don't have to. It's enough just to hear them."

Mike placed a reassuring hand on Charlie's shoulder and looked slowly around the tiny room, at the drawings and writings on the wall, at the altar and its offerings. In the light of day, in his office, he might have laughed at Charlie's story, but there, surrounded by darkness and rock and silence, he could actively believe there were beings – spirits – whatever they were, tunnelling through the earth.

He needed time to think, to reconcile what had happened since he had arrived in Colthorpe with his rational, logical mind. Even if he dismissed Charlie's tale, he could not discount the evidence of his own eyes. There was something frightening happening; he could no longer deny that it terrified him.

"Come on," he said quietly. "We'd better get out of here."

Chapter Sixteen

The altar room and its strange, humming atmosphere pressed against their backs as Charlie led the way back to the main tunnel. Mike was glad to be out of its confines. It had started to oppress him, standing there surrounded by those strange pictures with their twisted, inhuman figures. The air had a cloying dampness which caught at the back of his throat; several times he had the unnerving feeling that someone was standing just behind his shoulder.

The further they moved from the altar with its odd assortment of offerings, the more his mind dwelled on the tortuous crawl through the rat-hole. If he could have done anything to avoid it he would have done, but he knew he had no option but to endure it. He asked if there was another route back, no matter how long it took or how close it brought them to the main work areas. Charlie said if there was he knew nothing of it.

Mike's conversation dried up as he brooded on the trial ahead of him, but his morbid thoughts were suddenly disturbed when Charlie stopped sharply, anxiously scanning the tunnel.

"What's the problem?" Mike asked.

"It's just . . . there's another tunnel here and I swear it wasn't there when we came through before." He directed his helmet lamp to his left and outlined a side passage almost as large as the one along which they were walking.

"You probably missed it. Christ, the Prime Minister and two Page Three girls could have walked past us down here and we wouldn't have seen them."

106

"No. I know this area. I know it well. There's never been a tunnel there. Never."

"I know your colleagues are anxious to keep this pit open, but I don't think even they could work so efficiently they could dig another tunnel in the short time we were in that room."

"I don't like this," Charlie murmured.

The hairs on the back of Mike's neck prickled at the hint of fear which had rematerialized in the young miner's voice. As he stepped forward to investigate the new tunnel, Charlie edged backwards. "What do you mean?" Mike asked. "Are you suggesting this is connected to what we've been talking about?"

"I don't know," Charlie mumbled. "I just know it wasn't there when we came this way earlier."

"Well, I know we're not lost. Even I can see we've managed to retrace our steps." He turned to Charlie. "I think we should check it out."

"No!"

"What do you mean, 'No'? You want to see this resolved, don't you?"

"I don't want to go down there."

"Come on," Mike said, as lightly as he could. "You're not scared, are you?" If he had to admit it, he was a little scared himself, but the *need to know* was a powerful driving force.

Charlie licked his lips and stared wide-eyed down the tunnel, as if his gaze could pierce the darkness and reveal whatever was down there.

"Look," Mike continued, "we don't have to go far. I just want to see where it leads. If it was hidden before, then it must be important, right? There's a chance we might discover something that might help us. And we can always turn around and come straight back."

"I don't know . . ."

"Come on. We'll just take a quick look."

Charlie resisted for a second, then reluctantly aquiesced and followed Mike into the tunnel. "I'm not going to wait for you if we have to run." he said.

"Do you think I'm going to wait for *you*?" Mike countered.

The tunnel continued straight for several hundred yards

before it began to twist and turn along an erratic route; Mike also suspected it was gradually sloping downwards. There was little to distinguish it from any of the others he had passed along, although the walls were, perhaps, a little rougher and the ceiling slightly lower. Charlie became more himself with each few yards they covered and eventually he was talking normally, although in a hushed voice.

"How much farther are we going?" he whispered.

"Not much more. Are you sure you don't know this tunnel?"

"They all look the bloody same. I might have been along here before, but it doesn't look familiar."

"Have a lot of tunnels been sealed off?"

"Aye, quite a few. When they finish one area the seal it up and move on to the next. But even if this is one of them, it doesn't explain why I didn't come across it before."

"Let's not think about that at the moment. We'll give it ten more minutes and if we don't get anywhere, we'll head back. Okay?"

"Fair enough."

They had barely walked five paces before Mike held out his arm and brought them both to a halt. "What's that?"

"What? I don't hear nothin'." Charlie was suddenly tense and nervous.

"Listen. Somebody's digging."

Ahead of them they could hear the faint chink-chink of metal on rock. When Mike looked at Charlie, he saw in the lamp's beam that relief had spread across his face.

"I don't know where the fucking hell we are," he said happily, "but if one of the lads is down here we can't be too far away from the shaft. I thought this tunnel was taking us away from the face, but it must have doubled back. I reckon we should turn round so he doesn't see us."

Mike thought of the rat-hole. "No – it's too far. I'll just tell them I got lost down here and you found me and had to bring me back."

Charlie was reluctant, but eventually consented. They continued along the tunnel for five more minutes with the sound of the tool growing louder and louder, until they began to see a faint glow ahead of them. It was not sufficiently bright to be one of the powerful tunnel lights and it flickered and wavered strongly.

"Must be working with just his helmet lamp on," Charlie muttered.

The light was emanating from around a bend in the tunnel and at that close proximity Mike could tell the movement of the shadows signified an unguarded flame, not an electrical source. An unguarded flame: the anathema of miners. He knew Charlie was thinking the same from the expression on his face. As the young miner went to march around the corner and shout out, Mike snatched at him and held him back. There was an alarm screeching in his mind.

Charlie looked at him questioningly, but Mike put a finger to his lips and slowly edged past him to the bend in the tunnel. The noise was as clear as a bell now. Chink, chink, chink. A short period of scrabbling and then chink, chink, chink, again. Whoever was digging was making a distinctly half-hearted attempt.

Stealthily, Mike switched off his helmet lamp and peered around the corner. About thirty feet away he could just make out the hunched form of the digger, working to the pale light of a burning wooden torch. To Mike's surprise the figure was almost naked. His only item of clothing was a dirty loin cloth tied around his lower regions, offering scant protection against the underground chill. His pale, wiry body was streaked with sweat and dust, shimmering in the torchlight as his arm rose and fell, wielding a crude tool which chipped away at the rocks before him. The digger's back was to him, but even so, Mike could tell his mane of thick black hair was straggly and matted with filth.

There was something else – something about the light – which was not quite right. It was muted, its luminescence insipid as if filtered through several layers of gauze, and the more Mike concentrated the more it seemed that the figure itself was also wrong. When the light flickered a certain way, the digger seemed to be almost translucent, the edges wavering like a mirage.

Mike could feel Charlie at his side watching the scene intently. His body was tense, like a rabbit disturbed in a field. He was tugging at Mike's arm insistently.

"Shit," he croaked, almost under his breath.

At that moment, the digger slowly turned his head and stared directly at them, a malevolent, mocking grin spreading across his face. His black eyes were filled with evil and hatred; an emotion so powerful that Mike felt it leap between them like a lightning bolt.

An electric jolt of terror surged through him. He knew instinctively that if the digger had been alive once, he was no longer. He seemed to recognize Mike's fear. His grin was a slash of malice in his filthy face. He advanced towards them, with each step his body growing more solid, the edges hardening and becoming crisp and black against the torch's light. Mike could see the sinews moving beneath his skin, the steely fingers opening and closing.

Charlie was the first to move. He sprinted back the way they had come, his head bowed into the tunnel's dark. Mike followed, flicking on his helmet lamp as he ran.

Five paces later, their helmet lights winked out.

Darkness.

Total, impenetrable darkness.

Mike heard Charlie scream in fright somewhere ahead of him. For a second it seemed as if he was flying through space with no sensation of up, down or forward – then his momentum carried him heavily into a wall and he crashed to the ground in a daze.

It could have been seconds or minutes later when he stirred, but the full terror of the situation hit him instantly. He was lost far underground with little hope of finding his way back to the main shaft. Worse, whatever it was that they had disturbed was down there with him. He lay on his back, as still as possible, trying to make no sound. Then he raised his arm and tried to focus on it. Even when his palm was brushing the end of his nose, it did not register in the enveloping blackness. Carefully he switched his helmet lamp on and off, feeling the lead to the battery and checking that the coupling had not come loose. There was no power.

In resignation he lay back on the floor of the tunnel and considered his position. Looking around him he could see no trace of the flickering torch. Perhaps the digger, the spook, whatever, had returned to whence it had come. Straining his

110

ears he could not discern any sound whatsoever, apart from his own harsh breathing like a traction engine in the silence. Had Charlie managed to keep going in the right direction? At least he would be able to alert Bulmer, who would presumably organize a search party for him. But what if he was afraid to tell anyone he had been with Mike? No one else knew he was down there. Or perhaps he had stumbled in the darkness too, and was lying only a few feet away, too scared to move.

"Charlie?" he whispered.

No reply. He tried again, louder this time. There was still nothing but the ringing, endless silence. He realized, although he could barely bring himself to admit it, that he was wasting his breath; if he wanted to get out of the mine he would have to rely on his own instincts. He thought of the miles and miles of tunnels, traversing the area like an ant hill's tiny burrows, then he discovered that his fall had disorientated him so much he didn't even know which way to go to retrace his steps. He was in the abandoned section now. What happened if he wandered into a tunnel that was dangerous? Gaping holes in the floor? Roof liable to collapse?

Which way?

Which way?

He pulled himself up the wall like a drunk outside a night club, selected a direction at random and began to ease himself along, using the cold stone to guide him, testing the ground with each step. Even at a conservative estimate, he knew it would take him several hours to find his way back to the well-trodden areas of the mine. He steeled himself and blanked his mind for the trial ahead.

Despair was beginning to creep up on him. The darkness was almost hallucinogenic in its intensity, plucking images from his mind and playing them so lucidly in his head that they could have been happening before his eyes. With each step he wondered if he was about to plummet into an abyss. With each echo he wondered if there was someone – or something – behind him. It was impossible to judge the passage of time or distance in that swathing blackness. He could not see how far he had travelled, and the twists and turns of the tunnels and the occasional detours he had taken along side-branches had

111

left him clueless as to his direction. For all he knew, he could have been going round and round in circles. His right foot ached where it had been dragged along the wall in the hope that it might accidentally slip into the rat-hole that would allow him egress. He was searching for the proverbial needle in a haystack. Looking for a small hole in the dark of seemingly endless tunnels . . . it was almost laughable. He did not even want to consider the possibility that the rat-holes were the only exits from the abandoned section of the mine. With a belief that verged on religious faith he hoped that one of the large tunnels would eventually find its way back to the main area. He hoped; because if he didn't believe it, then he might just, perhaps, give up for good.

Quietly, he sat against the foot of the wall and rested. The tunnel appeared to have continued in a straight line for miles. Perhaps he had missed a branch tunnel on the opposite wall. He knew he had never walked this far when he had been exploring the newly discovered tunnel with Charlie. Perhaps he was no longer in the mine at all. Perhaps he had stumbled into one of those strange, empty tunnels that crisscrossed Colthorpe and a few yards further along he would find himself looking up into the deserted cottage. He could always dream.

What concerned him more than being lost was that Hannah would be frantic with worry if he did not return in the evening. That was the last thing he wanted to put her through. She had already suffered enough at the hands of his mood swings, his violent temper that forced him to hurt the one thing he loved the most.

For a moment, he considered what it would feel like to die down there in the dark; never to see her again, never put things right and create that idyllic, sharing existence that had always been their ideal. He could not imagine anything closer to hell. He blinked tightly and stifled a tear. It was the job that had ruined everything – the damned, fucking job! It had turned him into an angry, bitter hack with no career prospects, and it had cast a pall over their marriage. If he was not so scared, it would be laughable that it was the job that was now on the verge of killing him.

He pictured them all together: Hannah, Jack and himself,

walking through Kew Gardens on a balmy Sunday evening, just talking and laughing and enjoying life. Like a snapshot, he held that image in his mind, concentrated on it until fire ran through his veins and the tears fought their way on to his cheeks. He could not give that up. He would not let it happen.

How long it had been? He could see lights in the dark now, gentle will o' the wisps, that appeared and disappeared, danced and flickered. Or were they just his eyelids? His muscles ached. He was thirsty. He was hungry. He could hear things too: voices, behind the walls. But when he stopped and listened, they stopped too.

He had sat down several times to rest and each time the despair gripped him a little tighter; all he could do was try to keep moving, try not to think about his predicament. He kept repeating the gentle prayer that Charlie had made it back and that a search party was even now being formed.

Sure that was happening. He wasn't really going to keep walking on and on, until hunger and thirst brought him to a halt and a slow, lingering death!

"Come on, Mikey," he muttered, surprised at how pleased he was to hear the sound of his own voice. "One step after the other – that's the way to do it."

"Hello?"

He almost yelled out in shock at the sound of the voice echoing down the tunnel: gruff, barely audible, but a human voice nonetheless.

"Who's there?" Mike shouted. His fright was quickly replaced by total relief. "Christ, I'm glad to hear you. I've been wandering around down here for hours."

"Stay where you are." The voice was not Charlie's, but the accent was rich enough for Mike to identify one of the older miners. There was the sound of boots echoing along the tunnel towards him.

"I'm over here," he said anxiously, afraid they would pass in the dark. "I'll keep talking until you find me. I know it sounds stupid, but I got lost. These tunnels, they all look the same don't they?" He laughed. "Well, they all look the same when you can actually see them. It's . . ."

"All right, I'm here." Mike felt a hand grab at the arm of his

113

overalls and fumble downwards until it felt his forearm. He could smell the odour of sweat and coal dust, heavy in the cool, still tunnel air. A faint trace of tobacco wafted across his face.

"I thought I was going to die down here," Mike said, almost to himself.

"Aye. You're lucky."

"If you hadn't come along . . . why did you come along?"

"There's something wrong with the lights. Broke away from the others and just ended up wanderin'."

"So we're both in the same boat," Mike said. His hopes tumbled.

"I know where I'm goin'. When you been down here long enough, you recognize these tunnels. Even in the dark."

"Thank God," Mike said. "You can't imagine the things that have been going through my head."

"We better get going."

"Right. Lead on!"

"I'll keep a hold of you. Then we won't get split up."

"Sure. Whatever you say."

The miner started to lead Mike back the way he had come before taking a sudden detour down a side tunnel, which Mike had passed without even knowing it had been there. The slow, steady crunch of his boots on the ground was reassuring, as was the tightness of his hand round Mike's forearm. The fingers were like steel bands. The grip, the human contact, gave Mike strength to continue. His relief was as strong as the despair he had felt earlier. He had almost reconciled himself to the fact that he was going to die; Hannah always said he had a stubbornly pessimistic streak.

"You know, I thought I wasn't going to see my wife and son again," he added. The words tumbled out joyfully, a celebration of communication coming only moments after thinking he would never talk to anyone again. "That was more frightening than the thought of dying alone down here. Are you married?"

There was a pause before the miner replied. "I was."

"Then you must know what I mean. You stumble through life worrying about work and day-to-day problems and you never have time to think about the really vital things. Listen

to me! I sound like some fucking church magazine moralist."
He laughed again. "But it's true. I've got a lot of things to sort
out. A *lot* of things. I don't know how my wife has put up with
me over the last few years." Adding, "Still, there's plenty of
time to make it up to her."

After hours of walking aimlessly in the darkness, Mike was
happy to relinquish control and let himself be led. It was
comforting to put all his faith in someone else and let the
stress and tension slip away.

"Is it much further?" he asked, realizing how exhausted he
was. The muscles on his legs were trembling and his feet felt
as if there were at least four blisters erupting.

"No. Not much further." The miner's harsh voice held the
merest edge of annoyance. Mike assumed his rambling conversation, fuelled by the rush of relief, was starting to jar. His
rescuer was, after all, concentrating on following a complex
route in complete darkness. He restrained the urge to chatter
and focused his thoughts inwards.

They always returned to Hannah and Jack. With the
blinding insight of someone born again into a new life, Mike
could not believe how he had abused his position as husband,
lover and father through selfishness and the blinkered search
for a solution for his own minor problems. "It's amazing what
a little time to reflect in a quiet place will do," he muttered.

When he made it back he would sort things out. Fuck the
job! Fuck Whicker. There were plenty more things he could
do.

"I'm going to buy you a drink when we get out of here,"
Mike said. The miner's pace had speeded up. He presumed
they were getting closer to the main working area. "Shit, I'll
buy you a whole night's worth of drinks! That's after Bulmer
has bitten my head off. Christ, I'm not looking forward to
that. He's going to give me the biggest bollocking of my life."

Out of the corner of his eye he saw something glimmering.
A light.

"Hang on." He dug his heels in and brought the miner up
sharply. Down a tunnel to his right he could see the faint but
welcoming glow of an electric light. "Thank God. We've
made it."

He stepped towards the tunnel, but his rescuer did not

move. "Come on," Mike said, irritated. "What's wrong with you? Can't you see the light?"

The grip around his arm became tighter and Mike heard the rasp of the miner's breath. "You can carry on that way if you want, but I'm going down here," Mike continued. He tried to drag his arm out of the miner's grip, but the fingers bit sharply into the soft flesh of his forearm. "Ow!" Mike snarled. "You bastard! Let me . . ."

The miner began to drag him relentlessly along the tunnel away from the light. Mike's left hand had gone numb and there were lances of pain up to his shoulder. The light, the beacon that had comforted him, winked out as he passed the edge of the tunnel. The miner was forcing him to go back into the darkness, back into the earth.

Suddenly he was aware. An air-raid siren was wailing in his head, screaming at him to run to safety. How could he have been so stupid? It was no miner. *They* had got him. The Tunnellers.

And they were taking him . . .

Back . . .

Below.

Strength that he thought had eked out of him during his hours underground flooded back into his limbs. With a surge of adrenalin he lashed out and wrenched his arm free. The pain was excruciating, but he ignored it. Turning rapidly, he scrambled frantically along the wall until he found the tunnel. Behind him a howl of rage, bestial, non-human, convinced him that he had not made his escape a moment too soon.

Then, as the thud of boots began to draw nearer, he was running.

Ignoring the possibility of splitting his head open, ignoring the chance of falling and losing everything: just running. Towards the light.

Sounds of pursuit followed him, as instinctive as a wolf after a lamb, but he dared not look, dared not even think about what had been holding his arm.

The light grew brighter as he approached. After the bleak, hopeless cold of the dark, it was a brilliant gold, with all the security and warmth of a fire seen through a window on a winter's day.

116

If only he could reach it in time.

His foot skidded on the dusty ground and for a moment he thought he had lost his balance, but he righted himself somehow and kept running, running fast, with tears in his eyes and a lump in his throat and Hannah's face in his mind. There was something behind him that seemed to be howling and raging or perhaps it was silent and that was just in his mind and there was a clutching hand reaching out to grab his shoulder and yank him back on the brink of safety and . . .

He was there.

When he burst into the light it was like breaking through sheets of hanging cobwebs or thin films of gauze. He did not stop to investigate; he just kept going.

It was more by luck than judgment that he found the shaft. His footsteps had echoed through deserted tunnels for less than five minutes before he stumbled, weary and frightened, up to the closed doors and called the lift operator on the radio. It was all he could do to calm himself during the few minutes it took for the lift to trundle down to his level; his mind could barely comprehend how close he had been to some unimaginable horror.

With the last of his fading strength, he closed the cage door and pressed the button that signalled to the operator to kick the lifting gear into life, and then he slumped back against the mesh and let his exhausted eyes rest for a second.

The darkness behind his eyelids was more soothing than the harsh absence of light he had experienced in the tunnels, but he had little chance to enjoy it. Within seconds, his nostrils began to wrinkle at a foul smell that flooded into the cage like steam from a ruptured pipe. It was the thick, clinging odour of decomposition: a nauseating stench which summoned an image of a swirling mixture of rotting fruit and meat. He wanted to gag, but he held his breath and kept his eyes shut tight.

It wasn't over.

If he could just get to the surface; it couldn't be much further. Just a few more yards, please God!

Even without looking, he knew he was not alone in the lift. His nerves tingled, warning of other presences nearby. He could sense them: standing close watching him, waiting, perhaps, for him to look into their faces.

117

And what would he see then?

As the upward motion of the lift slowed, and the grinding of the gears signalled that the journey was coming to an end, the urge to open his eyes almost proved too much. His skin was gooseflesh. He could feel their gaze on him, willing him to look at them. The smell grew stronger and stronger, reeking of long dead flesh, loam and wet coal dust. Occasionally he thought he heard the slight movement of boots on the cage floor.

When the lift jolted to a halt, he automatically shut his eyes even tighter. When he opened them again he was alone.

As the doors opened, Mike almost fell into the arms of Bulmer. "Jesus Christ, man! What the fucking hell happened to you?"

Mike sat on the cold concrete floor and let his head loll back against the wall. He took one more look into the cage, just to be sure. Empty. Definitely empty.

"Tom, you wouldn't believe me," he replied.

"You're damn right I wouldn't," Bulmer raged. "What the fuck do you think you've been doing? What about safety regulations, eh? What about them? You're fucking management! You, of all people, should know!" The blood flushed into his chubby face and his mouth opened and closed in frustration. "How long have you been down there?" he snapped.

Mike shook his head; the muscles in his neck felt like string. "What time is it now?"

"Six o'clock."

"Hours," he sighed. It had seemed like much longer. "I went down at lunchtime."

Bulmer swore. "All right, I'll ask you again. What happened to you?"

"I got lost."

"Lost?" Bulmer spat out a stream of vulgarity. "If you worked for me I'd have you sacked! We're trying to improve our fucking accident record, not add to it!"

"I know, I know, and I'm truly sorry. I've got a good explanation." He glanced at the smirking face of the lift operator. "Let's go somewhere a bit more private and I'll tell you about it."

"You better have a good explanation," Bulmer snarled, "or you'll be on your way back to London tonight."

As he pulled himself to his feet, Mike suddenly remembered. "Charlie!"

"What?"

"Charlie Robson. He was down there with me. We got separated: no lights. Is he . . . is he back?"

He glanced at the lift operator, who shook his head. Mike's heart sank.

Bulmer slowly put his hand to his eyes and then gently massaged his temples with his thumb and forefinger. "So," he began, restraining his temper, "not only have you gone and flaunted all the fucking safety regulations in the book, you've also lost one of my men. I suppose we better get someone down there to look for him!"

"It's a bit more urgent than that, Tom."

Bulmer searched Mike's face curiously. "What do you mean?"

"I . . . look, just trust me. I fear for his safety. We've got to move quickly."

Mike could tell from the faint knowing spark in Bulmer's eyes that he would not question him further. "Shit!" the pit boss said. "It would happen at a time like this."

"What do you mean?"

"All the bleeding men are in a union meeting. Didn't you wonder why you hadn't bumped into anyone down there? Packard convened it urgently this afternoon. They're baying for blood in the canteen."

"They'll come, won't they?" Mike asked. "For Charlie's sake?"

Bulmer nodded. "They'll come."

It took Bulmer less than ten minutes to hand-pick a search party from the meeting. Mike kept out of sight of the men in the canteen. Tempers were running so high that they would probably have lynched him had he dared to set foot into the room. Bulmer's blunt charm quickly expounded the seriousness of the problem and the meeting continued as he and ten others strode out to the lift shaft where Mike was waiting. There was no anger in their eyes when they saw him. Bulmer

119

had told them there was no definite evidence for concern about Charlie's safety, but Mike knew they feared the worst.

When they radioed for an ambulance team an hour later, he guessed their fears had been confirmed. It was like a re-run of the evening he had arrived in Colthorpe, when Jakes' eyeless corpse had been brought to the surface. The atmosphere in the lift shaft building was tense; nobody spoke. All eyes were fixed on the lift doors. Bulmer's face was as ghastly pale as a death-mask. Mike wondered what was going through his head; what fears, what thoughts of hopelessness. He looked like a broken man who had given his all and who could summon no more strength for the fight.

They all jumped when the radio squawked into life. The lift operator answered it, mumbling his reply into the receiver in the operating booth. His expression changed instantly. "He's alive!" he yelled, one thumb aloft.

Bulmer's face creased with a grin of relief and a small cheer rose from the handful assembled. Mike smiled palely; he had no energy left for celebrations.

"Hang on a minute," the lift operator said, returning to the radio, before adding, "He's badly injured. Something about his arm. They want to get him straight off for surgery."

Bulmer's face lost its sheen. "What happened now?"

"This place is jinxed," another man added. It was not said with fear or anger, just a strange matter-of-factness that a burden had been shouldered and accepted.

When the lift reached ground level and the doors were thrust aside, all hell broke loose. "Make way," a stretcher-bearer yelled, "we're coming straight through. Is that fucking ambulance there?"

They came out of the lift like a train, carrying the stretcher between them, their faces taut and concerned. Charlie's own face was chalk-white and his head lolled from side-to-side, his eyes staring. A blanket covered him, but one side of it was drenched in blood, a purple patch that was spreading even as Mike watched. In their rush to get to the ambulance, the blanket slipped down. Mike saw with horror that Charlie's right arm was missing from the shoulder.

"Shit!" Bulmer said as he helped load him into the back of

the ambulance. "Didn't he know better than to get too close to the machinery?"

Charlie staring, pain-wracked eyes focused on him for a second. "Not . . . not the machinery. They got me . . . dragged me into the tunnels . . . kept pulling . . . pulling . . ." He sobbed at the memory. "They pulled it off . . ."

Mike was at his side, shouting, "*Who* did? Who got you?"

Charlie stared at him glassily without recognition, then the other men were pushing Mike away and closing the ambulance doors. As the vehicle roared off across the colliery yard, its blue light flared across the faces of the rescue team. Frightened faces. Terrified faces.

"He's delirious," Bulmer said, but his eyes told a different story. "Christ, losing an arm like that . . . it's bound to put you in shock."

"So where's his arm?" Mike asked quietly. He looked round at the men who found Charlie and repeated the question. "*Where's the arm*? Was it where you found him?"

They shook their heads, refusing to meet his searching gaze.

"He wasn't near any machinery, was he? He wasn't near anything that could have done that to him."

None of them answered. Bulmer interjected before Mike could ask any more questions. "This isn't the time for a post-mortem. We'll ask the questions later."

"What, when everyone's had the time to sit and think of a few good explanations?" he sneered. "I know what's happening here," he said directly to Bulmer, keeping his voice down so none of the men could hear him. "I don't know if you do, whether you're feigning ignorance or whether you just won't accept it. What is it, Tom? Burying your head in the coal dust?"

Bulmer's face remained empty for the briefest moment, then fire exploded in his eyes. "Don't ever talk to me like that again!" he hissed, his fists bunching so tightly that Mike thought he would lash out. "You know nothing. Nothing at all!"

"And don't talk to me like that," Mike spat back, barely restraining his anger. "At least I care enough to try to do something. I'm not going to sit back and wait for the next man

121

to die or be maimed. And you know what? I don't think it's going to end there. It's going to get worse, much worse, unless we stop it now."

Bulmer's face was less than a foot from Mike's, white in the yard lights, his eyes probing. Eventually he released the pressure in his fists and backed off. "We'll talk about this later," he said sullenly, "in my office. Tomorrow. It'd be better if we calmed down a bit, don't you think? Wouldn't want to say anything we regret." Then he turned on his heels and marched across the yard into the night.

The men around Mike dispersed quickly. Within seconds he found himself alone, staring at the wet, red line which ran from the lift building to where the ambulance had been parked. He hoped Charlie would survive the shock of losing his arm. He hoped he would live to marry his sweetheart and escape from Colthorpe before it was too late. He hoped – but he feared the worst.

There was a chill in the air, the first frosty greeting-kiss of winter. The land around the mine was as black as the tunnels beneath his feet, the tranquil fields hidden from view. He shivered again and jogged, despite his exhaustion, towards home.

Chapter Seventeen

"Mike! My God, what's happened?"

He was a shocking sight. His face was filthy with coal dust and dirt, streaked in bands where the sweat had run and he had wiped it with the back of his hand. His hair was matted and greasy. Beneath the grime his skin was chalky-white, bleached by fear, and there was a vague, wild look in his eyes. Hannah was astonished by his transformation, and at the same time scared. She had never seen her husband so . . . *broken*, was the word that sprang to mind, although that was probably too strong. Defeated, maybe. Punch-drunk? She could not link the figure before her with the man she knew: the one ravaged by a cancerous temper who railed loudly and bitterly against his lot in life.

He muttered something in reply, but the words were lost to her. All she could do was stare.

"I said, what's happened?" She reached out and touched the back of his hand. The skin was as cold as a fish.

"I got lost. Underground." His voice was small too, a pale, frightened thing. He wanted to unburden himself of the whole terrifying experience, but he knew that to do so would be to bring the dark thing out into the real world, delineate it with the fullness of life. And by keeping it buried, at the back of his mind, he could almost deny its existence.

"Oh, Mike . . ."

She put her arms around him, oblivious to the dirt that was smearing her clothes and skin. Her embrace gave him strength. He found in it something he had forgotten in the turmoil of the intervening years since they married. It was a feeling he liked very much.

"Don't worry, I'm fine. It was just a shock, that's all. I was scared I wouldn't see you again."

"Well, you're back now. Safe. How did it happen?"

"I was with that lad I told you about, Charlie. He was helping me find out what happened to Alec Jakes and he took me into an abandoned part of the mine. Something went wrong with our helmet lights and we got separated in the dark."

"Mike, you've got to be careful! It's dangerous down there. It isn't Oxford Street on a Saturday afternoon. You've got to stop acting like you're indestructible."

"I'm learning. Slowly." He squeezed her cheek. "I'm going to have a shower and try to get some of this filth off me. Then I'll cook you dinner."

"No, I'll cook *you* dinner. You take it easy."

He hated not telling her the whole truth, but he knew it was for the best. He wanted to protect her. The world was a tough enough place without adding to it an element of incredible horror.

At the sound of his father's voice, Jack came running into the lounge. "Daddy!" He stopped in his tracks when he saw Mike, his simple excitement suspended in a moment of surprise. Then he giggled. "Daddy, you're dirty."

"Yes, and he's going to get a smacked botty if he doesn't wash before dinner." Hannah pushed him mock-roughly between his shoulder blades.

"See, even I can't get away with being a mucky pup." Jack giggled again at Mike's expression. The laughter eased him, each moment sieving the thought of that cold, bony grip further into the depths of his mind. "And what have you been doing today?"

Jack bounced around gleefully. "I've been playing."

"Have you done any exploring yet?"

Jack thought carefully for a second and then replied. "No. I've been playing."

"He hasn't done any exploring because he spends all his time in his bedroom, don't you, you little monkey?" Hannah said sternly.

"What? In this lovely weather?" Mike picked him up and tickled him until he squirmed. "Well, this weekend we're going to go out and find some exciting places. Okay?"

124

"Okay."

Mike chased him back into the bedroom and horsed around happily before taking his shower. In the privacy of the bathroom, the memory of what had happened to him underground resurfaced. He remembered everything: the rasping voice, the feel of the fingers around his wrist, the way the flesh felt clammy, lifeless. He returned to Hannah as quickly as he could.

Later, after they had eaten, he lounged on the sofa next to her and fumbled for her hand. "I'm glad you're here," he said, realizing how much he meant it.

Hannah squeezed his hand in return. After a moment she said tentatively, "I'm a little bit worried, Mike."

"Why?" he asked, his eyelids lazily fluttering half-closed.

She chose her words carefully. She did not want to frighten him – or herself. "The little monster's been playing up a bit."

"What do you mean?" He started at the word "monster".

"I've been having a lot of cramps." That was an understatement. The pains had begun around noon and they had only subsided about an hour before Mike had returned, knotting her insides with the feel of undigested sour apples. At one point she had been convinced that the baby was clawing at her womb lining. "Maybe I'm on the wrong diet! I really thought I was going to be sick."

Mike suddenly became concerned. "I'm calling the doctor first thing tomorrow. He can come round here to see you."

"Mike, it's not that serious."

"Better safe than sorry, Hannah. You ought to have a full check-up. If there's anything wrong, you need to sort it out now, not later."

Comforted already, she gave in. "I suppose you're right."

"Of course I'm right. Now, listen to me. I want you to take it easy from now on. I've not been very fair recently." He held up his hand to silence her before she could interrupt. "No, I know it's true. I've been selfish. I've spent all my time worrying about my own problems when I should have been worrying about you. That's going to change."

"So I get to live in the lap of luxury, do I, with my own servant at my beck and call? Yes, I think I could get used to that." She lay back across the sofa. "I can see it now . . .

125

breakfast in bed. Gourmet dishes prepared for my delectation. Someone to type up my features as I lounge back and dictate them."

"Well, let's not go overboard," Mike laughed. "I was thinking more along the lines of not forcing you to fetch in sacks of coal for the fire!"

The laughter was a release that set the scene for a quiet, tender evening. After Jack had been put to bed, they revelled in the luxury of a few peaceful moments together, just sitting chatting, doing the things it seemed to Mike they had not done for a long time.

At eleven thirty, the tranquillity was broken by the sound of sobbing from Jack's bedroom. Hannah raised her eyebrows and sighed. "Sounds like he's having a nightmare."

"I'll go." Before he had time to cross the room, Jack's door swung open. He came stumbling in, tears streaming down his blotchy face.

"Hey, hey, what's the matter?" Mike swept him up in his arms.

Jack tried to speak, but the words were lost beneath sobs and gulps of air. He was trembling. Mike held him tightly and stroked the back of his head, whispering softly into his ear. Eventually he had calmed enough to talk.

"Did you have a bad dream, sweetheart?" Hannah said.

He swivelled in Mike's arms and looked at her despairingly. "Don't die, Mummy!"

She laughed dismissively. "I'm not about to, honey. Whatever made you say that?"

He took another deep breath and said, "The elves." Hannah's face dropped. "The elves told me you and Daddy were going to die. I don't want you and Daddy to die!"

"Come on," Mike said, jigging him up and down. "It was just a bad dream. It'll go in a few minutes."

"No, it was the elves," he added with certainty. "They *told* me."

"Well, whatever they said, they were wrong," Mike said. "We're not going to die and leave you. We're too tough. You tell them that the next time they speak to you."

Jack's lips puckered as he glanced from Mike to Hannah and back. He remained unconvinced, but after Mike had

126

walked around the room with him, whispering reassuringly into his ear, he slowly forgot whatever had been troubling him. Mike continued to stroke his head until his eyelids flickered and then closed. "Come on," Mike whispered. "Back to the Land of Nod."

Hannah watched Mike carry him gently through to bed, remembering the guttural voice she had heard in Jack's room the previous day. The elves were becoming almost as real to her as they were to Jack.

At four am, Mike woke with a start. A thin band of moonlight filtered between the curtains, lining the edges of the wardrobe and the chest of drawers. Although it was cold outside, his body was slicked with sweat. Sleep slipped from him swiftly with the realization that Hannah was thrashing in her dreams next to him, but he knew that was not what had woken him. From beneath the floor, near the bed, he could hear the unmistakable sound of scratching. It was louder than he had heard it before and uncomfortably close to the surface. With a growing feeling of anxiety, he crawled to the end of the bed and stared, as if he had X-ray vision which could see through the floor to whatever was beneath.

The scratching echoed through the quiet of the room: an irritating clawing that set his teeth on edge and put a chill down his spine. Was it moving closer to the surface – or was it his imagination?

It was not until he rolled over and tried to block out the disturbing noise that he noticed Hannah's dream spasms seemed to correspond to the bouts of scratching beneath the floor. He pulled the sheets back and watched her hands clutching at her stomach as if she were trying to stop some deep-seated pain.

It was, he thought with a mixture of curiosity and fear, as if the scratching was coming from within.

Chapter Eighteen

Bulmer was giving nothing away. The desk between them was an effective barrier that provided him with a resolute detachment. From the moment Mike was summoned in and told to sit down, like a naughty schoolboy before the headmaster, he knew it would be a struggle to achieve anything. He had hoped for a frank discussion about Colthorpe's secrets; he was convinced Bulmer knew more than he was saying. After the events of the previous day, his desire to discover what was happening at the colliery, and beneath it, had almost become an obsession. He *needed* to know the truth. He was increasingly sure of one thing: that the bizarre, unnerving incidents he had experienced were just the start of something momentous and ultimately terrifying. The incidence of strange manifestations was increasing with each passing day; the scratchings under the bungalow were now as regular a disturbance as the trundle of heavy lorries along the road past the mine. He had never believed in the supernatural before. Now it was as real to him as the slag and rock piled in the corner of the pit yard.

"Out with it then. What have you got to say?" Bulmer disrupted his thoughts bluntly.

"Tom, we've been straight with each other so far. I just want to know what's happening."

Bulmer's chair creaked as his heavy frame shifted into a more comfortable position. His coal-hard eyes never flickered. "What do you mean?"

Mike sighed in exasperation. "What is the point in playing a cat-and-mouse game? You know what I'm talking about. Do I have to spell it out?"

128

Bulmer nodded. "Spell it out."

"All right." Mike gritted his teeth. "I know there are things happening in Colthorpe which, to use a cliché, defy all rational explanation. I know there's an altar in a tiny room somewhere off the abandoned tunnels of the mine and I know it's been used by miners for hundreds of years. I know about the Tunnellers." He paused, watching for some flicker of interest in Bulmer's face. "I know they're real, whatever they are. Ghosts, spirits of the dead – God knows. I'm too scared to even think about it for too long. I don't know what you prefer to call the things that are roaming about your mine, Tom, but you can't deny their existence. They killed Jakes and they maimed Charlie Robson. And you're a fool if you think it'll stop there."

"If you said that to anyone they'd laugh in your face."

"You're not laughing."

Bulmer shrugged and glanced out of the window.

"I can't understand your position, Tom. Can't you see that if we don't do something this could blow up in our faces? I'm not some superstitious labourer, I'm an educated, intelligent person. But . . . I've seen things, Tom. Frightening things. I can't sleep at night. I have to believe in them, because not to believe would be to bury my head in the sand. Your men have awakened something down there. Those funny little exercises in superstition at that altar have got out of hand and there's going to be . . ." he shifted uneasily at his accidental joke, ". . . the devil to pay."

Bulmer grunted. "There's a strike brewing. The men are angry and talking about picket lines and God knows what. And this pit is about to close and put me out of a job that I thought would keep me well-fed till my retirement. I haven't got time for fucking ghosties and ghoulies."

"That's not the way to look at it, Tom," Mike pleaded.

"It's the only bloody way. There might be things happening down there that can't be explained – there might not. I've heard rumours, same as anyone else on this site, and I might have my own suspicions, but it doesn't concern you."

"Of course it concerns me," Mike snapped. "You seem to be ignoring the fact that I was sent here to look into your pit's appalling safety record."

129

"I'd like to see you put all this in your fucking report," Bulmer said icily.

"So it's better to come up with . . . shall we say, realistic solutions, even though they're obvious lies?"

Bulmer merely smiled.

"Tom – "

"Forget all this rubbish, lad," Bulmer interrupted, a faint glimmer of warmth appearing in his voice.

"I can't, Tom. It's important to me to discover what's really happening. I'm going to do it with or without your help."

Bulmer raised his hands. "It'll be without, then."

"What are you hiding, Tom? I know there's something stopping you getting involved. You're a decent bloke – you wouldn't allow this to happen if you didn't have a reason."

"I'm hiding nothing," he replied. "What you see is what you get."

Mike shook his head and made his way to the door. "I'm sorry you feel that way, Tom, but I've got a conscience, even if you haven't."

In his own office, Mike instantly dismissed Bulmer's inactivity; he was steeled in his own mind for decisive action of some sort and really did not care if Bulmer was with him or not. Knowledge was the key to the problem, knowledge of the enemy, and he knew just how to gain that.

The first thing he did was to call Hannah. Her condition had been preying on his mind and he knew, although she dismissed it, that it had been disturbing her too.

"Hi, honey, it's me. How did it go?"

"No problem. What did I tell you?" She sounded in good spirits.

"So what did the doc say?"

"One hundred per cent, tip-top shape. I don't think there were any tests left to give me when he finished. Heart, blood pressure, the works. It was a complete MOT."

"How did he explain the stomach pains? Christ, last night I thought you were . . ."

"What? Miscarrying? To be honest, that worried me too, but he says it was just a stomach upset. Sometimes when you're pregnant your glands start working overtime and you

130

produce a surplus of acid which gives you a real gripey tummy. Or so he says."

"Does it seem like he knows what he's talking about? We can always get a second opinion." Mike stared out of the window across the fields; there was a faint mist clinging to the hollows, but the sun was warm and bright.

"He's fine, Mike. Really. He's given me the number of the local hospital if I want to go for more extensive tests, but he said it would be best to wait and see if the stomach cramps come back. I'm inclined to agree with him. I admit I was worried last night, but the doctor didn't seem too concerned and he'd know if there was a chance of anything being wrong, wouldn't he?"

"I suppose so."

"So, how are things with you?"

"Fine. Dull. Bulmer's in a bad mood, so I'm going to take the rest of the day off."

"Coming to wait on your beautiful, heavily pregnant wife, then?"

"Love to, hon, but I'll have to take a rain check this time. I'm going to meet that reporter I told you about; Terry Richmond."

"Oh. Why?"

"I've just got a hunch he might be able to help me. He's one of those blokes who seem to know everything that happens, often before it even does. And at the moment I can use all the pointers I can get."

"Well, good luck. Pick me up a present!"

"Will do." He hung up, snatched his mac from the desk and headed out to the car, filled with a new sense of purpose, a fiery confidence. He caught sight of Bulmer through the window, but the colliery manager turned away brusquely. *Fuck him.* Mike thought. If he needed an ally, and he had not convinced himself that he did, he was confident he would find one in Terry Richmond.

Chapter Nineteen

"It's not much further." Richmond lit another cigarette and coughed fitfully.

The road from Burton-on-Trent, where Mike had collected the reporter from his office, had plunged them straight into the heart of the countryside. At first there had been rolling green fields on either side, interrupted every now and then by ancient cottages with fading red brick and dark wooden beams, but as they progressed clumps of trees, copses and small woods began to appear at increasingly regular intervals. Soon the trees had clustered in around the road until eventually, ahead of them, he saw the thick line of the forest, tall, dark and brooding. It leaned menacingly against the road.

"Needwood Forest," Richmond said. "Ancient woodland, all of it. One of the last great unspoilt forests in Britain. Duchy of Lancaster owns most of it, I believe."

Richmond had known immediately what to do when Mike had called him with a request for in-depth information on the history of Colthorpe. One phone call had arranged a meeting with a local academic. His books were renowned, Richmond had informed him. The reporter had wanted to know exactly what Mike was looking for, but a promise of a full explanation at a later date had deflected his questions for the time being.

Professor Eric Williams' house stood on the edge of the thickest part of the forest, the last boundary post between humanity and nature. On either side the trees were packed so densely that only dark shadows lay between them. Several times Mike felt there was someone within watching him, but he dismissed it as an inevitable reaction to the experiences of the past few days. The house was square and sturdy, two storeys high, but small enough for Mike to think it was a lodge for some larger hall hidden behind the trees. The gardens were neatly tended with large, overblown pink and yellow roses at the front. A thin line of white smoke drifted up from the chimney.

"He doesn't go out much," Richmond said. He opened the garden gate and allowed Mike through first. "He's getting on a bit, I suppose. He must be seventy-nine or eighty, if he's a day, but he's still as sharp as a needle."

A small, grey-haired woman with a piercing gaze and a broad smile answered the door. "You must be the gentlemen from the paper," she said. "He's in a good mood today. He's been looking forward to talking to you."

She led them through to a study at one corner of the house. There were windows on two adjoining walls, but the encroaching forest was so impenetrable that the room was filled with a permanent gloom.

"He's in the garden at the back. I'll just go and fetch him." The woman, his daughter or housekeeper, ushered Mike and Richmond to a well-used sofa.

The study's walls were lined with old books on rich, dark, mahogany shelves. There were hundreds of them – leather-bound and cracking, fabric-bound and splitting. The room was filled with the luxuriant aroma of old wisdom that reminded Mike of hushed school libraries. A small fire crackled and spluttered in the grate, occasionally showering an army of red sparks up the chimney. The dry, lazy tick of a hidden clock hung in the air.

Williams had a brightness about him that belied his age. Although his face was lined like a weather-beaten outcropping, his eyes sparkled with youth and vitality. "Hello, Mr Richmond. How are you? And you are . . . ?" His voice rumbled with the local inflection, but a university education had papered over the cracks.

"Mike Leary. British Coal."

"Ah, yes. Indeed. Would you both like tea? Mrs Whittaker, could we have a pot of tea, please," he said loudly through the door before he closed it. He lowered himself into a high-backed leather chair next to the fire and proceeded to

133

clean his spectacles. "Now gentlemen," he continued, "what can I do for you?"

Richmond replied. "As I mentioned on the phone, Professor Williams, Mr Leary is very interested in the history of this area. The history of Colthorpe and the mine in particular."

"Oh, really?" Williams raised one silvery eyebrow. "Are you interested in anything special?"

Mike thought carefully about what he should or should not say. His indecision must have been reflected on his face, for Williams said, "Come, come, Mr Leary. I may be old, but I'm still busy. Surely you don't expect to keep me waiting all day?"

"I'm sorry, Professor. It's just that I find it very hard to put into words. Look, I'll come clean with you. Some odd things have been happening at the mine over the last few weeks. It's my job to look into the situation there and I'm grateful for any information that will help me."

"What kind of things?" Williams stare was unwavering.

"One man dead underground in mysterious circumstances. Another injured in a terrible accident yesterday. I don't think it would be too melodramatic to say that both of them are inexplicable."

"Nothing is truly inexplicable," Williams replied. "It all depends on how good we are at reading the information, doesn't it? And how much of an open mind one has."

"I didn't know someone was injured yesterday?" Richmond blinked at Mike quizzically through his glasses.

"We were a little more cautious this time. We told the police and the ambulance service not to release any details." Mike turned back to Williams. "Why did you say that, Professor?"

The old man's eyes sparkled. "I think you're playing games with me because you don't want to seem like a fool." He laughed quietly. "A superstitious fool."

Mike was suddenly sure Williams had some perception of the frighteningly unreal things that had taken place at Colthorpe. How he knew it, he had no idea, but recognizing that knowledge in him was like finding a kindred spirit. He turned to Richmond. "Terry, you most promise me that

134

everything said in this room stays in the strictest confidence."
He tried to make it seem like a request. "At least for the
moment."

"That's fine by me," Richmond replied sourly. "I'm only a
reporter, after all."

"You'll get a good story in the end, believe me." Mike was
confident that everything that had happened would seem too
fanciful ever to be published. He felt it safe to continue.
"Professor, what is *wrong* with Colthorpe?"

Williams rested his head on the back of his chair and closed
his eyes for so long that Mike thought he had dozed off. But
when he opened them, they were dark and scared. "I can tell
from looking at you that you've seen the things that happen
there. But I doubt you've seen it all. You wouldn't be sitting
here . . . you wouldn't be in this county if you had. I don't
want you to think I'm an old fool, Mr Leary. I'm not. I'm
just . . . aware. There are many things I could tell you, but
the most important thing is this: if you believe in your soul,
your immortal soul, you will keep away from Colthorpe. Is
that enough? I doubt it. You are an intelligent man with an
inquiring mind. I would guess that you *need* to know – in the
samew way that I *need* to know. Am I right?"

Mike concurred.

"Well then, I must go on. To say it is an evil place would not
be an overstatement. That may sound a little melodramatic,
but believe me, Mr Leary, it is not."

"Do you mind if I smoke?" Richmond asked. His mind was
already wandering.

"Yes, I do," Williams snapped.

They sat in silence as Mrs Whittaker brought in a trolley
and poured the tea out into china cups. After she had left,
Mike said, "Tell me about the Tunnellers."

"So it *has* started again." Williams covered his eyes. "It will
not end with one death, Mr Leary. There will be more, many
more. Who knows, maybe you will be one of them? The
Tunnellers exist." This time he stared at Richmond, his cold,
unflinching gaze daring him to disagree. "They are souls. Lost
souls. They have been trapped there since the first people
settled in the village. Spirits that are still being trapped to this
very day."

135

"How do you know?" Mike asked.

"I know." He gestured at the shelf-lined walls. "Some of the evidence is in these books. A few of the volumes date back three hundred years or more."

"And the other evidence?"

Williams ignored him. He eased himself to his feet and walked slowly to one of the shelves, rubbing his chin thoughtfully as he perused the titles. "Where is it now? Ah, here. This," he said, holding a thin book aloft, "is a history of the area written in 1790 by Stebbing Shaw." He flicked through the pages until he found the paragraph he wanted. Then he began to read. "'The area is a dreary waste which chills the view, interrupted only by a coal mine, and the smoke of a small pottery for common brown ware.' An image of desolation, indeed. There was mining even then, and hundreds of years before. The Phillipps Charters recorded deeds to mines from the thirteenth to the seventeenth century. Colthorpe was always popular for mining because the coal outcropped to the surface in many places. The area was littered with the medieval equivalent of drift mines. In the years after that, bell pits were dug out and eventually, as the industry progressed, deep shafts were sunk to the coal seams. There is a fine history of honest toil here." He replaced the book, smiling wanly. "In the seventeenth century, when coal was vital to the economy of the country, Colthorpe was a prime site because the seams were relatively close to the surface. That meant pumping engines were not necessary to remove the water settlement which caused massive problems in lower strata."

Richmond coughed politely. "Professor, Mr Leary asked about the Tunnellers . . . ?"

Williams brushed his query aside with a wave of his hand. "Yes, yes, but you need to know it all, don't you see? No, of course you don't. How silly of me." He spent several minutes pulling a selection of books from the shelves and carrying them over to his chair by the fire. Mike helped him. "I apologize," Williams said. "I forget things sometimes. I forgot that I know things of which you have no idea. But you must understand the history of Colthorpe – because it is filled with secrets . . . hidden things . . . death."

"What secrets?" Mike stared at him.

"I need to show you the whole picture before you can see. There's no point baldly stating conclusions without providing the evidence that led me to them. Now, listen carefully." In that dark room, with the fire crackling in the background, Mike felt like a child once more, listening to the weavings of a storyteller. There was no doubt that Williams could create such a spell, with his expressive, resonant voice, but Mike sensed something else adding to the atmosphere: a darkness closing in around his words, a darkness at the centre of Williams' very being.

"Colthorpe, more than many other areas, is a product of its history." Williams continued drily. "Insular, close-knit, intractably linked to the coal industry that gave it life. The village expanded as the coal reserves were developed. At the start of the coal boom, the staple diet for most villagers was potato, fat mutton and haver cake – a very unpalatable kind of food, believe me. With the influx of money, the standard of living rose and a richer middle class developed. This resulted in tension in village life. The newer, richer classes who moved to the area were appalled by the behaviour of the labourers: those who worked on, and under, the land." He tapped the leather hide of a book in emphasis. "They were little more than animals – drunken, violent, anti-social. The well-to-do complained ferociously about the terrible standards. They claimed that it was purely the result of a lack of religion. Naturally, that caught the attention of a local vicar, the Reverend Arnold Collett, who took it upon himself to build a church with his own savings." Williams traced a line in a book with his finger. "He said this was a 'means of producing a reformation in the habits and morals of many of the inhabitants'."

There was a detailed drawing in the text of a high-domed man with piercing eyes, hollow cheeks and a pinched expression. Wisps of silvery hair protruded over his ears. He stared out of the page with a cold power that stretched across the years. A hard man for hard times.

"Is that the church that stands in the village now?" Mike asked.

Williams nodded. "Reverend Collett's church remained

137

empty for the first two weeks, but slowly, in dribs and drabs, the congregation began to increase. His reputation as a fiery preacher reached far and wide and he was held in high regard by many of his contemporaries for undertaking a mission in such an area of degradation. Although he condemned the immoralities of the time with passion, he could do little to staunch the less savoury habits of Colthorpe's working class. In a pamphlet which he published privately, he said, 'Colthorpe is a dark and dreary place. There is a badness in the earth which seeps up and into the hearts of the bitter and oppressed and makes them turn their eyes from God. It is my mission to stop this black tide, and although the road is long and arduous I will not shirk from my task. Some say the land itself is foul and that in all of God's Earth it is the one spot where the devil has sown his seed. Whether that is true, I know not. It is true, however, that many of the people are a foul, godless lot, much taken to drink, gambling and wantonness.'"

Williams looked across at them and repeated, "'there is a badness in the earth'."

Mike felt something knot in his stomach. "Even then . . ."

Williams smiled wanly. "Although Collett obviously wielded a tremendous influence in Colthorpe, he mysteriously disappeared one night from his home next to the church. The villagers said the devil had taken him because of his forthright views, but the book suggests that, faced by the awesome task of turning Colthorpe's residents into God-fearing folk, he upped and left for an easier calling. That is a much saner explanation, don't you think?" The irony in his voice was unmistakable.

There was a loud retort from the fire as a log split in two. Richmond started nervously. "It's a bit early for ghost stories, isn't it?" he laughed.

"The point I am making, in a very circumlocutory way, is that the people who live in Colthorpe are open to a very strange, and very individual influence."

"What? Radiation?" Richmond said.

"No, but whatever it is operates in a similar way. It pollutes the minds of the living. It brings out the dark side, the bestial. And it holds on to the souls of the dead like a magnet."

138

Richmond laughed, then stopped when he saw he was alone in his amusement.

"Most people in this area have been touched, in one way or another, by it," Williams added cryptically. He lifted his cup to his mouth. "This tea is cold. Would anyone like something else? Something a little stronger?"

"The sun hasn't set yet," Richmond said.

"If the sun had set this conversation would not be taking place. I think we deserve a little sustenance, if only to get us to the end of our little chat. It is not really a subject that should be tackled without a degree of fire in the blood."

He went over to a small antique cupboard in one corner of the room and opened it to reveal a row of sparkling crystal glasses and a cut-glass decanter of golden liquid. He poured three healthy measures of whisky and handed them around. After he had returned to his seat he continued: "Terry, do you remember when you called me the other day for information about the history of strikes at the pit?"

"My contacts told me there's another strike brewing now. I was writing a background piece."

"You remarked at the time how they seemed to come in cycles. That is true. And there are also corresponding cycles of public violence, drunkenness, immoral behaviour."

"There's a link." Mike stared thoughtfully into the fire. It glowed a dull red.

"I believe," Williams said, holding his glass high to catch the light, "that whatever power there is in Colthorpe is given life by the angry, charged feelings of the miners. Imagine what emotions could be generated by a fight to save your livelihood, your family, your very existence!"

"This is beyond me," Richmond said with growing irritation. "No one believes in this balderdash any more."

"In the mine, in a tiny room in an abandoned section, there's an altar," Mike said. "It's been there for years. Hundreds of years. I was told that the miners prayed there to . . . to something. Not a Christian God."

"I've heard about that altar," Williams said. "A conduit. What better way to channel feelings?"

"Tell me about the strikes," Mike asked. "What happened then?"

"In the 1790s, miners were paid two shillings and sixpence a day with a beer allowance. That's well-documented. For years it never improved. The first major strike was in 1842. It failed dismally. By 1867, the miners' conditions were far worse than those of any of their colleagues in surrounding areas. Although the practice had been made illegal in 1831, wages were still paid in public houses run by the mine owners, and a proportion of their wage had to be spent there before the remaining cash could be obtained. The truck system, which was also illegal, was still in operation too. This meant that wages were paid, partly or wholly, in goods supplied by the pit owners at whatever price they chose to ask. By 1870 Colthorpe's miners had had enough. They went on strike for eight months to try to better their conditions. It must have been a harrowing experience. Can you imagine the suffering? They were finally defeated by strikebreakers from nearby counties and a national depression in the coal trade. The strike left a legacy of anger and bitterness in Colthorpe which remained for many years. And as they had failed to rid themselves of the oppressive system, it was compounded by the fact that the grievance remained. The miners' failure in these disputes meant Colthorpe stayed backward in terms of hours, conditions and mechanization well into the twentieth century."

Williams paused to prod the fire and throw another log on to the embers. The air was heavy with words and thoughts; Mike could feel the weight of hundreds of years pressing down around him. Richmond jerked as his head nodded down to his chest; he smiled apologetically.

"While the strikes took hold," Williams continued, "lawlessness blossomed. At one point the locals, who were still trying to live genteel, civilized lives, were forced to petition Parliament to try to get their own police force." He opened another book and ruffled through several pages. "This is what the petitioners said: 'There is a prevalence of vice and immorality in this realm generally, and in the neighbourhood particularly. On the Sabbath, all sort of gambling, card-playing, dog-fighting, drunkenness and debauchery much prevail, and that to such a degree, that the well-disposed and peaceable inhabitants cannot go out of their houses, even to attend places of worship, without insult; and that females, especially, of decent habits and character, can hardly shew themselves on that day with safety to their persons, for the brutal attacks of the drunken and dissolute, who are to be found standing by the roadside, at the doors of beershops, or in the vicinity.' The petition was unsuccessful and Colthorpe had to wait another thirteen years before a police force was established in the county."

"I can see what you're driving at, Professor," Richmond said, in a way that suggested he had no comprehension of what was being discussed, "but you keep swinging between superstition and hard fact. I haven't heard much . . ."

"I am just getting to that, Mr Richmond," Williams snapped irritably. "You must see the whole picture. You must see the subtleties before I get to the heart of the matter." He held up the last book in his pile. "Here."

It was a leather-bound book with a worn, dog-eared covering and yellowing, parchment-dry pages. On the cover, in faded, gold letters, was the title *A Guide to Leicestershire by Gregory Huxtable*. "This was published in the eighteenth century. Huxtable had already made a name for himself with several guides to areas around the Midlands. He was an author who relished gossip and contumely as much as hard facts. He loved bawdy tales of sex-crazed squires and village girls. Buried in this slim volume, however, is the key to the problem. There is one brief mention of Colthorpe which he introduces with the words 'Beware. 'Tis a haunted place.' He recounts the tale of a village boy's encounter with the ghost of his father who had died in a mining accident several years earlier. Huxtable says the father had joined 'a strange and ghostly troupe' called the Tunnellers, who lived beneath the village. The ghost tried to entice his son to join him underground, but the youngster kept his wits about him and escaped to the sanctuary of the church."

Mike's wrist tingled where unearthly fingers had grasped it tightly. His shoulder ached where it had been strained by an inhuman strength.

"He finishes his account with these words: 'The land is sour. It conjures shades and spooks and bogles and imprisons them on Earth. Over the black well, milk sours

141

in the churn and no crop will grow. God-fearing men, pass by.'"

Williams closed the book. Outside the sun was close to the horizon and what little sunlight remained cast long shadows across the room, illuminating motes of dust which hung in the air. In that half-light, Williams' face looked heavy with age. The lines were deeper, the cheeks hollower and his eyes had lost their sparkle. "Is that what it is? A black well? Polluting the people? Polluting – souls?" He looked directly at Mike, ignoring Richmond who shifted uncomfortably in his seat. "The mine is sited on a spot which is somehow tainted. It is a haunted few acres, casting a spell over the villagers and in turn becoming activated by their negative thoughts like a key opening a door to another world. Hate, despair and anger are a powerful fuel."

"How do you know?" Mike asked. "How can you have such conviction?"

"How?" Williams laughed a little too loudly. "Because they told me."

"Who told you?"

He merely smiled in reply and then glanced at his watch. "Wait a while longer and you will see."

And so they waited. They sat quietly, drinking whisky and listening to the crackle of the fire and the rush of wind down the chimney. Williams' housekeeper bid them goodbye and left for the evening. Richmond tried a few times to make conversation, but lapsed into silence after a feeble response. Mike knew that he doubted the argument Williams had made; he prided himself on his rationality. But Mike believed. He believed totally and he wished he did not. As the minutes ticked by, the shadows grew longer, and then night came, turning the forest into a wall of ultimate darkness.

Eventually Williams broke the silence with a single word. "Soon."

"What the hell are we waiting for?" Richmond asked impatiently.

Williams ignored him, levering himself to his feet with cracking joints. He stood at the window for five minutes, staring out into the depths of the forest before he said, "Come here." The words were quiet but charged with tension.

Mike looked over Williams' shoulder. He could see nothing. The trees thrashed wildly in the wind, but beneath their tops and between their boles was a blackness as deep as space. "Where?" He tried to sound confident, but his voice was a hoarse whisper.

"There." Williams pointed one pale, bony finger.

Mike strained until he could just make out something moving – a shape marginally lighter than the darkness around it.

"They like the forest," Williams said. "The shadows remind them of being underground."

A cold hand touched Mike's heart. "What is it?"

Williams' throaty chuckle was humourless. "A Tunneller, if you want to call them that. The dead. They wander the forests at night. I've been seeing them more and more over the last week or two."

The shape moved a little closer. Mike could just make out a white face with dark shadows where the eyes were, but the features were hidden to him. It seemed to be staring at them. There was other movements further back into the forest, brief shimmers but without substance.

"Don't worry. They won't come any closer while you're here, although I admit they are a little braver than usual tonight. Shortly after they first appeared I asked Mrs Whittaker to stay to see if she could see them. They never came. I fear she thinks senility has set in."

Richmond was aghast, his own face as white as the thing in the trees. "You said *they* told you . . . ?"

"A few nights ago. I ventured outside, not daring to go beyond the circle of light from the window. I heard their voices calling out to me. Pleading with me to join them. Horrible, horrible voices." He choked slightly. "They said it was cold underground and they wanted my warmth. They're jealous, you see. Very, very bitter."

"Stop it," Richmond said.

"One of them . . ." His words faltered, but Williams' gaze never left the shape in the forest. "One of them came forward. Close enough for me to see. There was so much pain in his face, and a terrible hatred for humanity; I was in no doubt that it wanted me dead. I spoke to it and it answered my questions with dull, flat words. It told me that the souls of men who died in Colthorpe, in the mine, even in the village, were trapped there. There was something underneath the land that held them fast. They were suffering, denied eternal rest."

"Stop it," Richmond said.

"That's a lot of souls," Mike whispered.

Williams nodded. "Over the centuries. A lot of souls."

The movement was increasing, brief glimpses flashing beneath the trees then disappearing – and there were other things, occasional pinpricks of light like will o'the wisps deep in the woods. And behind the wind which was raging around the house Mike thought he could hear something else: a howling and shrieking of a multitude of voices in agony.

"What is keeping them here?"

"I don't know," Williams replied, "but I cannot see much good in it. And whatever it is, it wants to come out. They told me. They said the time was right. They are coming to the surface."

The shapes shifted around the house, a stone's throw away; every now and then there was a sparkle like starlight. After almost an hour they faded back into the trees.

"Is that it?" Richmond asked. "Have they gone?"

"For the moment." Williams returned to his chair and stoked the fire high. "I thought at my age that I had left fear behind me, but I must admit that I'm afraid now. I fear for my soul. Do you understand?" Mike nodded. "They have killed one man already. There will be more before it is over. As they emerge into this world, like worms from beneath the earth, they will drag the living down." Williams stared deep into the flames. His voice became barely audible. "*It told me.*"

"Come with us," Mike said. "You can't stay here."

Williams declined, his voice small and sad. "This is my home. I don't want to leave it. I don't think they will touch me for the moment. They're not strong enough yet."

"But what happens when they are?"

He thought silently, then replied. "We shall see."

Mike heard the bolts slide across the door behind him when

he stepped out into the chill night. Within seconds the house was ablaze with brightness. Williams was moving from room to room, switching on lamps, lights, in the kitchen, pantry, bathroom, bedroom. Richmond could barely contain himself. He ran down the path to the car and turned the ignition before Mike had left the doorstep. As they drove along the winding lanes to Burton, he thought several times that he saw faces in the trees on either side. He kept his eyes fixed firmly on the road ahead.

Chapter Twenty

They pulled the car up outside a quiet pub on the High Street in Burton. They needed normality. Richmond appeared to be in a state of mild shock, his firmly-held belief in logic and rationality badly rattled by what he had seen in the shadows of the forest. For Mike, the situation was as bad as he had feared. He was surprised at how calmly he had come to accept things which, only a few weeks earlier, he had thought existed only in nightmares. That acceptance strangely pleased him; he felt good in himself, strong, despite the looming presence of the unknown. His only real concern was for Hannah and Jack, for their safety. His stomach knotted when he thought about them. For his own peace of mind, he wanted them as far away from Colthorpe as possible.

After a brief call to ensure they were both okay, Mike and Richmond settled at a table at the back of the pub. It was early and there were only a few drinkers scattered around the lounge, mulling over their glasses in silence or chatting in hushed voices. The barman, a youth who looked barely old enough to drink himself, whistled tunelessly, his expression one of utter boredom. A juke box played "Four In The Morning" by Faron Young to an inattentive audience. Richmond had the jitters, fumbling for his lighter with nervous hands. He wiped a film of sweat from his brow and downed half his pint in one draught, before lighting a cigarette and inhaling deeply.

"Are you okay?" Mike asked.

"I'm not cut out for this," the reporter replied. He choked back a cough and the smoke billowed up and made his eyes water.

"Yes you are. I need you."

"Need me? What for?" Richmond lowered his eyes, expecting the worst. "What are you planning to do?"

"We've got to do *something*, Terry. Didn't you feel the air of menace out there? The evil? They *wanted* us. You could almost taste it."

"Well it's a long way away now. I'd rather forget it."

"You can't forget it, Terry. You heard what Williams said. It's not going to go away. In time, maybe soon, they're going to come out on to the surface. Whatever force is driving them is going to come out and it's going to wash across this area. Then what are you going to do?"

Richmond considered the question, drawing the smoke deep into his lungs. "Move away?" he ventured.

"Give up your job? Try telling your wife your reasons for moving. She won't believe a word of it. You're stuck here. So you can either bury your head in the sand and accept the consequences, or . . ."

"All right, all right," he snapped. It was the first time Mike had seen him register annoyance. "What do you suggest?"

The question gave Mike pause. What could they do? What chance did two normal, everyday people stand against such an incomprehensible force? And why did he feel the urge to get involved when it would be so much easier, saner, as Richmond had suggested, to walk away? He was no hero. His mind could not even grasp the depth of the threat sufficiently to formulate any kind of effective plan. How could you plan against the unknown? Still, he had to try: if only to convince Richmond that he was needed. "If the emotions of the men are acting as a catalyst," he said tentatively, "maybe we could keep them away from the pit, away from the source of it all."

Richmond grunted derisively.

"For God's sake, Terry, be a bit more constructive. One person has died – another has been dismembered. Doesn't that mean anything?"

"Don't be so fucking condescending." Richmond's face had turned scarlet; his cheeks were blotchy with passion. "Who do you think I am, Leary? I'll tell you: I'm an overweight, second-rate reporter who just wants a quiet life and a

147

happy retirement with his wife and his garden. Why does it have to be up to us?"

A young couple were arguing at a table nearby. There were tears in the woman's eyes and anger in her voice. The man was leaning across the table, stabbing a finger an inch from her face. Mike thought of Hannah and all the arguments they had had over the years. He remembered how it used to be. "I'm not a good man, Terry," he said quietly. The beer lubricated his dry throat. "I always thought I was, but it went wrong somewhere down the line. I don't know why. You wake up one day and look in the mirror and you think, 'Who's that bad-tempered, selfish bastard?'. But I do want to be good, I really do, and I think I can do something here. I'm not going to force you to help me and I don't want to blackmail you emotionally. But I can't do it alone."

Richmond finished his pint and dabbed the moisture from the corners of his mouth. He looked frightened; uncertain and disturbed at the same time. "You bastard. How can I not help you?" His smile was grim but supportive. "The room underground that you mentioned. We could move the altar, destroy it. That might do something."

"Perhaps." Mike thought of the tiny tunnel, the rat-hole, and shivered inwardly. "It's worth a try."

"Dare we risk going underground? To the very heart of it?"

Mike ignored the question. "There's another reason, Terry. Another reason why I've got to do it."

"What's that?"

"I think they're after my wife and child."

Richmond raised a querying eyebrow.

"I don't know why I think that." Mike chewed his knuckle. "It's a gut feeling, a premonition. Sometimes I feel like I've plugged into vibrations that no one else can hear and they're telling me that we're on the lip of an abyss."

"Very poetic. You should have been a journalist."

"Anything's better than what I'm doing now. So when do we do it?"

"Three days. I've got a day off then."

"Three days. That's a long time. What happens if the shit hits the fan before then?"

"You ask too many questions. That's supposed to be my

job!" He stood up and slipped his arms into his mac. It was a size too small for him. "I better go. My poor old wife will be worrying about me. You know," he added thoughtfully, "I normally like to stay up late and read after she's gone to bed. I don't think I will tonight somehow."

Mike clapped a hand on his shoulder: a gesture of support, a recognition of a bond. "Thanks, Terry." He didn't know what else to say.

"Don't thank me. I don't feel like I'm being noble. I just feel like I haven't got any choice. Lord, I hope this isn't going to ruin my Christmas."

They shook hands warmly at the door and Mike walked along the quiet High Street to where he had left his car. The night was cold and there was a smell of hops in the air from the town's breweries. The shop windows were bright, illuminating their displays for drinkers who would not remember what they had seen the next day. Mike was grateful for the light. He wondered if he would be looking over his shoulder and into the dark of alleyways for the rest of his life.

Five hours earlier, Hannah had settled on to the sofa with a glass of water (since her pregnancy, coffee made her retch), a chocolate bar and the phone. Her day had been quiet. She was relieved that there had been no repetition of the cramps which had wracked her stomach the previous day – not even a twinge of pain or a dull ache. Perhaps it had been something she ate after all. For the first time that week she felt fit, healthy and relaxed; her only remaining problem was the boredom. With Mike working every day, including weekends, she had little chance to escape her routine or the confines of the bungalow. All she really wanted was to have her own possessions around her and to be in easy reach of a place she knew.

That craving for the security of old times prompted her to reach out for the phone and, on a whim, she dialled the office of her former magazine and asked to be put through to Jacqueline Evans. She still missed the hectic days, the tensions and deadlines, even the office politics. As the dull, clicking sound of her call being connected hissed down the line, she wistfully remembered the old times. At least her freelancing kept her in touch with all her friends. Jackie had been the one she could turn to whenever she needed advice, or when a feature had to be written quickly or particularly well. One day she would make a good editor, and there was no one more pleased than herself when Jackie was promoted to deputy editor after her own resignation.

Jackie's voice sounded work-weary when she eventually picked up her extension. "Hello."

"Jackie, it's Hannah."

"Hannah! You haven't called me in ages."

"Mike's working away again, in the Midlands, and with the baby so close I decided I'd rather be with him than on my own in London."

"That's the spirit! Don't let him get away. He'd only be lounging around with his feet up."

"Yes, this way he gets to wait on me hand and foot. Lucky old Mike." A laugh rose from within her. She felt the tremendous urge to giggle uncontrollably, releasing all those repressed emotions that had built up inside after the stress and strain of the previous few days – of the previous few months. It was almost sufficient to know she *could* still laugh. There was something liberating about being able to chat with her friend without carefully choosing her words, without expecting a curt reply or angry words. They talked easily for a while, discussing work, office politics, people the knew. Eventually, as Hannah knew it would, the serious subjects arose.

"So how are you and Mike getting on?" Jackie asked nonchalantly enough, but Hannah knew she was probing. After all she was the only person outside the marriage who knew the history of the problems they had been experiencing on and off for years.

"That's just it," Hannah replied. "I don't know. For the first time in months I can't really tell what's happening. Everything is in a complete state of flux The rows we had when we first arrived here were major. And I mean *major*. I thought we were getting to the stage where everything was going to break down completely."

"Was it work again?"

"Isn't it always? But this time it was worse. He was losing

150

his temper . . . and I mean *really* losing it, as well as his perspective, his balance . . . everything. He was so wrapped up in himself. Then . . ."

"Then?" Down the line, Hannah could hear the faint clatter of someone tapping a keyboard and the constant ringing of phones. She caught at her breath, fearing that if she said it, it would suddenly make it untrue.

"Then he changed."

"What? Just like that?"

"Just like that. Unbelievable, I know, but true. God, I can't believe it. Well, it's not that he's changed, it's more that he's *been* changed in some way. I'm his wife, I can tell these things; but, as usual, he keeps everything bottled up inside him and I can't get to the bottom of it. Whatever it is, I should be thankful for it. He's been so caring, just like he was when I first met him." A shiver of emotion returned with the memory. "Romantic. The sex is better than ever, even with my bump getting in the way. He hasn't had any of his moods, no fits of temper – nothing. He doesn't even seem to be bothering about work."

"That doesn't sound like Mike."

"You're telling me! Maybe I'll even talk him into giving it up and looking for something that he actually enjoys."

"Don't hold your breath. Hang on a minute." Jackie's voice drifted off into a garbled conversation about page proofs and layouts to somone nearby. Hannah felt a slight twinge of loss. "Sorry about that. They can't do without me here! So how are you feeling?"

"I'm fine at the moment." She subconsciously touched her belly.

"At the moment?"

"Well . . . I did go through a bad patch. I had terrible stomach pains the other day – the ones that double you up. The doctor said it was nothing . . ." Her voice trailed off.

"But?"

"But I couldn't get it out of my head that there was something wrong with the baby."

"The doctor is the expert, Hannah."

The pressure returned, forcing things back inside her. A lump suddenly rose in her throat. "I know that. Sometimes

151

you get a . . . feeling. It's . . . God, I don't know how to say this."

"Just take your time."

Hannah was comforted by the concern in Jackie's voice. "It felt like the baby was scratching me. Clawing at my womb." There, she had said it.

"That can't happen, Hannah."

"I know, I know." She hadn't had any alcohol since she found she was pregnant, but she wanted some right then. Vodka – to numb the thoughts. "Jackie, sometimes I feel the baby hates me. Sometimes I think it's a monster that just wants to rip its way out of my stomach."

"Don't talk like that, Hannah!" Jackie said sharply.

"I'm sorry, Jackie. It's just this place. There's an atmosphere here. I don't think Mike notices it, but there's an air of . . . I don't know . . . darkness. Something oppressive. Not all the time, of course. Sometimes it's almost idyllic. There's peace and quiet and green fields and birds, and all that. But there are creepy things too. Scratching noises under the floor, like there's rats down there or something. And, God, we saw a girl . . ." She suddenly could not bring herself to describe the image of the young girl slipping the package containing the body of her dead child into the black waters of the pool. "It's just – weird."

"It sounds to me like you need a good dose of London pollution. Why don't you come back and stay with me? We've got plenty of room and you know John would love to have you. It won't be long before Mike's back."

It was inviting, but she could not accept. "Thanks, but I can't. It would be wrong to leave Mike at the moment. He needs me around. And we're getting on so well, I don't want to jeopardize that. I've got to keep him in line, you know." Jackie laughed, but the concern was still there. "I know I'm being silly, Jackie. You worry about the most outrageous things when you get low."

"Well, any more worries and you get on the first train down here."

"Thanks, Jackie. You're a pal."

They spoke some more, returning to comforting trivia, before Hannah reluctantly ended the conversation. It had

152

been a cleansing experience for her, flushing out bad experiences and worse thoughts. Everything had been put into perspective. Of course the baby was not a monster! Of course she had nothing to worry about. It was just the ridiculous fantasies of someone with too much time on their hands.

For the first time in days, she took out her writing pad and began to sketch out some ideas. It gave her a thrill to think about writing again. With all her worries, it had fallen by the wayside, but she felt revitalized and ready for work once more. Within an hour she came up with ten solid ideas that would keep her working for three months at least.

Amazed at her creativity, she closed her eyes and drifted instantly into a soothing sleep.

Chapter Twenty-One

The pain was almost too much to bear. Knives in her ears, a dagger in her heart.

Like Theseus in the maze, Hannah staggered along dark corridors. Sweat slicked her body, her vision blurred. Nausea needled her stomach.

She was drawn by the sound of the child: the terrible, frightening sound. Its cry encompassed more than just fear or pain, sweeping up through its body like a black wave, drawing despair and complete loneliness in its wake. All Hannah wanted to do was to find the source of the piercing wail: to comfort the child, ease its pain, free it from suffering. The noise undulated, high pitched and ready, speaking volumes.

It said: *"I have known no suffering like this. I want to die."*

The closer she got to its origin, the more she wanted to claw at her ears to cut off that awful sound. But there was no respite, just a dolorous flow of suffering that seemed like it would go on forever.

Along the twisting, turning corridors she ran, pausing only to catch her breath, desperation pushing her heart to a frenzied jackhammer pounding. She had no idea where she was, or why it was so dark. Only one thing was important – and that was saving the child.

Droplets of stinging sweat seeped into the corner of her eyes, oozing down her spine so her shirt clung to her back. How much further? She was the only one who could save the child, but time was running out. She didn't know how she knew that. She just knew it.

Her footsteps echoed like shotgun blasts off the walls of the never-ending corridors. Every time she rounded a corner she thought she had reached the source, but then the cry faded and became distant once more, drawing back as if she had mysteriously returned to her starting point. It was a torment without end, she thought as she ran. Why was she being punished?

Then, suddenly, she was there. At the far end of the corridor, stairs led up to a bottle-green door, a bedroom door, which was slightly ajar. Immediately in front and above was a bare light bulb swinging slowly, its brilliant white glare strangely unable to pierce the deep surrounding darkness.

"Thank God," she whispered. She shielded her eyes. There were tears in the corners, mingling with the sweat.

As soon as the words left her mouth, the cry stopped, winding down to a softly juddering sob, interspersed with gulps of air. Then there was silence.

Quietly she approached the stairs, creeping forward on tiptoe, afraid of disturbing what lay behind the door or of finding she had arrived seconds too late. The walls to each side, dank and dully gleaming, seemed to be breathing – in, out, in, out – each movement matching a beat of her heart.

Trepidation gripped her. She placed a foot on the first step, forcing herself to continue. At the top of the steps she paused, listening to the sound of her laboured breathing, her hand hovering over the metal handle. From behind the door came a soft whimper. Stealing herself she grasped the handle and wrenched it, but although she put all her strength into the action the door swung open as if it were in a film running at half-speed.

Somewhere distant she could hear a low throb like hulking machines inexorably grinding, pounding eternally at some mysterious task. She stepped over the threshold and looked around. The room was huge, much bigger than she had expected, and it was lined with candles; hundreds of them flickered gently, the shadows dancing madly with each slight breeze. There was an overpowering odour of hot wax and smoke. Beneath it, she could smell something else. Something distasteful.

Hovering in the centre of the room was a strange haze, merging with the soft golden glow that radiated from the

155

candles. Beyond it, when she strained her eyes, she could just make out a small shape huddled on an ornate oaken chair.

Walking forward slowly, she saw the shape was a baby girl, smiling at her with twinkling eyes. The throbbing of the machines intensified slightly, pumping out a steady rhythm, occasionally fading to reveal another, stranger noise, a gentle sighing which occasionally passed her ears like a breeze.

She ignored them both, concentrating on the baby.

"Don't worry," she said soothingly, "I'll look after you now." She could barely contain her joy at finding the child unharmed. Her cry had threatened so much. "Are you all right?"

Bending down, Hannah plucked the baby from the chair and cradled her in her arms, resting her cheek against its warm, pink head. A comforting wave of motherhood swept through her. "Baby," she whispered. "My baby."

But when she glanced into the child's face and saw its eyes her blood ran cold. Within them was reflected every conceivable horror, every dark thing which crawled through every nightmare – and hate, immeasurable hate, like a huge black ocean stretching into the distance of an endless night. The pounding of the machines grew louder still and she felt the ground vibrate beneath her feet, their operators stepping up the speed of their mysterious task.

Slowly, she held the baby up to her face, unable to comprehend what she saw in its eyes. It smiled. Then, in a deep, rumbling voice, that seemed ancient yet ageless, it said, "Charles Robson is dead."

Hannah screamed.

The baby, its smile fixed, lashed out furiously with hands that were stronger than an adults', clawing savagely at her face and hair.

"Charles Robson is dead," it repeated calmly.

Pain wracked Hannah as her flesh opened beneath the baby's nails. She screamed louder, in agony and despair, and then she realized the cry she had been following had not been the child's.

It had been hers.

Mike grabbed hold of her arms and tried to hold her tight, but her thrashing was so frenzied that she threw him off.

156

"Hannah," he yelled anxiously. "Wake up."

He had found her asleep on the sofa, feverish and sweating, clutching at her stomach in such agony that he wondered if her appendix was about to burst. Tears were streaming down her cheeks and she was mumbling incomprehensibly in the throes of a nightmare.

He shook her again, harder, as the panic overcame him, and this time her eyes flickered open.

"Charles . . . Charles Robson is dead," she gasped.

"What? What did you say?" Her glassy stare looked straight through him.

Her hands continued to clutch frantically at her stomach, kneading and probling anxiously. Fearing she would hurt herself even more, Mike pulled them away and began to strike her belly. He stared into her face for some flicker of recognition.

"Come on, Hannah," he whispered. "You'll be okay. I'm here."

Suddenly he felt a movement beneath his fingertips like an electric shock that forced him to snatch his hands back. Surprised, a little scared, he peeled back her blouse to reveal the pale skin of her rounded stomach.

The skin was raised, as malleable and semi-transparent as the rubber of a party balloon. Five ridges slowly traversed the length of her belly before starting the journey again. It seemed to Mike that nails were clawing at the thin wall from the other side.

Shock and fear clutched at him. It was too much. He hastily pulled the blouse back down. As he stood back and looked at her moaning in pain on the sofa, a feeling of crippling impotence came over him. What was wrong with her? What was wrong with their child?

He knew, of course. The answer was simple. Horrifying, but simple.

"Daddy, is Mummy all right?" Jack had wandered from his bedroom to the edge of the sofa, his face concerned and frightened.

"Get back to your bedroom, Jack," Mike said, his concern making the words unduly stern.

He dropped to his knees and grasped Hannah's hand,

157

rubbing it gently, hoping it would somehow magic her awake. "Hannah, honey, talk to me," he whispered in her ear. His heart pounded with worry. Was she going to miscarry? "Come on," he said, the frustrating futility of his actions making his voice louder. "Hannah!"

Slowly her eyes flickered and focused, then she was staring quizzically into his face. "What . . . ?"

"Sssh," he said, silencing her with a finger to her lips. "Thank God. How are you feeling?"

"My stomach hurts," she replied weakly. "Oh God! I think I'm going to be sick." She staggered to her feet and as quickly as she could manage on shaking legs, she pushed past him to the toilet.

By the time she had emerged, Mike had phoned the doctor. He was horrified by her appearance. Her hair, matted with sweat, clung to her forehead. Her face was sallow, with dark rings around her eyes and along her cheekbones.

"Don't look at me," she mumbled, dropping her head. "I look a right state."

"Don't worry about that. Tell me what's wrong."

She slumped on to the sofa and lolled against one arm. "I've barely got the energy to stand," she said. "God, what is happening to me?" She rested her head in her hands dejectedly. "I had an awful nightmare about this baby and . . . oh, my stomach."

"Just stay calm." Mike sat next to her and held her hand. "The doctor will be here soon. We're going to sort this out once and for all." He paused. "I saw something on your stomach . . ."

"What?" Her eyes widened fearfully.

"Some kind of movement . . . it looked like . . . like the baby was . . ."

She stared at him struggling to describe what he saw and then burst into tears.

She had calmed herself by the time the doctor arrived looking concerned but efficient and confident. While he was examining her in the bedroom, Mike phoned Bulmer at home.

"Tom, it's Mike. Any news on Charlie Robson?"

A pause. "He died an hour ago. The hospital just called."

A pause. "He never recovered from the shock of losing his arm. Spent the last couple of days in a coma and then just slipped away."

Mike felt his stomach flip. How could Hannah have known? "Did the hospital call anyone else?"

"Just his family, I think. Why?"

"No reason. I'll miss him. He was a good guy."

"Salt of the earth. I won't mention that he'd still be alive now if you hadn't dragged him away from the main tunnels."

Mike bit on his lip; it was a low blow, but he knew it was only Bulmer's way of coping with the loss. "Any sign of his arm?"

Bulmer grunted. "Not yet."

"I bet the doctors were pleased about that."

"They realize the mine is a big place. They know we're doing everything we can to find it," Bulmer replied coldly. "They'll be the first to know once it's located."

"*If* it's located." The doctor emerged from the bedroom and waited politely by the door for Mike to finish his conversation. "Sorry, Tom, got to go. Hannah's not too well. I'll see you tomorrow."

Mike hung up and turned to the doctor, a tall, thin man with black hair that was streaked with silver. "How is she, doctor?"

He handed over a prescription. "I've told her to rest. I can't find anything seriously wrong with her. She's just run-down, stressed." He pointed at the prescription. "That's just for some paracetamol, between you and me; a placebo. She just needs to relax; that's really all I can say. Breathing exercises, yoga, it all helps. The simple solution would be to take her away from the source of the stress, but you know all about that. For some reason, Mrs Leary won't talk about it. I can't prescribe anything stronger because of the baby."

"But her stomach pains . . ."

"A symptom of stress, nothing more. The stomach is one of those things that responds very quickly when the body and mind is overloaded."

Mike shook his head. "It's more than that. The baby . . ."

"The baby will be okay, Mr Leary," he said reassuringly.

"Doctor, would it be possible for the baby to be . . . scratching her? You know, in the womb?"

He laughed. "Not at all. Apart from the stress, your wife's fit and healthy – and the baby is too. Just make sure she takes it easy up to the birth."

After he had gone, Mike sat on the sofa and massaged the tendons on the back of his neck. They were as tense as elevator cables. He wished he could take comfort from the doctor's words, but after seeing with his own eyes the scratch marks on her stomach he could no more accept his diagnosis than he could take heed of Bulmer's pleas to let well alone at Colthorpe. But what could he do? What was wrong with her? The memory of the pain etched starkly on her face would not go away and he was suddenly filled with an overwhelming fear that he might lose her. He could not cope with that. She meant more to him than the world.

"Daddy? Can I come out now?" Jack's subdued voice stirred him from his maudlin thoughts. When he turned and saw his son's pale, worried face they were instantly replaced by a powerful feeling of love.

"Sure," he said with a weary smile. "Come here." He held out his arms and Jack ran across the room and leapt into his lap, nestling his head in the crook of Mike's neck. "Sorry I shouted at you, shortie. I was worried about Mummy."

"Will she be all right?"

"'Course she will. And you'll get your new brother or sister on time, just like we spoke about. Are you looking forward to that?"

"Yes." He held Mike even tighter, for some reason afraid to let go. Mike wrapped his arms around him and tried to draw strength from the tiny form. Outside, an owl hooted forlornly in the still of the night. He wished it was all over and the three of them could go somewhere where they could forget all the pressures and just enjoy life. It was a dream that had become increasingly vivid. Perhaps the feeling of danger, of darkness closing in, gave him a deeper sense of what was important. He carried Jack in his arms as he bolted all the doors tightly. The locks did not seem strong enough. The owl hooted again, the jarring eeriness of its call reminding him how far from London they were. For once he ached for the proximity of neighbours, for the feeling of people crowding in all around him: people he could call out to for help if he needed it.

He could not resist a peek through the curtains; the night was still, peaceful.

He checked the locks once more.

Chapter Twenty-Two

The explosion woke Mike at twenty minutes past six.

Dawn was barely tinting the sky on the horizon when the bedroom window burst inwards, showering jagged shards of glass across the floor in a glittering rain. Mike made it out of bed and halfway to the shattered window frame before Hannah had swung her legs from the bed. A bitterly cold wind whipped the curtains wildly and through the gap between them Mike could see an inferno of scarlet and golden flames. His nostrils wrinkled at the strong smell of petrol and rubber which had flooded into the room.

"What is it?" Hannah yelled fearfully over the thunderous roar of the fire.

He knew before he had reached the window. Treading gingerly over the carpet of glass, he leaned on the window ledge and looked out. He could feel the red heat of the flames on his face, even though the fire was more than twenty feet away.

"It's the car," he said. There was a slight note of bitterness in his voice, but little surprise.

By the time the fire brigade had arrived, all that was left of his virtually new Nissan Silvia Turbo was a blackened, twisted lump of metal. It was still too hot for him to get close enough to see inside, but the firemen were oblivious to the heat as they poked and prodded the remains. Hannah had bundled herself into a thick dressing gown and was sipping tea with Jack in the lounge. He was excitable, almost feverish with the adventure of the moment. It was, as he pointed out, more exciting than the A-Team, Thundercats and Ninja Turtles put together.

162

Mike had dressed quickly before the fire brigade arrived, pulling on his thickest jacket to keep out the bite of the wind. Now he wandered around the front of the house in the growing light, listening to the deep, rumbling voice of the fire chief.

His first question confirmed Mike's suspicions. "Got any enemies, then?"

"You think somebody blew it up?"

"You don't reckon this kind of thing happens by accident, do you? It's not one of our regular trips out, you know . . . dealing with cars that spontaneously explode when most good folk are tucked up in their warm beds thinking of their Scot's Porridge Oats."

"What was it? A bomb? *Here*?"

The fire chief's blue eyes sparkled in the growing light. Mike was slightly irritated that he seemed to think the total destruction of his car was one of the most amusing things he had encountered in years. "Oi, Joe!" he yelled suddenly. "Wash down around it, make sure there's no petrol leakage." Then he turned back to Mike and repeated, "Well, any enemies?"

"None I could name," Mike replied. "I'm not going to win many popularity awards at the moment."

"Ah. That's it then. Come over here." He swivelled on the spot like a sergeant-major on the parade ground and walked towards the still-smoking hulk of the car. "Still a bit hot, but when it's cooled down you'll be able to look inside and see what caused it. You'll find the remains of a bottle, a lemonade bottle. I believe, on the back seat. Some of it is scattered around here." He pointed at minute fragments in the black pools of water. "You had a friendly visit from somebody with a Molotov cocktail. A petrol bomb. Easy to make – you just need any old bottle filled with petrol and an old rag stuffed in the top. Light the rag, throw it at your target and . . . whoof! – Bob's your uncle. Instant inferno."

"Bit of an extreme way to show your feelings."

"The police will want to know about it," the fire chief said.

"And they'll have a big chance of finding the culprit," Mike replied sarcastically. "There's a whole pit full of suspects."

He walked back into the bungalow. Behind him, the

163

firemen doused gallons of water over the car and driveway, sloughing petrol, charred rubber and twisted remnants of plastic down to the gutter. Hannah greeted him with a smile, but it was lost in her pale, fragile face. He could read the signs; she was frightened.

"Any idea what went wrong?" she asked.

Mike nodded gravely. "Petrol bomb, they say."

"What?" Her eyes widened.

"It appears our friends at the mine have finally decided to voice their objection at British Coal messing with their lives."

"But that's ridiculous! It's got nothing to do with you."

"I represent the company – that's the way they see it. They can't strike at some nebulous organisation, so they have to go for its representative."

"But a *petrol bomb*! We could have been hurt. Or killed."

"It's stupid, yeah, but they're getting desperate. I never thought they'd go this far, though."

Her eyes filled with tears. "What will they do next, Mike? If they start off with a petrol bomb, where do they go from there? What if they do something to hurt Jack?"

He put his arm around her shoulders and pulled her close to him. "It was a warning, that's all. I'll make sure Bulmer puts it around that hurting me or my family won't change British Coal's view. And you've got to remember that it's probably only a handful of them that are going to this kind of extreme. Most them are decent blokes."

"I still don't like it, Mike. I'm scared."

He was scared too. They were getting caught up in a whirlpool of madness that brought violence closer and closer to their doorstep. He thought carefully, then said, "Hannah, I want you and Jack to go away until this blows over."

She shook her head adamantly. "No, I'm staying with you. I don't want to be on my own, especially with the baby so close."

He tried again and again, but his attempts at persuasion fell on deaf ears. Eventually he compromised. "Let's wait until I've spoken to Bulmer before we make any major decisions. He'll know the mood of the men and he'll have an idea if things are likely to get out of hand." The mood of the men, perhaps: but simple, human emotions, however charged, were the least of his worries. It was the things he could not explain that terrified him more.

"It seems like everything's going wrong at once," Hannah said wearily. "Your job, my stomach cramps and now this. Life's gone off-balance."

"It just happens like that sometimes. Your life gets turned on its head and you think everything is doom and despair. Then it slowly rights itself and things are better than they were before. Don't worry."

"Always the optimist," she said with a wan smile.

Behind his brave face he was deeply concerned. If what Williams said was true, the emotions of the miners and whatever dark power lay beneath the village fed each other. Colthorpe was a pressure cooker. The men would fight to the bitter end to stop the mine from closing. What effect would that have on the black well?

Mike arrived at the mine early and went straight to the canteen for breakfast. Almost every table was filled with raucous men, their jeers and japes, shouts and laughter adding to the din of the sizzle of bacon and eggs and the clink of cutlery. The salty aroma of cooking soothed him. The woman behind the counter served up a large, high-cholesterol meal with a cheeky wink and an overly-cheery line in conversation. Mike laughed politely and carried his tray to one of the few free tables near the heavily steamed windows.

Normally he would not have eaten with the men. He was acutely aware of their thinly-veiled antagonism, their mistrust and anger enveloping him whenever he walked by, and during his brief stay he had always tried to ensure he did not aggravate the situation. After the attack on his property he was determined to make a point, to show that he was not afraid. It was easy to ignore the cold, threatening stares, but the strong undercurrent of hatred in the room was more difficult to dispel. It made him feel uncomfortable, but he refused to let it show on his face; he chewed his food with complete detachment, staring through them to the far wall.

Soon Mike became aware that three men at a nearby table were laughing at him. They looked away when he glanced over, but he could overhear snippets of conversation which were undoubtedly meant for his ears. He did not remember seeing them before, but that was not unusual. They were uniformly mean-looking, their faces quick to sneer, their laughter mocking. The ringleader was rotund with a mottled, ruddy face and wiry grey hair like a terrier. His eyes were stupid, sheep-like.

"Anybody want to buy a new car?" he said loudly. "It's a good runner. Goes like a bomb."

Their braying laughter spread to other tables; the news had obviously travelled quickly.

The youngest miner at the table, a teenager with rodent features and lank brown hair, broke into a brief chorus of a song. Mike recognized the chorus from the Madness record, "Driving in my Car", before it devolved into embarrassed laughter. Mike smiled, he would not allow them the satisfaction of seeing his irritation.

Finishing his meal in a leisurely manner, he deliberately left the canteen by a route which passed close to their table. They shifted nervously as he neared them, their bravado fading instantly. Mike stopped next to the one with wiry hair and stared at him impassively; the miner did not meet his gaze.

"Is Bob Packard around?" Mike asked calmly.

"Aye. He's over there." Without lifting his gaze from the bottom of his tea mug, the miner pointed to a table near the door.

"Thank you," Mike said. "I've got some very important business to raise with him."

Packard agreed to meet Mike in his office before he went on his shift. When he arrived, his hatchet face was hard and uncompromising as ever. He was the kind of man who did not care if others knew he did not like them; in fact, he preferred it that way. His handshake was crushing, but there was no sincerity or friendliness; it was merely the thing to do.

"What can I do for you, Mr Leary?" he asked coldly.

"Sit down, Mr Packard. Or can I call you Bob?"

"You can," he replied grudgingly, as he pulled up a chair on the other side of Mike's desk. "I ought to say now that we shouldn't really be talking. The union only recognizes Tom Bulmer as the official representative of the management. We can't negotiate with anyone else."

"I don't want negotiation, Bob, I just want to talk. Man to man. I thought that's how you dealt with things up here."

Packard's eyes gave nothing away. "Mind if I smoke?"

"Sure," Mike replied, declining the offer of a cigarette.

"I don't mind talking," Packard continued, "but I'll tell you, there's nothing you could say that could interest me."

"Maybe. But there's a few interesting things you could tell me. Like who set fire to my car this morning."

Packard's puzzled expression told Mike immediately that he knew nothing about what had happened.

"Somebody threw a petrol bomb at my car today. Blew it to smithereens."

"Who are you accusing?" Packard snapped.

"Don't play games with me," Mike said. "We both know the only people around these parts with a grudge against me work here."

Packard chewed on his lip while he considered the statement. "Can't deny that. If it was some of the blokes here – it's a big if – then it was a bloody stupid thing to do. We've got a tough fight to save our jobs and something like this . . . it'll do more harm than good. Anyway, I don't condone violence. We had enough bloody trouble when Scargill had his monkeys at the gate trying to stop us working back in '86. We're not about to start using their bully-boy tactics."

"I just wondered if I could be expecting any more early morning calls from the fire brigade."

"I'll see what I can do," Packard said. "But if they go off and do things like that off their own backs, it's out of my hands. I can just advise them how daft it is. And if I find out who it was I'll make sure they get their arses kicked."

"That's all I'm asking. I realize everybody's tempers are running a bit high. I don't want to see things getting out of hand." He added, "You might not believe it, but I've got a lot of sympathy for you. The last thing I want to see is anybody losing their job."

For the briefest moment, Packard's mask slipped, revealing the drained face of someone who carried a crushing burden on his shoulders. "We made a bloody big mistake not fighting when Scargill said. He told us the pits would be shut down within five years, but we thought we knew best. We thought he was just some loud-mouthed leftie who was only bothered about overthrowing the Government, so we all scabbed and threw away our principles – and for what? Here we are fightin' the same bloody fight, only this time we've got nobody on our side." The steel returned to his face. "The difference is, now we're going to win. Because if we don't Colthorpe will die and all the villages around'll die. It'll be the end."

Mike nodded grimly. Packard's words made him think of Whicker's callousness; he didn't care if a whole community was made to suffer for the sake of a good balance sheet. He didn't care, full stop.

"If that's all, Mr Leary, I'm getting back to work. I'll have a word with a few people, but in the end it's up to them."

"That's all I'm asking, Bob."

After Packard had departed, Mike picked up the phone and called Whicker. He was not looking forward to hearing his weasel voice.

"Mikey! We'd almost forgotten you were still alive!" Even his opening sentence carried the implication that Mike was surplus to requirements. "How's it going there in Hicksville?"

"Fine. I'm making good headway."

"Good to hear it." Whicker put his hand over the receiver and Mike could hear a muffled conversation with someone else. "Sorry about that, Mikey. Some of us have to work for a living while you're lazing around up there, y'know." Mike knew Whicker would be saying exactly the same thing to their superiors, but without the sickening pretence of humour. He was dangerous and he had Mike just where he wanted him; far enough away for him to have a free hand in sticking the knife in.

"It's not exactly lazing around! I'm supervising a major investigation here."

"Ha, ha. Just joking, Mikey. So how much longer will we be without your invaluable services?"

"A week – two at the most," Mike lied. A full report on Colthorpe's operational problems was the furthest thing from his mind. "I just thought I'd check in so you didn't forget me. I'll be able to give you a full update on my work in maybe a couple of days' time."

"No rush, Mikey. Just keep me posted."

Mike had timed the call perfectly. Any earlier and it would have appeared that he couldn't cope on his own without the advice of Head Office. A day later and Whicker would have been able to go to the executives to say he was slacking because he had not been in touch. As Whicker signed off, Mike noted with relish the disappointment in his voice.

The rest of the day passed quickly. He had a brief meeting with Bulmer to discuss the attack on his car and then spent the remainder of his time deep in thought, frequently making calls to Hannah to ensure she was okay. One thought repeatedly preyed on his mind. He remembered reading a magazine article about a place called Borley Rectory which they had called The Most Haunted House in Britain before it inexplicably burnt down. It had exhibited much of the strange phenomena of Colthorpe, from apparitions to automatic writing on the walls and strange noises that seemed to come from nowhere.

The article had concluded that the site of the rectory was the reason for its mysterious happenings. There was something in the earth itself, in that particular spot, it suggested, which made the unlikely and supernatural more likely to happen. "A ghost magnet", it had been called, with the implication that there was no consciousness behind the events at Borley. It went on to suggest the theory that there were other places around the world with some strange quality in the ground which opened a door to unnatural forces. Mike's attempts to draw comfort from the article's argument – that Borley's apparitions were a natural force, neither good nor evil – floundered every time he remembered that grip on his wrist. Every time he pictured Alec Jakes' face, or Charlie Robson.

At seven pm, when most of the office staff had already departed, Mike finally decided to go home. Through the window, he could see the scattered lights of Colthorpe village, a few spots of illumination in an inky sea. The wind had increased during the afternoon and now it howled across the fields and into the mine yard, carrying the occasional splatter of raindrops onto his window. The sky was an impenetrable black, devoid of moon and stars. The thick clouds piled up overhead, threatening a storm.

Bulmer's secretary was fastening her coat as Mike passed the doorway. She smiled at him coquettishly and proceeded to flirt quite openly when he stopped to make smalltalk. Mike needed to see Bulmer before he left to ask him the results of two crucial meetings he had had with Packard and the UDM during the afternoon, and he was relieved when the secretary told him he was still around. Mike wished her good night, declining her request for a brief drink after work, and headed over to the next block.

It was brightly lit within the complex, quiet and deserted, the long corridors and rooms up to the shower block devoid of the usual throb of activity. One shift was already underground and the next was not expected for a few hours. Mike paused at the main entrance to see if he could hear Bulmer's voice booming through the building.

"Tom?" he yelled. "Are you there?" His voice echoed through emptiness. "Tom?"

Mike walked along the corridor towards the lamp room, checking each room as he passed. To his annoyance, they were all empty, nor was there any sign of him in the locker room and the shower area. He retraced his steps, swearing under his breath. If any industrial action was likely to intensify rapidly he wanted to know in advance, so he could get Hannah and Jack out of the way.

Back in the lamp room, he leaned against the wall and rested, considering if he should phone Bulmer at home that evening. It was then that he noticed the floor. There seemed to be a faint glow emanating from the tiles in one corner. It was not instantly obvious, barely brighter than natural light, and he would not have noticed it had he not been staring directly at it. As he watched, the glow shifted slightly, although there was no apparent source. He decided it was in some way coming through the floor itself. His thoughts instantly leapt back to the terrifying moment when he had seen the faces pressed against his office floor.

The hairs on the nape of his neck prickled in warning. Cautiously he walked across the room until he was within a yard of the bright spot. For a second nothing happened. Then, as he watched, writing started to appear in the same form as the jumbled scrawl he had seen on his arrival at

170

Colthorpe. It manifested gradually to begin with, but then the messages appeared more rapidly, as if several hands were writing at once.

WE ARE COMING.

COMING UP.

COLD DOWN HERE. A pause, then, AWAY FROM THE LIGHT. Another pause.

GIVE US LIGHT. GIVE US LIFE.

Much of the scrawl was unintelligible, meaningless words or phrases, but occasionally parts of it stood out so clearly, Mike wondered if they were messages meant just for him.

COME WALK WITH US IN DARKNESS.

And then the final message that froze Mike's blood;

CHARLES ROBSON IS HERE.

A whirling pit of blackness, of bleak despair and terror, opened up before him and he felt he could plunge into it and fall for ever. Dazed, he turned away the moment the words formed and half-walked, half-ran out of the block and into the cold night air where he leaned against a wall, breathing deeply.

"*Charlie,*" he whispered, the word instantly snatched away on the wind.

His soul, his immortal soul . . . he could not complete the thought. Lights twinkled with a harsh light in the darkness: homes no longer filled with warmth and life, just blank spots in a universe of madness. In his head he thought he could hear mocking laughter.

Charlie Robson was dead and he was still suffering. Who would be next? Mike's head was spinning.

Who would be next?

Chapter Twenty-Three

That night a storm of frightening intensity raged across the area. The rain came in sheets, flooding the gutters with black, churning water and filling the sewers until the drains were gushing. Mike awoke in the small hours from a dream of Charlie Robson's pleading face. The thunder crashed overhead and white flashes of lightning illuminated the bedroom in stark strobe bursts. For once Hannah was sleeping peacefully, her face relaxed, contented, her chest rising and falling slowly and regularly, it was a sleep of innocence, free of worries; Mike envied her. There had been no scratchings at all that night for the first time in days, as if the elemental fury of the storm had cowed the restless spirits underground.

The sound of the storm rolling around the house reminded him of his first night in Colthorpe and the aching loneliness he had felt. Seeking reassurance, he reached out and touched the warm skin of Hannah's shoulder. She murmured in response and he leaned over and kissed her softly on the cheek before going back to sleep.

The next morning the storm had blown itself out, but there was still the threat of more bad weather in the air. From the kitchen window, the unruly garden at the rear of the bungalow appeared to have been buffeted by a hurricane. Branches, leaves, plastic bags and mysterious pieces of litter had been strewn across the thick, sodden grass and black soil like toys discarded by an angry child, dangling messily from shrubs and trees and hedgerows. A large pool of brackish water had formed in the centre of the lawn.

As Mike absently stared out, cupping a steaming mug of tea

to warm his chilled hands, he noticed a strange sight in the field beyond the garden. Where there had once been a gently rolling meadow, filled most afternoons by a herd of grazing cows, there was a mud and water-mottled field with a gaping black hole at its centre. Sometime during the evening, an area the size of two large, detached houses had disappeared.

"Look at that!" he said to Hannah. She was sleepily pouring milk into a bowl of muesli behind him.

"What is it?" she asked, following the line of his pointing finger. "Oh."

"Must be subsidence," he continued. "All that rain last night – all those tunnels running around underground – it must have collapsed." He turned to her and joked, "Makes you wonder how safe this place is, doesn't it?"

"Well, thanks a lot, Mike," Hannah replied with mock annoyance. "You'll be laughing out of the other side of your face when you come home tonight and find your doting wife and son and heir have disappeared into a yawning chasm."

"Don't worry. They do surveys every year to make sure they're not causing too much disturbance." He added, pensively, "But I've never known land to cave in like that because of subsidence. Normally it's just a gradual drop."

Hannah put her arms around his waist and peered over his shoulder. "Well, I don't like the look of it. What happens if Jack decides to go out and play there? He could tumble into it. God forbid he should ever leave his bedroom of course!"

"You're right. I'll mention it to Bulmer when I get to work. He'll make sure it's roped off."

"Daddy?" Jack's voice interrupted their conversation. He had wandered in from the living room where he had been eating his breakfast. He seemed on edge, distracted. "Daddy, can I go out to play today?"

"I don't believe it," Hannah said. "I could barely get you out of your bedroom for the last few days and now all of a sudden, after the worst storm for years, you want to play outside."

"You can go into the garden as long as you don't go any further," Mike said, squatting on his haunches to look him in the eye. "You mustn't go into the fields because it's dangerous after the storm last night. Do you understand?"

173

"Yes, Daddy." Jack smiled, then he turned on his heels and ran to his bedroom.

Hannah stared after him in surprise. "I just don't believe him," she repeated. "Is he doing this to wind me up?"

"Oh, you know what kids are like. Naturally bloody-minded. I bet you were the same when you were younger."

"I was not so. I was a very mature little girl, I'll have you know."

"And now you're a mature big girl." He patted her stomach. "Just keep an eye on him. If I was a kid I'd want to have a look at a mysterious hole. And my dad telling me not to would only make it more enticing."

"What do you mean, *if* you were a kid? You're the biggest kid I know!" She smiled victoriously and flounced through to the lounge with a giggle.

Mike's plans for the day were put to one side the moment he arrived at the mine. Bulmer was waiting for him in his office, looking agitated and irritable, his round face more florid than normal. Late on the previous evening, Packard had called him to tell him industrial action was definitely going ahead and that the men would meet that night to discuss their plan of action. There had been a full ballot of union members and the response had been unanimous. Packard had warned Bulmer in advance because they were old friends, but he told him there would be no punches pulled; it would be a fight to the death.

"There goes my fucking job," Bulmer snarled bitterly.

"It can't be helped, Tom," Mike countered. "It's just . . ."

"I know it can't be helped. It's been on the cards for a long time. That doesn't make it any better. All I bloody wanted was a quiet time. Why does this have to happen now?"

"Don't they realise they're fighting a losing battle?"

Bulmer laughed in the way that adults do when they pity a child's inability to grasp an obvious fact of life. "If your whole life depended on the decision of a bunch of people a hundred miles away who you'd never met, you'd fight too, wouldn't you? What do you expect them to do? Touch their forelocks as they walk out of the gate to a life on the dole? At least this way they feel like they're doing something."

174

"Even if they're wasting time when they could be looking for a new job?" He realized how lame the comment sounded as soon as it had left his lips.

"Your naivety is frightening, lad. Even supposing there were enough jobs around here – which there aren't – how do you expect a lot of blokes in their forties and fifties to compete against hungry young school leavers? It's just not real. When they get out of here, a few might pick up the odd job, part-time maybe. The rest of them will be sitting on their arses waiting for the pub to open."

Mike knew he was right. Survival was a much more basic struggle in Colthorpe than in the capital, where the options were endless and enterprise culture provided a myriad avenues of escape.

"That's the problem with the bloody politicians," Bulmer added. "They forget what it's like outside London. They should get up here sometime, learn a few basic facts."

Mike spent most of the day in regular contact with the office in London. Whicker thankfully passed him over to another department where he talked to someone called Guy Lynch, an expert on industrial relations. Lynch spoke with a clipped, well-educated accent. The general consensus was that Mike should do nothing for the moment, waiting until the men had firmly played their hand. The company was adept at handling strikes and they felt the dispute was unlikely to spread to other pits. They also had the insurance that the UDM had signed a no-strike agreement and if the worst came to the worst they could crush any action in the courts. A team of top-level negotiators were standing by if necessary.

Whicker came on the phone later in the day to tell Mike what a great responsibility he had and wasn't it lucky that he was in the right place at the right time. The tone of his voice suggested that luck had nothing to do with it and that it was not the kind of responsibility that anybody else would have wanted. For once Mike did not care. He agreed with Whicker in all the right places and then hung up without losing his temper.

Throughout the day, an air of tension hung over the mine. It was not exactly electric; more like a raging black stream flowing deep underground. From his window, Mike could see

175

it etched on all their faces. There were no smiles; their features were as expressionless as stone. In the canteen, the only laughter came in nervous bursts, quickly stifled. Everyone knew that things were coming to a head.

At half past five, Mike called Hannah to tell her he would be late. He had to wait until the outcome of the union meeting was known.

The havey bank of gun-metal clouds had not shifted all day, but the threat of another storm had not been realized. As the afternoon drew on, they grew darker and darker until, by the time night fell, their blackness was as deep as space. The wind was intermittent, but its sudden bursts carried the knives of winter. Even next to the radiator in his office, Mike shivered.

At seven pm, when the darkness had reached its peak, the night came to life. Fires exploded at regular intervals around the perimeter of the pit yard. The shadows danced and the dark receded, giving up its ground reluctantly. In the red glow of the flames, Mike thought the scene resembled some pagan festival, a tribute to Beltane to keep summer alive and the icy clutch of winter at bay.

Within ten minutes, the men began to assemble. They trudged into the yard sombrely from all corners of the colliery, heads bowed, hands thrust deep into pockets, summoned by some clarion call that Mike could not hear. It was an image that bore no relation to the twentieth century. Its gravitas harked back to another time when the world was a much darker place, when the weight of existence had to be endured instead of ignored.

It took barely a quarter of an hour for the yard to be filled. Everyone was there, every miner, from the freshest sixteen-year-old apprentice, to the hoariest, wrinkled old hand, all eyes fixed on the oil drums and planks that would serve as an impromptu stage. On each side of it, two dustbins blazed brighter than the other fires as a group of miners heaped wood and rubbish into them.

Mike sneaked out of the office door, wrapped tightly in his mac and scarf, and hurried around the edge of the site to a vantage point at the back where he could watch the proceedings and listen to the speeches without being seen. Despite the huge crowd, there was almost total silence as they waited

176

for their leaders to take the stand. Eventually, Packard and three others appeared from the shower block and walked through the men to the stage. At their appearance, the atmosphere changed palpably. A few men clapped, a few more shouted encouragement, others cheered raucously. By the time the union officials had clambered on to the makeshift stage, the workforce was yelling as one, their fists jabbing the air aggressively. The tensions had mutated into resentment, anger, pride. The din of their voices would have been audible for almost a mile around.

Mike moved closer into the shadows of a brick outbuilding. With the mood of the crowd as it was, he did not want to risk being seen. They would undoubtedly think he was spying on them for the company, when his loyalty towards it was in fact diminishing with each passing day. It was the charged atmosphere that attracted him; the passion that crackled through the air. He had never experienced anything like it.

The men fell silent when one of Packard's deputies began to speak, haltingly, without the skills of any great orator, but in a language they could understand. He explained formally why they were there and what the union committee had discussed. There was little passion in what he said – it was more like an account of a council meeting by a parish clerk – but the men applauded appreciatively. He was followed by another official, tall, thin and sombre like an undertaker, who explained the union's options in a resonant voice. It was obvious the miners were waiting for Packard.

When he eventually rose another huge cheer followed him to his feet. He silenced them with one hand, his large, thickset head a dull red in the glow of the fires. He had eschewed the smart suit he wore for official business for the uniform worn by the men, the dark overalls and boots that showed he was one of them, united in opposition to those who would do them harm. His hair had been slicked back, giving him a flinty, powerful appearance. Everything about him suggested confidence and commitment.

When he spoke, his words carried clearly and easily to where Mike stood, his broad Midlands accent giving them a granite reality. "The time has come," he said to a hushed audience, "to stand up and be counted. Once before, seven

177

years ago, we met like this. That time we made the wrong decision. I don't mind admitting it. I voted with you when we decided we'd rather work than stand with our brothers. It wasn't an easy decision. We didn't agree with the way they put their case, but there was some support for united action. But then we had to put food on the table, pay the rent, look after our families. That came first.

"You remember what happened. The picket lines. The insults. The violence. The bitter arguments that set friend against friend and father against son. It split the union in two. We set up the UDM because we wanted moderation. We wanted to be able to work for a better life for all of us. We didn't care about the NUM and their Socialist Workers and Militants and anarchists. But you know what? They were right? When Scargill said the Government and the NCB were going to systematically shut down the pits and put us out of work, he was right!"

A loud cheer went up.

"Round here we've seen Cadley Hill and Rawdon and Donisthorpe and Measham go – and now Colthorpe's the top of their list. They've not made any announcement yet; oh no, they wouldn't do that until it was in the bag and we didn't stand a chance. But documents I have in my possession, documents on British Coal paper, say we've had our cards marked. In a year's time, Colthorpe won't exist." He paused. "If we sit down and let them!" An angry murmur ran through the crowd. "But we won't, will we?" The murmur became a shout. "Will we?" The shout became an angry, rebel yell, drowning Packard out for a moment. He quietened them again with one simple gesture before continuing. "Oh, they'll offer us a lot of money to make us lie down and let them do what they want. But we're not whores, are we? We're clever people. We're smart. We know that forty thousand pounds might seem like a lot in one lump, but it's not going to last for the rest of a working life. And what happens when it runs out? That's right – the dole. If you think you're going to find another job round here, you've got another think coming. They don't want miners any more. They don't want people who work with their hands. They want computer operators. Accountants. Technicians. They don't want miners! You better believe it."

178

Packard was whipping them up into a frenzy, but Mike couldn't dispute what he was saying. The men could not take their eyes off him, their faces contorted in anger, shifting from foot to foot because of the repressed feelings that were building within them, fiery, violent feelings that needed an outlet before they exploded. The crowd was one beast, a seething entity, ready to rampage across the land devouring everything in its path.

And still Packard spoke, wringing every last drop of emotion from his audience. He played the situation like a master, manipulating feelings, choosing exactly the right words until he had the response he wanted, until they were bordering on the edge of a riot.

At that moment, Mike saw something which chilled him to the bone. Just outside the circle of fires, where the shadows were deepest, there were now other things standing; things which Mike did not want to acknowledge, but faced with the evidence of his eyes could not deny. He squinted, trying to distinguish the forms which shifted as if they were wisps of smoke every time the wind stirred the flames. He knew, of course, what they were.

They were wearing the same clothes as the men – heavy boots, helmets, dark overalls – but they were mildewed from years underground, tattered and torn. Where the cloth fluttered in the breeze Mike could see through to white bone or mouldering flesh. The helmets shadowed their faces, but Mike could still make out bare, white cheekbones glinting in the firelight, tombstone teeth where the lips had shrivelled and pulled back and hosts of sores and lesions across what grey skin remained.

There were scores of them, mute, unmoving, blankly staring at Packard like some grim parody of the living miners. The men, wrapped up in their own passions, did not see them.

Mike had not noticed them arrive. One moment there was nothing beyond the crowd apart from a deep, unrelenting darkness, the next moment they were there. Were these the things that had been standing in the lift when he had refused to open his eyes after he had been lost underground? He remembered the smell.

The smell of dead things.

179

What had called them there? The moment the thought had entered his head, he knew the answer. He looked at the men, their angry voices still drowning out Packard. He saw their powerful, seething emotions: their hate, their fear.

Now even Packard could not control the men, his simple hand gestures ignored, and he was forced to speak louder and louder until he was bellowing like a wounded animal.

"The time has come to fight back! The time has come to strike!"

As the men heaped more wood and paper on to the fires and the flames and smoke licked higher into the night sky, Mike realized the union meeting had become a ritual of awakening, both of the men's own struggle and whatever was beneath Colthorpe. It had called it forth to the surface. Mike could not help but feel that this was just the advance guard, and now that it had tasted freedom it would not rest until the remaining darkness had crawled out on to the earth.

Packard sat down, drained and shaking with the emotion he had expended, and the first union official took his place on the stand, calming the men and telling them to go home and prepare for action. When Mike's attention returned to the peripheries of the crowd, he saw that the shades that had been there had gone.

He became aware that his fingers had been biting into the brick of the wall, clinging on painfully as if it was his only link to reality. As the crowd broke up and the men loudly drifted away from the mine, his heart ceased to pound so violently and his shallow breathing returned to normal. He ran back to his office, to the security of electric lights, knowing in his heart that events had reached a turning point. He took refuge behind his desk, staring blankly at the far wall, listening to the dwindling sounds of rebellion.

Chapter Twenty-Four

The night was alive. A red glow, visible for miles around, radiated from the colliery yard where the bonfires slowly burned down, throwing up clouds of pungent smoke to blank out the few stars that pierced the thick cloud cover. Packard felt a wave of exhilaration sweep through him as he watched it. An adrenalin high had gripped him, his pulse jackhammering triumphantly. It was a moment to be savoured. The air was almost singing, crackling with electricity that left an iron taste in his mouth, and he was filled with the almost religious conviction that anything could be achieved.

It had been the best performance of his life. The words had leapt to his lips unprompted, the passion drawn in from somewhere outside of him. It was almost as if he had been possessed.

The night was alive. He turned to Alan O'Brien and told him.

"You did fucking brilliant there, Bob," O'Brien said, slapping his back resoundingly. "You're wasted here. You should be a fucking politician."

Packard nodded soberly. He thought so too.

"The lads are all going to the pub. We should be down there with them, show them solidarity before the fight starts."

"I reckon we're going to win, Alan." Packard surprised even himself with his own certainty. At that moment the universe was open to him with an amazing clarity of insight. "I can feel it inside me."

If he had been truthful to himself he would have used the word *hear* instead of *feel*. The voices whispered to him over

181

and over again, but he was not perturbed. He knew they were just the voices inside his head.

A clamouring gang of workers caught him up and buoyed him along in their flow to the pub. It was a moment he knew he would cherish, whatever else happened.

In the bar of the Colthorpe Arms, the atmosphere was vibrant and excitable, charged with the anticipation and confidence of a Wembley crowd on Cup Final Day. When Packard stepped through the door, a cheer went up so exuberantly deafening that even he was taken aback. He shook hands until he was bewildered by the emotions on show. Finally he was led to a table in the corner where a pint was presented to him.

"They're behind you all the way, Bob," O'Brien said. "They're putting their jobs and livelihoods on the line. It's a fucking big responsibility, but everyone knows you're the only man who can take it on and win."

Packard smiled and sipped his beer. Within, he was in turmoil. He had always been a simple, down-to-earth advisor, who could point out paths and obstacles and ways to overcome them with the easy dexterity of an Indian trail guide. He had never set himself up to be a Messiah. What had come over him out there in the mine yard?

The celebration in the pub continued apace, although the men gave Packard enough space to drink in peace. As the evening passed, during the lulls in O'Brien's limited conversation, he realized there was a certain desperation in their revelry which occasionally manifested itself in dark looks flickering across faces in unguarded moments when the drinking and jokes briefly abated. Sometimes gazes would meet, seeking support, trying to convince themselves that the things they loved were not irretrievably slipping away. Then someone would laugh raucously, freeing them from introspection, and they would all hastily join in.

By ten pm Packard had drunk enough to dull any doubts he had. Instead, his attention wandered from face to face, group to group, observing the tiny dramas, the courting rituals and petty rivalries which were all the more obvious in the face of their situation.

One particular scene had caught his eye several times during the previous two hours. As they became slowly drunk, a husband and wife sitting at the table near the open fire had been arguing more and more vociferously. She was in her mid-twenties with a hard, provocative face, emphasized by sullen lips and long, dark hair. He was a few years older, thick-set, with a beer belly that quivered when he spoke and heavy, muscled arms, colourfully tattooed. Occasionally his hand darted to smooth down his hair which had been slicked back and tied in a short ponytail. Packard knew him vaguely. He did not like him. Everyone called him Griff, and in Packard's eyes he was the closest thing to an animal. Quick to anger, his cruel eyes perfectly reflected a character that would always pick on the weak.

Every time he went to the bar or the toilet, his wife smiled at a taller, handsome youth standing near the dartboard, half-closing her eyes and pouting in a manner so sexually flirtatious that it was virtually an open invitation to take her to bed. As the evening drew on, the harsh words between Griff and his wife grew louder. She began to take risks, flirting over her husband's shoulder while he was staring at the table or the bar, but always managing to look away when his eyes strayed back to her.

Packard could not tell what was the source of their argument, although it was causing amusement in the couple's vicinity. Occasionally the woman's words would strike home and Griff's cheeks would flare momentarily. It only made his eyes grow darker.

O'Brien saw Packard staring. "That's a recipe for disaster," he said. "Look at her knocking back that brandy and port. There's going to be trouble."

Twice she almost slipped off her stool in her jeering and once her insult was so cutting that he grabbed her wrist until she squealed in pain. His warning to her was inaudible.

"They've always argued, but I've never seen them like this," O'Brien continued.

"It's not just them." Packard point out other, less passionate arguments that had flared, receded, then flared again. "Must be because everyone's wound up."

As he reached the bottom of his pint, the situation boiled over. She jumped to her feet, almost tipping the table over,

183

and snarled, "You're worse than useless. You can't even fucking get it up any more." Then she snatched her handbag and stormed out, with cheers and laughter following her. Her husband flushed and trembling with rage, stared firmly ahead of him. Packard saw one thing that the others missed. As she left, she paused in the doorway and nodded her head outside in invitation to the youth at the dartboard. He grabbed his coat and followed the moment Griff picked up his empty glass and went to the bar.

"She's gone off with young Pete Myers," Packard said curiously.

"What, Myers and her? Never." O'Brien shook his head in disbelief. "He's got a steady girl. He wouldn't touch an old slapper like Tracey Griffin."

"He'll be touching her in a minute."

Griff returned to his table and took two sips of his beer. Then he left the glass on the table and walked out of the pub.

"Oh bloody hell," Packard said. "There's going to be trouble. Come on." O'Brien had no time to look puzzled. Packard hooked his hand under his collar and pulled him to his feet. Outside, the night threatened ice and snow. Packard's breath clouded and plumed up towards the pub light. He pulled up the collar of his overcoat to protect his ears, desperately searching the quiet street for any sign of Griff, his wife or Pete Myers.

"What's going on?" O'Brien asked.

"Griff's gone after them. He's got blood on his mind and trouble like that's the last thing we need at the moment. We'll find him and calm him down."

"I don't know what's bloody come over people," O'Brien muttered sourly. He followed Packard into the night.

Mike sat in his office watching the walls change colour from red to black as the fires in the yard died down. The acrid odour of smouldering rubber permeated the room, even through the closed window, and there was a thin layer of black ash coating the glass. Every few minutes he looked out, searching the shadows for spectral figures. The yard was deserted. The only movement came from half-burnt newspapers plucked up by the wind and swirled across the black expanse of tarmac.

A cold foreboding overcame him in the aftermath of the union rally. Time was running out. His first response had been to call Hannah and her voice, although a little weary, had lifted his spirits. He did not tell her what he had seen, but he did make one more attempt to persuade her to leave the area. She told him she had no intention of going without him and that she would not succumb to intimidation. Her only concession to his pleading was to keep the bungalow's doors and windows locked at all times. Mike did not know how effective that would be, but it did give him some small comfort.

If Hannah would not go, he knew the onus was on him to act. His resolve was shaky, but it was sufficient. He did not feel heroic when he picked up the phone to tell Richmond they would be confronting the darkness sooner than expected, although he was disappointed when it rang out dull and flat, mocking his good intentions. He quickly dismissed the notion of going underground alone; there was little hope that by himself he could achieve anything.

As the last of the flames crackled and winked out, he concluded that he had no choice but to wait until Richmond's return. And if that was in the morning, then so be it. If nothing else, he would at least feel braver in the cold light of day.

The clouds parted when he stepped out into the night. The pole star cast its unfriendly light fleetingly above the horizon, and for one moment Mike caught sight of a gibbous moon, bright and hungry. He was suddenly aware of the vast sweep of the heavens, distant galaxies moving coldly through the barren, unfathomable void.

Smoke caught at the back of his throat. He coughed and the sound echoed across the yard like a gunshot. It served to emphasize the stillness that lay across the countryside; no trees or grass rustled, no vehicles rumbled in the distance. Although several cities lay within an hour's drive, it was as if the motorways and major roads that linked them had cut off the rest of the countryside, herding people to the bright lights, turning the villages into barely-disturbed backwaters.

Mike hunched into the breeze and headed along the road off the site. For the first time since his arrival, the mine was

185

devoid of life. The canteen lights glared brightly, but the room was empty; even the catering staff had departed. There was no one in the offices or the machine shop and lorries and vans had been parked haphazardly and abandoned. An eerie quiet clung to the squat buildings. He turned right out of the gates, avoiding pits and holes in the cracked pavement with a necessary skill learnt during his stay. The first night he had left the site he had almost broken his ankle when he had slipped into one of the deeper holes.

Somewhere a dog barked, three times. In the quiet, the sound travelled with remarkable sharpness, and Mike found it impossible to tell if it was near at hand or on a farm in the far reaches of the village.

The road dipped down into a dark hollow. There was an iciness at the bottom, colder than the surrounding air; Mike pulled his coat tighter around him. It was then that he heard the voice. It carried out across the fields to his right, low and reedy and barely audible. He recognized it instantly.

It was Hannah.

There was a moment of brief panic – the kind that flashes when a plane lurches and starts its descent – and then he was moving off the road and up to the hedgerow. His mind was a jumble of thoughts. Had she come out looking for him? And why had she left the house when only a half-hour earlier she had promised to lock the doors and stay safely inside until his arrival? A more worrying thought was that something had happened to Jack and that she had been forced to flee the house to find help.

He clambered over a rickety gate and jumped down on to the scrubby grass of the field. The soil was wet and heavy, but not unduly muddy. He resisted the temptation to call out to her; there was a small voice in the back of his head warning him to remain silent. Steeling himself, he set out across the field, keeping to the perimeter where the shadows were thickest. The clouds had closed back across the moon, drawing a heavy veil across the land. Hannah could have been a few feet away from him and he would not have seen her. His ears ached from the strain of listening. Nothing. He realized he was sweating, despite the cold; a thin sheen of perspiration prickled his face.

The clouds shifted again and a sickly beam of moonlight formed a spotlight, highlighting a figure twenty feet away from him. He started suddenly, aware in an instant that it was not his wife.

The smell told him what his eyes would not believe. It drifted towards him, heavy and cloying with the odour of loam and dank, dark caverns, and of other, more unpleasant, aromas.

Its face was white, its eyes lost in puddles of shadow, hollow, sunken. It was clothed in a miner's work gear, old-fashioned overalls, torn and filthy, speckled with mould, and boots that were cracked and mud-encrusted. Mike could not take his gaze off its face. It radiated hatred and malevolence so powerful that it forced him to take a step back. There was a scowl on its bleached, dead features that seemed to have been carved in stone. He knew, as surely as he knew anything, that it wanted him to die, agonizingly, in torment. His blood was cold, his skin in goosebumps. His desire to run was over-powering, but his legs were rooted and his eyes sealed on its dark stare.

Then, like the shift of a mirror at a funfair, his whole world skewed. There was a sensation of falling and the sharp tang of ozone as the figure, the countryside, the night, turned in upon itself. When his vision had cleared, he was presented with a scene of such madness that he thought he would faint. There was Hannah before him, slumped on the ground, her face chalk-white. She was dead. Her eyes had been gouged out. A scream built within him, but it would not escape, it would not release the pressure.

The scene skewed again and he was back in the field. But things had changed. During his brief dream, or vision, the spectral figure had moved closer. It was now less than ten feet away, its hands raised slightly from its side.

Another flash, exploding in his head. The ground slipped away and this time he looked at Jack, buried to his waist in the earth, worms burrowing into his dead flesh. It was like a sharp punch in the face, and this time he did scream, but it was a weak, pitiful thing.

The seesawing of reality and nightmare swung back, unbalancing him. His head was spinning and nausea played with his

187

stomach. When his eyes flickered open, he was horrified to see the white face inches away from his own. Its eyes were visible now, staring wildly, deep into his own. All madness and horror was there, screaming for his blood, for him to be ripped limb from limb. Its skin was taut and peeling, the odour drifting from its mouth rank and foul. Although he could see nothing apart from the face, he could sense its hands moving upwards, higher, higher . . .

He broke the spell with a tremendous effort of will, then scrambled backwards, almost falling, and ran frantically for the road. The gate was vaulted with one bound, his hands sliding on the rotting wood. There was dread in his heart. He had looked into a world of corruption and evil, of eternal death and suffering, and he had been only inches from being dragged into it. His breath was ragged and his heart pounded at the thought of how close he had been. At the thought of that ghastly dead face.

He did not stop or look back until he reached the crossroads. By then, he knew where he had to go.

An hour later, Packard and O'Brien walked over the crossroads towards the mine in pursuit of Griff. In the quiet of the night they could hear the harsh click of the metal segs on the soles of his boots ahead of them. Packard led the way, while O'Brien grumbled quietly behind.

"Why can't we leave them to it. Bob?"

"Because it's not going to be very good for morale if that bastard kills young Myers."

"Ah, he wouldn't do that!"

"Wouldn't he? You saw the look on his face. He's out for blood."

"Well you can get between them, then. It's your bloody funeral."

The beer brought a flush to Packard's face and a shiver to his limbs. At that moment he wanted nothing more than to be in bed with his wife, but he had a duty to perform, and was a firm believer in shouldering the obligations of his office.

They paused in a dip in the road not far from the entrance to the colliery. They could see Griff standing next to the hedge, observing something in the field beyond. Moving

188

closer, they were able to manoeuvre into a position where they could see his wife and Myers without drawing attention to themselves. She was leaning against a cattle trough, passionately kissing her young lover while ripping at his clothes with frenzied hand movements. Myers was pawing at her body and grunting like an animal. He had tugged her knickers halfway down her thighs. A howl of bestial rage roared from Griff's mouth as he clambered over a fence into the field, his whole body trembling with anger. Myers and Griff's wife were oblivious, too locked into their own passion to hear his approach.

Griff's momentum sent the couple sprawling. "You bitch!" he yelled, his pace bullish, relentless. "I'm gonna kill you!"

"Griff," she pleaded, struggling to pull her skirt down. She climbed shakily to her feet. His blow caught the side of her face and she stumbled backwards into the icy water of the trough. Before Packard and O'Brien had chance to move, Griff raised his sturdy work boot and powered it into Myers face. There was a sickening thud and blood spurted from Myer's nose. Griff snarled in triumph and turned his attentions back to his unconscious wife, her head submerged in the water. Rolling up his sleeve, he dunked his hand into the water and dragged her up by the hair before flinging her face-down on to the ground. Then he turned back to Myers, his eyes blazing.

"Don't do it, Griff." Packard had moved silently to his side.

It took a second before any intelligence returned to Griff's eyes. When it did, he looked bewildered, as if he were surprised to find himself in the field. "Stay out of this, Bob. It's nothing to do with you."

"You're right, Griff. I just don't want to see any violence that you're going to regret later."

"I won't regret it!"

Packard's intervention had come at the right moment. Myers had had time to recover and stem the blood which was streaming from his nose. While Griff's back was turned, he quietly stood up and sprinted across the field.

"Come back, you cowardly bastard!" Griff yelled after him.

"Let him go, Griff. It'll be better to sort this out in the morning when everyone's got a clear head."

He grunted and looked down at his wife, who was rubbing her face where he had hit her. "And what the fuck am I going to do with her?"

"Just take her home, Griff. Don't hit her again." Packard was tense. He knew if Griff raised his hand to the woman he would not be able to stop himself from defending her.

With surprising tenderness, Griff helped her to her feet and supported her. "She's a stupid cow," he said to Packard, "but I don't want to hurt her. I don't know what came over me." Then he turned away and led her back to the road.

"That was close." O'Brien lit a cigarette and watched Griff and his wife until they had disappeared into the darkness.

"This place has turned on its head," Packard said in bemusement. "It's sending people crazy. There's too much tension in the air."

"There's going to be a lot more of it. When that picket line sets up tomorrow morning . . ."

"I know. But it's got to be done." He looked around him, over the dark fields, past the lights of the village to the red warning lamps on the mine's overhead conveyor belt. "If we fuck up, all this will be gone in a few years. Colthorpe won't be able to carry on without the pit; people'll just drift away, looking for jobs, looking for lives. We've got a lot of people counting on us."

"Can we win?"

Packard didn't reply. He knew the answer, but he would not admit it, even to himself. His earlier confidence had evaporated.

"Wait. What's that?" O'Brien half-turned away, his head to one side, listening.

"What?"

"A voice. I could hear a voice calling out to us."

"Is it Myers? He was in a bad way."

"I don't know. It was over there."

The wind keened across the field suddenly, rustling the trees in the hedgerow. O'Brien and Packard took a few steps towards the centre of the field, lowering their heads into the icy breeze, and when they glanced up they saw they were not

190

alone. Several figures surrounded them, their chalky, hollow faces slightly bowed. The wind carried the smell of dankness, of corruption below the earth.

"Where the fuck did they come from?" Packard growled to O'Brien. Then louder, "Who are you?"

There was no reply. The wind died down once more and the stillness of space, of cathedral-like caverns far underground, descended upon them.

"Have you seen their faces?" O'Brien hissed. His voice cracked.

Packard turned slowly. In their faces, he saw his own fears reflected. He saw his own death. Their stone stares were hungry for life and he knew, somehow, that they were jealous of his life above ground, of his warmth. "*Tunnellers*," he whispered.

"No!" O'Brien dropped to his knees. He was staring into the face of one of the figures as it moved slowly forward, seeing some horror that Packard could not comprehend. "They hate us," he moaned pathetically.

Packard turned to run, but found his boots were mired in the mud of the field. He tugged at them, but they would not come free. It was only then that he realized he was sinking.

O'Brien became aware of what was happening at the same time. His yell was loud and high-pitched. When he used his hands to try to lever himself upright, they disappeared up to his forearms. The field around them seemed to ripple like water and Packard had the strangest sensation that he could see through the grass and the topsoil as if he were looking through mist.

He shouted, bellowing furiously until his throat was raw. Futility made him mute when he felt the pressure of the earth around his chest.

O'Brien went first. Packard heard him gargle and choke, his screams strangling in his throat, his mouth filled with grass and soil. He watched in horror the last wisps of his grey hair disappear beneath the turf.

And then Packard followed, wracked with loss at the thought of his family, wondering in terror what lay ahead. He spat out grass, but the soil continued to surge into his mouth and down his throat. The last thing he saw was a white face snarling like a beast and the mine's red lights blinking on and off, on and off.

191

Chapter Twenty-Five

The scotch cradled in Mike's hands was at least four fingers deep, and it had the rich, peaty flavour of a malt for connoisseurs. The glass Bulmer had served it in caught the gleam of the coal fire, shimmering with an inner golden light. The drink helped take the edge off Mike's nerves. Bulmer had disappeared through to the kitchen, leaving Mike alone in the comfortable, sleepy lounge of his house on the outskirts of Colthorpe.

Like Bulmer himself, it was a mass of contradictions. The fire and its tiled surround, the battered coal scuttle sitting in the hearth and the threadbare rug in front of it hearkened back to a different era, of hard work and poverty. But the scotch, the state-of-the-art TV and video recorder and the CD player in the corner spoke of someone sophisticated, tasteful, with a reasonable income. The room was suffused with a smell of homeliness; of warmth, coal, books and thick carpets.

"Now are you sure I can't get you a sandwich or something, love, before I get off to bed?" Bulmer's wife, Eunice, poked her head around the door, smiling benignly. Behind her glasses her eyes sparkled warmly.

"No, thank you, Mrs Bulmer, I'm fine." Out of politeness, he tried to instil some vigour into his voice, but the night had left him drained.

"Well, don't go letting him get you too drunk. He does love his whisky."

Mike smiled wanly. "I won't."

Bulmer walked through a moment later, his shirt sleeves

rolled up and an even larger glass of scotch in his hand. He eyed Mike suspiciously and then said, "I know I said you were welcome to drop in for a drink, but I didn't expect it to be this time of night."

"I'm sorry too, Tom. Believe me, I've got a good reason." Mike felt the fire from the whisky course down his throat to dissolve the icy chill that had collected in the pit of his stomach.

"You look bloody awful," Bulmer said. He sank into a well-used armchair which allowed him easy access to rest his feet on the hearth. "And from that look on your face, I don't think I'm going to like this conversation one bit."

"You could be right." Mike stared at him thoughtfully, trying to read his face. But Bulmer said nothing, sipping his drink slowly while the fire crackled noisily and threw showers of orange sparks up the chimney.

"The next time you do a head count of the men you might find you're a few short." He continued to watch for a reaction.

Bulmer merely raised a bushy eyebrow in interest. "What do you mean?"

"I told you it wouldn't go away, Tom. I told you burying your head in the sand wouldn't solve anything." He gripped the arm of the chair, mentally steadying himself. "I *told* you!"

Bulmer looked at the bottom of his drink. He swilled it around and then drank almost half of it in one mouthful.

"There will be more deaths, Tom."

His stare levelled at Mike lazily as if they were discussing the weather or the state of the economy, but Mike could see hints of fear and despair hidden deep within it.

"I saw something tonight, Tom, and it wasn't buried deep underground. It was on the surface." He closed his eyes and massaged the corners, trying to prevent the memory resurfacing. "A ghost. A spirit. Something that was dead, something that shouldn't have been there. And it was walking around like it was on a fucking moonlight stroll. This wasn't just a colourful, harmless piece of folklore, Tom – I could feel its hatred. I knew that it wanted to kill me." He let the words hang in the air. There was silence apart from the soothing crackle of the fire. "It showed me things, Tom . . . about Hannah . . . and Jack. I can't stay here long. I've got to get back to them."

Bulmer slammed down the rest of his scotch and fumbled the empty glass nervously from hand to hand. "Do you want another one?" he asked, heaving himself out of his chair and heading to the bottle on the table near the window.

Mike shook his head. "No. I just want to know why you're trying to deny all this is happening."

"Because," Bulmer said angrily, "I don't want to think about it. I don't want to turn my fucking life and everything I've worked for on its head. You wouldn't understand that, you young bastard. Wait till you get to my age!"

Mike stayed calm. "If we don't do something to stop it, there'll be more than your lifestyle at risk."

"Stop it!" Bulmer sneered. "How do you think you can fucking stop it!"

"We've got to do something. We can't just let it carry on. How many more people have to die?"

"You don't seem to understand," Bulmer said, filling his glass. "We're talking about something here which you and me could never understand. We're talking about something which is beyond life and death. You want to do something about it, you get to that church and pray."

"I prefer to do something a little more positive than that."

"Like what?"

Mike shrugged. "I have a few ideas. There's some force underneath Colthorpe, Tom. I can't think of any other way to describe it, but it's not good. And it's coming to the surface."

"I can't talk about this kind of thing – it's beyond me."

"You must have known about it, Tom. Tell me, for Christ's sake! It might give me some clue as to what to do."

Bulmer sighed deeply, drawing on some deep well within him. "I've not spoken about this before," he said, almost to himself. "It's been so long." His words were beginning to slur, but when he looked at Mike there was a brightness in his eyes. "I never knew exactly what was down there, but I knew there was something, and as long as it didn't bother us then we wouldn't bother it. I was scared, I'll admit that. It's not a weakness – not when you're up against something like that."

"Of course it's not a weakness," Mike added, supportively. "I'm scared, too."

"I've lived with it all my life. All my life. I first came across it when I was a lad; 1947, it'd be. A good year. The industry was building up for the boom ahead after all the hard times of the war. We knew there was a bright future in front of us. We never had any doubt about that. I was seventeen, a bit green, a bit innocent, but I was a good worker. I'd already been down the pit for a few years. I left school at thirteen, like a lot used to do at that time. There was no point sitting in a classroom when you could be out earning a crust. It was a good time, all right, but I wasn't scared then. That's something I've learned to live with."

Outside the wind raged through the trees and shook the windows relentlessly. Mike was glad he was inside by the fire: warm, secure. His thoughts fleetingly turned to Hannah; he was relieved he had called her to tell her to lock the doors. He was desperate to be back at her side, but he needed to hear Bulmer out first. He needed to discover what he knew.

"It happened one November night," Bulmer continued, his voice droning in the still of the room. "It was so long ago, I've pushed it to the back of my mind over the years, but I remember it clearly. I'd finished the day shift, had me shower and all that, and I was walking home. My family lived in the terrace opposite the pub at the time, so it wasn't a very long walk. I remember how cold it was. We had a terrible winter that year and it had already set in. There was snow in the air and ice on the roads. I was shivering inside my jacket like I didn't have a stitch on and I was walking as quick as I could to get back to my mother's fireside. I wasn't far away from the lights of the crossroads and there were a couple of lads going into the Colthorpe Arms for a drink. I can see it as clear as if it was this morning."

He paused and took another long sip. There was a heaviness which lay upon his shoulders, bowing them to his seat. Mike was surprised to see how old he looked at that moment.

"It wasn't all good, I suppose," he continued. "Times were tough and a lot of people died young. My brother was one of them. Jim was only twenty-one, but we'd lost him the year before. Conditions down the pit were hard, primitive. It was dangerous, a lot worse than it is today. Jim was a decent lad, always one with a joke, but he was a bit headstrong. He'd take risks. He just took one too many. We never found out exactly

195

what happened to him. He'd gone wandering off on his own; that's one reason why I lost my temper when you did the same thing. Anyway, there was a tunnel collapse and Jim was in there when it all came down. We don't know what caused it, don't know anything . . . but the poor bastard caught the lot. We buried him a week later."

Bulmer's chin dropped on to his chest and Mike wondered if the warmth and the whisky had lulled him to sleep, but when the firelight glittered on his watery eyes, Mike realized he was just remembering.

"That all happened a year before," he continued. "And that night, when I was walking home, I saw Jim again."

The baldness of the statement was like a slap across the face. Mike leaned forward, hanging on his every word.

"I heard my name called, so quietly I thought I'd been fooled by the wind. But then I heard it again. Tom, Tom,' just like that, soft and gentle. I thought maybe it was one of the other blokes taking the piss, but I decided to check it out anyway. It was coming from a small copse in the field next to the road, so I climbed over the fence and thought I'd sneak around the edge and give whoever it was a fright. It took me a few minutes and then I ran into the copse yelling and whooping like an idiot. When I saw Jim standing in the centre I thought I was going to die of shock on the spot. He looked just like he had before he . . . before he died. There was something different – something in his eyes and the way he looked at me. But apart from that he was the same old Jim. I was terrified, but I just ran forward and threw my arms around him and cried. He was cold, so cold, and he smelled of . . . dirt, damp. His skin didn't feel right either. You know, he was my brother and everything, but it – it revolted me. I stepped back quickly and just stood watching him. He didn't blink, he didn't smile, he just said, 'I'm lonely, Tommy.'" He finished his drink in one draught. "'I'm lonely.'"

Bulmer looked away into the fire. It was several minutes before he spoke again. "It was like I was in a dream. I knew Jim was dead, I'd stood at the side of the grave when they put the coffin in, but all I could think about then was that I'd got my brother back. I started to cry like a bloody girl. He said he

196

didn't want to be on his own any more down in 'the cold and the dark'. Those were his exact words. I asked him what he wanted me to do and then he said, 'Come with me. Keep me warm. Be my friend like you used to. I need you.' I can hear him now." He drifted off again. "I didn't know what to say. Here was my brother, twelve months in the ground, telling me he wanted me to go with him. I don't know why I didn't just turn and run then, but I wanted to look after him, make him warm again. I probably would have done as well, if a car hadn't gone by at that moment. It just brought me to my senses and I said, 'Jim, you're dead. I can't come with you.' He asked me again and he held out his hands, trying to get me to hold on to them. His voice started sounding more desperate, and that was when I began to get worried. Right then, it didn't sound like him at all. It sounded like someone else, some*thing* else, in his body. I started to back off, just thinking about running out of there. That's when it happened."

Suddenly there was such black fear in his face that Mike shivered. "What happened, Tom?"

"He changed. At least, I think he did. I just ran out of there screaming all the way home. My mother and father couldn't do a thing with me – they thought I'd gone mad. I spent the next day in bed just trying to forget. Everyone asked me what had happened, but I wouldn't talk about it. I couldn't! I really would have gone mad if I'd dwelt on it. I just put it to the back of my mind and pretended it never happened."

The wind slammed against the windows as if it were trying to break in, and Mike was suddenly aware of the darkness around the house, the night spreading out across the empty, lonely fields. "What do you mean, he *changed*?"

"It was like . . . like . . . he turned himself inside out. I can't describe it any better than that. It happened so quickly. One minute he was pleading with me to go with him, then when he realized I was going to run off . . ." He made an exploding gesture with his hands. "It was like his face and skin and clothes all got sucked in and something else came out to take his place."

"What was it?"

Bulmer struggled to find the right words, shaking his head as the description of something beyond his comprehension eluded him. "All I can say is, it was like a darkness. Like space, black but with things inside it like stars, and I thought I saw a mouth and . . ." He stopped and put a hand across his eyes.

"Don't worry, Tom. At least you got away." Mike struggled to find the words to comfort him. "Others weren't so lucky."

"Oh, I got away all right, but I still carry the fucking scars." He suddenly stood up and unbuttoned his shirt. There, in the lurid orange glow of the fire, Mike could see five white scars running across his torso from his left shoulder to his hip. "It lashed out at me before I had a chance to move. If I hadn't already been backing away it would have split me open from head to foot."

"Jesus." Mike thought how close he had come to a similar fate.

"When I got home I was soaked in blood. My mother was hysterical. She thought I'd been attacked with a knife."

"You were lucky."

Bulmer grunted. "Despite what happened, despite him trying to kill me . . . he was still my brother. I felt like I'd let him down."

"That wasn't your brother, Tom, you said it yourself. It was just something that had taken his shape for a while. Something that's been living under Colthorpe for centuries."

"I don't know about that. I just know what I saw." He slowly fastened his shirt. "I saw him once more after that. It was years later – I was underground, on my way to the face with old Horace Simpkins. I happened to glance down a side tunnel and there he was at the end, just watching me. He looked as young as the day he died. There wasn't a mark on him. No lines or wrinkles or anything. But I could tell he was sad, terribly sad. It was like he was a broken man. Old Horace didn't see anything, he just kept right on walking. I stopped and I could see he was pleading with me to go with him again, silently, like, but this time I just turned away. That was the last time I saw him."

A lump of coal on the fire sent sparks showering into the hearth. Bulmer leaned forward and threw more fuel on, rattling the ashes with a long iron poker, before putting his feet even closer to the warmth.

198

"What do you think would have happened," he asked reflectively, "if I'd gone with him?"

"You wouldn't be here now." Mike rose and stood with his back to the fire, warming his legs. "Don't keep thinking it's your brother, Tom. It's something malignant. Something that kills."

"I hear what you say, but how do I know for sure that it's not Jim? Maybe what's down there is holding him back, holding all the ones that died back. I don't want to think that Jim's still there. He should be at peace . . . he should be resting, not suffering." He looked up at Mike with watery eyes. "He should be resting."

"I'm going to do what I can, Tom. There's got to be an answer somewhere."

"What do you think you can do?"

"I'm going to go down there. I'm going to try to confront it."

"You're fucking stupid!"

"I probably am. But for once in my life I've found a purpose, some responsibility. I've even got a few ideas about what might work." He thought briefly about mentioning Richmond, but then decided against it. "I just don't want you to try to stop me, Tom."

"You want to fucking kill yourself, go right ahead." Some of the fire returned to his face. "I still think you're mad, but you've got my blessing."

Mike nodded. There was no need to say any more. "Look, I've got to get back to Hannah now, but I'll keep you posted."

"You do that. And . . . be careful on your way home."

"Don't worry. I'll be running so fast, my feet won't touch the ground." Mike pulled on his coat and scarf and thanked Bulmer for the whisky. He looked brighter than he had done earlier, but there was still a heavy weight on his shoulders which Mike knew would not be removed until the affair was over.

There was a hint of rain in the air when he stepped out of the front door into the chill face of the wind that roared around the house and tore at the few remaining leaves on the stately trees that hung over Bulmer's front garden. He felt apprehensive at the thought of the journey home. The moon

199

had once more disappeared behind the clouds and the night was black and cheerless. Bulmer slapped him on his back to send him on his way and then he was off and running without a backward glance.

Bulmer closed the door and bolted it, rubbing his arms at the cold. Back in the lounge, he poured himself another whisky and drank it quickly. His memories had disturbed him and he knew he would sleep uneasily that night; a few drinks would at least keep the nightmares at bay. In the distance he could hear the thunder begin, just a dull grumble at first, but it was followed by a white flash of lightning which seeped around the edges of the curtains and then another, louder, rumble. Soon the rain would begin in force.

He walked over to the window to watch the storm approach from the warm security of his own house, but when he pulled back the curtains he was shocked to see someone standing on his front lawn staring directly at the house. Another flash of lightning sharply illuminated the face of a young boy with pale, innocent features and high cheek bones beneath a flicked-back fringe of brown hair. His eyes were ringed darkly, but they were filled with an intense, pleading sadness.

"Jim," Bulmer whispered, as the glass slipped from his fingers and shattered on the floor.

The youth held up his arms in a beckoning gesture, the rain and wind lashing and buffeting him. Bulmer stroked the window pane gently and bit his lip, one tear welling in the corner of his eye. His brother, just as he remembered him. Eternally youthful, eternally sad. There was a hint of a smile on the youth's face. Bulmer turned away, his decision made.

Chapter Twenty-Six

Through the howling night, Mike ran, his chest pounding, his breath searing his throat. Icy rain bit into his face and numbed him to the bone. Wind sliced through his coat and gnawed into his ribs. The storm was terrifying; screeching and screaming across the land with thunder bellowing and lightning crackling, tugging him into hedgerows, throwing him into the road, laughing at his feeble efforts to make headway. And through it all, he was gripped with the fear that something was hiding around every corner, behind every tree, ready to step into his path and rip his life into shreds.

A car hurtled by, soaking him with a wave of filthy water from a rapidly growing roadside pool. He stopped, cursed loudly, and then continued, driven by the need to get to his wife's side. A mantra was chanted repeatedly under his breath: that Hannah would be safe in the relative security of their home, that he didn't have too far to go; just down an incline to the crossroads and then right, up to the bungalow. Not far at all. He could see the lights ahead of him. All he had to do was keep . . .

Running. She had been running for what seemed like hours, days even, along winding corridors that seemed to have no end, distant machines throbbing in her ears. Had she been here before? She thought so. Coming to an abrupt halt, Hannah rested against the wall which felt unpleasantly like flesh. She looked back the way she had come; it disappeared into impenetrable darkness only a few yards away. And in front, the same. She had no idea what she was running from or where she would finally arrive. This time she was going down deeper, much deeper than she ever had before, and perhaps she would never come back.

Mike sprinted up the drive, relief struggling with exhaustion within him. His face and hands were numb from the freezing bullets of rain that had been driven relentlessly into him. His clothes were sodden through to his skin. The wind tried to hold him back on the last leg, as he negotiated a pool of black water outside the door, tugging at his clothes and hair. And then he was there. Safety. He hammered on the door, once, twice, three times. There was no reply. Panic set in instantly and he regretted his foolishness in leaving Hannah alone while he chatted to Bulmer. *Anything could have happened to her*, he swore under his breath. Anything. In frustration he began to kick savagely at the door, with little result. Finally he decided to put his shoulder to it to try to break the lock.

While his arm was still aching from the first assault, he heard a movement on the other side. "Who is it?"

"Jack."

He gave a silent prayer. "Jack, it's Daddy. Can you open the door?"

Another roll of thunder clattered directly overhead and when it had subsided he heard Jack fumbling with the bolt and then the sound of the lock drawing back. He burst in and slammed the door behind him, locking it instantly. Jack stood in the centre of the room, scared and distressed by Mike's frantic movement. Mike caught his eye as he stripped off his soaking overcoat and smile reassuringly. "Don't worry, I just wanted to get out of the rain. And what are you doing up at this time? Where's you mother?"

"She's asleep, Daddy. I heard the banging on the door. It woke me."

Asleep. In relief he swept Jack up in his arms. "Come on, let's go and find her."

"The elves said she'd sleep for a long time."

"Well, the elves know these things, I suppose." He carried Jack through to their bedroom, but when he saw Hannah's feverish state, he hurriedly put him down and rushed to her side. She was mumbling incomprehensibly and there was a

202

thin film of sweat across her forehead. Mike grabbed her hand, but it was clammy and when he let go, it fell limply to the bed.

"Shit. This is all we need," he muttered. Then, turning to his son, "Jack, Mummy's got the flu. I'm going to tuck her in. You nip back to bed and I'll come through and kiss you good night in a minute."

Later, when Mike sat on the edge of his bed, Jack asked in a small, lonely voice, "Will Mummy be all right?"

"Of course she will. It's just a spot of flu, like you had last year."

"The elves say she's going away, Daddy. They say you're both going away."

"Well, this time they're as wrong as wrong can be. Mummy just needs a good rest, that's all. She's been under a lot of pressure recently."

Jack smiled, but his eyes were scared. Mike pulled the sheets around his neck and kissed him on the forehead. "Sleep tight. I'll see you in the morning."

In the stillness of their bedroom, he listened to the frenzy of the storm, the staccato sound of the rain on the window and the tumultous double act of thunder and lightning; it did not seem to be abating. He felt weary, drained of all feeling, all emotion. He could not even bring himself to worry. His muscles were aching and sore. Stiffly, he lowered himself fully-clothed on to the bed next to Hannah, the pillow comfortingly puffed up behind his shoulders, and watched her stir in the throes of a fever dream. He would cleanse himself with a purifying sleep and then tomorrow they would talk and he would persuade her to take Jack and move away until all of it was over. Tomorrow.

Hannah stopped and listened. She was right . . . there was something . . . several things . . . following her. No, not just following . . . hunting. She knew that as clearly as she knew she was pregnant, but how she knew it was a different matter. That wasn't relevant. She just had to stay ahead.

Moving as hastily as she could along the long, dark corridors with the repulsively warm walls, Hannah could hear them far behind her, but drawing closer, howling like hounds with the scent of a fox. Her heart began to beat faster. What were they? What did they want with her? Breathlessly she ran, sprinting now, her hand occasionally trailing against the wall. And they were getting nearer.

The corridor twisted and turned. Its endless byways had the familiarity of well-travelled streets, but that was not important. The howls behind were growing louder, more like lost souls than animals.

And then she was out into a wide open place, a cavern, cathedral-like in its enormity with walls that towered high above her head to a vaulted roof. A strange luminescence seeped out of the rock or whatever the walls were made of and the noise of the mysterious grinding machines throbbed louder, but dully, the vibrations grating at the base of her skull. She ran out into the dull light, searching for an exit, becoming more frenzied with each passing moment.

"Where am I?" she said softly, and them much louder, "Where am I?" Her words spiralled up towards the distant roof.

She was surprised to hear an answer to her rhetorical pleading from somewhere near at hand, although she could not make out the words. It was guttural and coarse and it cut through the still air of the cavern as if the speaker were at her elbow. "Who's there?" she asked, strangely unafraid. Looking around, she saw a dark shape silhouetted against the slightly lighter gloom. She headed towards it. The machines shifted up a gear.

Before her, on top of a pile of rocks which reached a foot above her head, was a tiny baby, pink and smooth, with sparkling eyes and an innocent, beatific smile.

"Hello," she cooed, thinking she had seen the child somewhere before.

"Hello," the baby replied. Her voice was that of an old man, throaty and deep with a rough edge.

"You can speak!"

The baby did not reply. It merely smiled and waved its arms and legs in the air excitedly.

"How can you speak? You're only a little baby."

"I am only a baby," she said, "but I am old. Older than you. Older than many things." She coughed, an old man's cough,

204

fetching phlegm from deep in her throat and then spitting it out over the side of her rocky seat.

"Oh. Then who are you?"

The baby chuckled deeply. "I am you and Michael and one other."

"I don't understand."

"No. You don't understand. And now it's too fucking late, you senseless cow." The baby lifted itself up on its tiny, pink elbows and looked into her face. "Stupid fucking cow."

"Don't talk like that. You're a baby!"

She laughed, the coarse laugh of a man who had seen years of toil and pain and sweat. "We brought you down here to see me, Hannah," she continued. "To see how sweet and beautiful I am. But now you're here, you can't go back. No, not at all. You must stay in the cool, soothing darkness. Forever."

Hands grabbed her, clawing at her face, her arms, her chest, pulling her back, away from the child and its malevolent grin. She struggled to turn to see who her attackers were, but her head was clamped firmly so that all she could focus on was the receding figure of the child, standing on the pile of rocks and waving its arms ecstatically. "The time has come," the baby bellowed deeply, "to see the light."

Hannah tried to scream, but there were grey, mottled fingers in her mouth. They were pulling at the corners of her eyes so that tears welled up, and they were biting into the soft flesh of her underarms. Back she went, back and down, and the darkness of a multitude of bodies closed over her head.

Mike woke at first light, fully-clothed and shivering in the chill of the room. It was still raining outside; he could hear the constant pitter-patter on the window pane, but the storm itself had blown itself out. He stretched slightly, feeling his shirt pull from his skin where it had dried on him, his aching muscles creaking.

His first thoughts were of Hannah. She was in a deep sleep, her dreams playing across her face in twitches and tics while her lips mouthed conversations with her dream partners. Her brow, though hot, did not seem as feverish as the previous evening, although her hair was matted with sweat. Mike carefully brushed the strands from her face and kissed her on the cheek; he would let her sleep for a little longer.

Three hours later, there was still no sign of her awakening and Mike's concern was beginning to mount. He had decided to wait until she was up and about before he went to see Bulmer about the latest developments in the dispute at Colthorpe, but by noon he knew he should try to rouse her himself. He was surprised to see that her position had barely altered since he had left the bedroom that morning; she was still lying on her back, head rigid in the centre of the pillow, although occasionally it lolled from side-to-side when the dreams took hold. Her arms lay limply at her sides, her lips dry and sticky.

"Hannah, honey, it's time to get up," Mike whispered in her ear. It had no effect. He shook her gently, but her body merely rocked like a rag doll without even the slightest flicker of her eyelids.

"Hannah," he said a little louder, "time to get up."

Her pallid appearance and the slackness of her limbs was so disturbing that Mike automatically checked for a pulse, even though he could see her chest slowly rising and falling. "Hannah," he shouted, grabbing her shoulders and shaking her roughly. Her head slipped to one side and a thin trail of saliva drooled out on to the pillow.

Anxiously, he grasped her hand. "Come on, Hannah," he muttered, repressing any urge to diagnose what was wrong with her. "You've got to keep on going. For the baby's sake."

His words reminded him how close she was to completing her pregnancy and with a growing fear he gently pulled back the sheets to reveal the pale flesh of her belly. As if in response, her head moved slightly and her mumbling became more frenzied.

Mike was not prepared for what he saw. He was afraid he would see the long, pink scratches on her skin that he had found earlier, the ones that seemed to come from within – but what he discovered was much worse.

All over her stomach, the flesh was erupting into words and phrases, red tracings like the scrawled messages that appeared on the floor of his office. They rose briefly, again as

206

if the skin was being raked from within, and then faded before breaking out on another part of her belly.

They appeared faster and faster, too quick for him to read, until they were bursting out over her skin like a speeded up film of lesions and boils erupting on the flesh of a leper. At one point, he brushed his fingertips across her stomach, but the sensation was so repulsive that he snatched his hand back as if it had been burnt.

Finally, three words remained constant in the centre of her belly.

SHE IS OURS.

Sickness knotted in his stomach. He made one more futile attempt at waking her before pulling the sheets back up to her neck. With a feeling of impotence, he sat on a small wooden chair in the corner of the room and watched her, praying silently that she would suddenly sit up and speak to him.

As he waited for the doctor to arrive, he stood in the kitchen and stared out across the fields, trying to put the chaotic jumble of his life into some kind of order. The warm security of his family was collapsing rapidly, the props maliciously whipped out by a hidden enemy. At the same time he was being assailed from the outside by a frightening, mysterious world that was beyond his comprehension, which threatened to end, not only his existence, but everything he held dear. "Why me?" he asked silently. "What have I done to deserve this?"

He noticed absently that the rain had opened up more holes in the ground. They were dotted randomly in the fields around the house, like evidence of a plague of giant moles. Mike made another mental note to tell Bulmer, but the thought was lost as soon as he had registered it.

Jack crept quietly in behind him. Mike thought his face had the red blotchiness of a long period of crying, but his smile was as broad as ever.

"When are we going to have lunch, Daddy?"

The normality of the question cheered him slightly. "Soon. I'm just waiting for the doctor to come to see your mother."

"Is she poorly?" His smile faded.

"She'll be okay, don't you worry." Mike put on a brave face

207

and tickled Jack under his arms, but his son gave a lacklustre response. He stopped pretending and placed his hands on Jack's shoulders. "Believe me, she'll be up and around in no time. Have I ever lied to you?"

"No."

"That's right. And I'm not lying this time. What do you fancy for lunch?"

"Don't know."

"Beans on toast sound okay?" I'll cook it in a little while. How does that grab you?"

Jack ignored his false humour and said earnestly, "Daddy, the elves say it's time for me to go to play with them now."

Mike was relieved that the conversation had moved away from Hannah; he didn't think he could hide his concern any longer. "That's good. Just don't go too far and make sure you're back for lunch. Okay?"

"Okay." Jack skipped off with newfound enthusiasm.

Mike turned back to the window. The swirling grey skies that looked set to turn to rain at any moment perfectly captured his mood; he was gripped by an engulfing melancholy that dulled his inspiration and prevented him seeing any way out of the complex, dangerous maze into which they were heading.

A flock of gulls suddenly rose cawing and screeching into the sky, disturbed by some movement in a field. Or beneath it. He retreated from the window and went to await the arrival of the doctor.

Hannah lay perfectly still. Darkness was all around her. She could have been floating in the cold depths of space, if not for the feel of the rock on her back. And her shoulders. And the soles of her feet. And the top of her head. And the tip of her nose. She was trapped, buried and forgotten, just waiting for death to come. Strangely, she could accept her fate calmly. In fact, it would be quite peaceful, were it not for the distant laughter, the harsh, barking, old man's laughter coming from a baby girl's mouth.

Chapter Twenty-Seven

The doctor sighed, shook his head, and looked at Mike with a mixture of exasperation and puzzlement. "Your wife is in labour, Mr Leary."

Mike stared back, dumbfounded. His jaw sagged and he was aware that he probably looked ridiculous, but he had no idea what to say.

"The contractions are well under way and her waters have broken." The doctor looked as baffled as Mike. "It's true."

"But . . . she's early!'

The doctor nodded sagely. "Indeed. But that shouldn't be a problem."

"That still doesn't explain why we can't wake her. Does it?"

The doctor shook his head, his face dark and thoughtful. "No, it doesn't explain it. I'll be honest with you, Mr Leary – I don't know what's wrong with your wife. I can't see any reason why she should be acting in this manner. It's not as if she's been traumatized. All the signs show that she's not comatose; in fact, she seems simply to be asleep. There's plenty of REM activity to suggest she's dreaming, so there's no reason why we shouldn't be able to wake her."

"So why can't we?" Mike heard the frustration and worry creep into his voice.

"I don't know," the doctor replied. "It's beyond my under-standing. I'm going to try to get a specialist over here as soon as possible. In the meantime I don't think I want to risk moving her. We'll have to deliver the baby here."

"Is that safe in her condition?" Mike felt a brief flutter of panic. "I mean . . . the baby's premature. What happens if you need an incubator, or a respirator, or something?"

"I'm having emergency equipment brought over from the surgery, if that's what you're worried about. And if the baby does have to go into hospital, we can keep it safe until the ambulance gets here. Mr Leary, I could have your wife sent into hospital now, but she's already nine centimetres dilated. I don't want to risk moving her at this stage. It could do more harm than good, as we don't have any idea what is causing her lack of consciousness. I've palpated her and the baby is in the right position for a normal birth. Of course, it will have to be a forceps delivery without your wife awake to push, but, again, that's not a problem. A midwife will come over and help me. Childbirth is a function that the body can carry out on a very subconscious level, even when the mother-to-be is totally anaesthetised. I'd feel happier if we did it here. Unless you have any specific objections?"

Mike shook his head. He wanted to say *Yes, I object, because we're right over the top of some frightening and dangerous supernatural activity that I already think has affected the child in the womb and I'm afraid, Doctor, I'm afraid that what is going to come out won't be any son of mine. Won't even be human.*

As the doctor went into the lounge to make his phone calls, Mike returned to the kitchen to put the kettle on. His nerves were electric, his breathing erratic; he could feel the stress lying across his shoulders like sacks of lead. It seemed someone was doing everything possible to break him, to make him give up in the face of the massed forces of adversity. Now he had to cope with the dread and worry of his wife going into labour while she was unconscious. And what was the child going to be like? Would it be blind, pale-skinned, like a creature that had spent its existence in the impenetrable darkness of a dank cavern far beneath the earth? Would it come out clawing and rending and scratching and digging? The thoughts turned over and over in his head, running away with him, punishing him with darker and darker fantasies. For no particular reason he could name, he felt that it was all his fault. Somehow Hannah was suffering because of him.

As he filled the kettle and plugged it in, he happened to

glance out of the window. What he saw was like a slap in the face, shocking him into instant action. Jack, bundled up in his thick coat and scarf and wearing his red wellington boots, was clambering over the fence at the bottom of the garden, the one that formed the boundary with the field containing the now giant hole where the topsoil had slipped into a gaping abyss.

"Jack!" Mike yelled, although he knew there was no chance he could hear him. He dropped the kettle and ran out into the garden. "Jack!" he bellowed again. By then his son had already disappeared over the top and Mike could see his small form skipping gleefully across the grass and mud to the hole.

He ran after him, splashing through the pool that had replaced the lawn, across the mired flower bed to the fence. In his haste, he clambered over it awkwardly, ripping the back of his hand open on a rusty, broken nail; the blood welled up but he did not feel the pain.

"Jack!" He was surprised how quickly his son had covered the distance between the fence and the hole which was several hundred yards away. As he watched, Jack hovered on the lip, jumped up and down excitedly, then disappeared into the gulf. "Jack!" The sheer volume of his shout tore at the back of his throat, his voice breaking with pain.

Suddenly it all became clear to him. The elves – the supposedly imaginary voices – it was the Tunnellers, the spirits, talking every day to his son, seducing a lonely youngster with promises of secret friends and play. And now they had called to him and he had answered.

Mike ran as fast as he could, slipping and sliding on the mud, falling full length, picking himself up and running again. They might have dragged his wife down, he thought; they wouldn't take his son too.

He careered straight over the lip of the hole without stopping, sliding rapidly down the steep incline, feeling the thick brown mud coat his body and cake under his fingernails. He came to a halt halfway down. Through the tears of frustration in his eyes, he could see Jack had disappeared. Swivelling round, he began to crawl head-first down the slope, calling out constantly, but hearing nothing in reply. At the bottom it

211

narrowed to the size of a manhole. Mike dove straight into it without even considering the risk. There was no sign of Jack; the only thing that marked his passing was the imprint of the child's wellingtons in the cold, wet clay. He had crawled barely four feet into the sloping hole when he realized he could not progress any further. The tunnel narrowed quickly until it was no longer wide enough to take his shoulders, although there had been room enough for Jack to scramble through. The cold draught on his face carrying the smell of the deep tunnels told him all he needed to know; that further on it widened out into the dark network of the Tunnellers. He stifled a cry of rage in his throat when he realized he had been beaten.

For one terrifying moment, he thought he was trapped there. The incline was so steep and the clay so slippery that he could not back up. However much he pushed and forced himself, there was no leverage to ease himself out. Then, just as the panic was about to take hold, he gave a heave with his aching arm muscles and slid back six inches, enough to allow him room to use his elbows.

The climb out of the hole was exhausting. The mud made it almost impossible to get a foothold, but after sliding back half a dozen times he finally pulled himself over the lip to lie face down in the wet grass in defeat. The tears came freely then; tears of loss, frustration and despair. He cried quietly for a moment until it was out of his sytem, then he wiped his face and steeled himself for the task ahead.

Back at the house, the doctor stopped in his tracks and gaped in horror. Every inch of Mike's skin and clothes was covered in brown mud and he was shivering with the cold. But it was the haunted, beaten look in his eyes that made the doctor think Mike was on the verge of a breakdown.

"My God," he exclaimed. "What in heaven's name happened to you?"

Mike repressed the almost overwhelming urge to give up. "It's my son, Jack," he said faintly. "He's run into one of those subsidence holes in the fields behind the house. I couldn't stop him . . ." His voice trailed off.

"But . . . where is he?"

"The hole leads into the tunnels." Mike was talking to

himself by then, his eyes staring blankly at his hands. "He's gone in there. It was too tight for me."

"We must call the police at once," the doctor said, running to the phone. "They'll organize a search party. We'll have him out in no time."

"You do that," Mike replied. He knew what he had to do. "Then look after Hannah. I'm going to start looking for him."

"Don't go down there on your own," the doctor warned.

"I won't." Mike knew it was futile starting at the hole in the field. He would have to go directly to the tunnels.

After the doctor had spoken to the police, Mike picked up the phone and called Richmond. When he heard the reporter's dry voice, he said, "It's Mike Leary. We've got to do it today."

"So soon?" He sounded hesitant. Mike feared he had changed his mind.

"The situation's changed. It's got to be now."

"I've got a council meeting to cover. And . . ."

"If you want to come with me, get your arse over here. I'm going down as soon as I've got a few things together. If you don't want to help, get off the phone. I've got things to do."

There was a slight pause. Mike could hear the sound of raised voices and then Richmond said, "I'll be right over." He went on to say, "I hope this doesn't cost me my job," but Mike had already put the receiver down and was beginning to scour the bungalow for the things they would need.

When Richmond arrived in his old, dirt-streaked Ford Fiesta, Mike had filled a small bag with a torch and spare batteries, some rope and gloves. He had changed his clothes and washed hurriedly, but there was still mud caked in his hair and around his wrists. Richmond eyed him curiously, but said nothing.

"We haven't got time to hang around," Mike said after exchanging greetings.

"What's the rush?" Richmond lit up a cigarette. He was wearing his cheap work suit and tie, Mike noted: not really suitable for a journey underground, but he would have to make do.

"They've got my son." His words were clipped, harsh.

Mike did not even want to think about the repercussions of that bald statement, because he knew that if he considered what it really meant he would break down. "They called to him and he went," he continued coldly, "down one of those holes in the fields at the back. He's in the tunnels now."

Richmond blanched. "My God! Do you think we can find him?"

"We've got to. I've got nothing to lose now. I'm going right to the heart of it, once and for all." As he slung the bag over his shoulder, he halted, then turned back to the reporter. He looked uncomfortable. "I understand if you want to back out. This could be dangerous. This *will* be dangerous. If you'll feel better out of it, then say now."

Richmond shook his head. "I'd never forgive myself if I didn't go with you. There's got to be a great story in this!" It was obvious his bravado was false; the fear in his eyes shone like a beacon.

Mike nodded slowly. "Okay, you go on to the car. I'll be out in a minute."

Apprehensively, he walked into the bedroom. The nurse, a middle-aged woman with doughy arms and a kind face, had arrived a few minutes earlier. She was in deep conversation with the doctor. "How is she?" Mike asked.

"She's fine, love," the nurse replied. "Don't you worry."

"I don't want to leave her alone, but our son . . ."

"That's okay. We understand." The nurse smiled reassuringly. "She'll be in good hands here."

Mike nodded. "I know." He knelt down at the side of the bed and watched the changing patterns of his wife's troubled, sleeping face. It was a terrible choice. He wanted so much to be there with her, helping her fight. Looking down at her, he knew he would never be able to live with himself if she died while he was away. The prospect seemed far too real at that moment. Gently he held her hand and squeezed it before kissing her on the lips. "Fight them," he whispered. "You're strong. You're stronger than me. You can do it." Then he turned and walked out of the room without saying another word.

Before they had got within half a mile of the mine entrance they were forced to pull the car over to the side of the road.

214

There was a huge crowd of men milling around the gates. They had successfully turned away one of the lorries which took the coal to a nearby power station and, as it passed, Mike could see the angry, red face of the driver.

"Pickets," Richmond said. "We'll never get past them."

There were at least eighty men in front of the mine, talking, smoking or warming their hands over a fire that blazed in an old dustbin. A few had makeshift banners and signs which said, "UDM – Official Picket" and "Keep Colthorpe Open". Mike could not see Packard, but there was a group of other union officials; unlike the rough clothes of the other men, they were wearing expensive car coats and woollen overcoats, hands thrust deep in their pockets against the chill. It was obvious they would not let Mike and Richmond on to the site. His heart sank.

"What are we going to do?" Richmond asked.

"Drive on," Mike said, chewing the nail of his little finger in thought.

Richmond sighed, slipped the car into gear and pulled slowly up the hill. As they neared, one by one the men turned and stared, trying to recognize the occupants of the car. When the first one saw Mike's face, the word ran through the crowd like wildfire, the whisper turning quickly to a jeer, then barks and abusive yells. Mike was taken aback by the intensity of the anger and the hatred on their faces. A missile hurtled out of the centre of the crowd and clanged noisily on the roof of the car. As another one followed it, Richmond did not wait for instructions from Mike and spun the car round in the road, speeding off quickly the way they had come. A jubilant cheer rose up behind them.

"I'm not trying to drive through that mob," Richmond said with a note of finality.

Mike remained silent, desperately trying to think of a way around the problem. Finally it came to him. "I've got it," he snapped. "Keep driving and turn right at the crossroads."

Two minutes later, Mike told Richmond to bring the car to a halt outside the deserted cottage on Colthorpe's fringes where he had first started to believe in the power that existed beneath the village. Nothing had changed since his last visit; the door still hung open, just as he had left it when he had

215

bolted out. There was no sign that anyone else had been anywhere near the building.

"Why are we here?" Richmond asked. He threw an empty cigarette packet into the back seat.

"Because this is our back door into the tunnel system. Those tunnels seem to cover the whole area. At certain points they're very close to the surface and the earth has collapsed in on them – like in the field behind my house, like in the graveyard and like here."

"So we can just climb down and get straight in there?"

"Exactly."

"What are these tunnels for?"

"Who knows? They probably date back hundreds of years, maybe longer, right back to when men first started to dig in the area."

Richmond looked nervously at the cottage through a thick cloud of cigarette smoke. "Well," he said finally, "shall we be on our way? I'd like to be back by the time the pubs open."

Mike led the way up the path and into the house. The bare living room was permeated with the underground smell, but the odour of decomposition which he had experienced previously was no longer around. The kitchen door opened and closed slightly in the breeze and the wind around the house rushed loudly through the trees and hedgerows.

"There's going to be another storm," Richmond said, as he stared at the black circle in the centre of the kitchen floor.

"We'll be in the right place for it," Mike replied. "You won't have to worry about raindrops falling on your head down there."

He dropped down on one knee and peered into the hole. "How far down do we have to go?" Richmond asked. His cigarette stub was crushed under his heel.

"Ten, maybe fifteen feet. I've brought a length of rope so I can lower you down."

"Then how do you get down?"

"It's not very wide. I can brace myself against the walls with my back and feet."

"I suppose we better do it then," Richmond sighed. "Can I have the torch?"

Mike handed it to him and he shone the beam down to

216

reveal the tunnel just below. As Mike lowered a wheezing Richmond into the pit, he started to feel a growing sense of apprehension. Only there, on the edge of the dark, underground world, did he finally start to comprehend the monumental task that they faced. The thought of those long, lonely tunnels was enough to make him consider turning back. Then he remembered his son.

Quickly, he followed Richmond down on the first step of their journey into the depths.

Chapter Twenty-Eight

The tunnel sloped downwards steeply, empty in both directions. As they walked, Mike fought back a wave of despair which threatened to engulf him. All he could think about was Jack, lost and alone in the darkness, and Hannah, unconscious in her bed. If he believed that they had been taken because of his refusal to leave well alone, that he was culpable in the suffering that lay ahead for both of them, then he would not be able to continue. He would not be able to live with himself.

Behind them, the tunnel ran close to the surface, so they had chosen the route which descended rapidly. Richmond had grown quiet and edgy since they had left behind the shaft of grey light which signalled their entry to the network. They walked silently, side by side, following the torch's beam which showed the way ahead was free of debris or any further shafts, but did little to hold back the surrounding darkness. Occasionally Mike would let his hand stray to the knife he had placed in his jacket pocket. Its main use was for carving arrows in the tunnel walls at junctions to mark the way they had come. Although he knew it would provide a poor defence, he took small comfort from the feel of cold steel against his palm.

"I think we're going upwards again," Richmond said, his voice echoing around them.

"You could be right. This tunnel is following an erratic path."

"They don't make them like they used to. I wish I knew where we were. I get comfort from little things like that. Do you have any idea what part of the village we're under?"

"No, it's deceptive. We could be curving around the out-skirts or going directly under it to the mine."

Richmond touched the wall. "Good workmanship."

Mike wished he had some idea where they were going – some plan that he could cling to for support – but his only aim was to walk the tunnels until he found Jack. He was relieved that Richmond had had the good manners not to point out the futility of it.

The tunnel rose and fell without taking them down as deep as they had expected and with each step the heavy odour became more overpowering. Sometimes roots protruded through the walls and ceiling, thick and snaking, throwing shadows that leapt monstrously in the light of the torch. At one point, a tunnel ran off to their left, but when they began to explore it they found it was blocked by a heavy fall of earth. Mike guessed their location before they had retraced their steps and turned back on to the main passageway. Hanging above their heads in front of them was what appeared to be a lump of rotting wood.

"What's this?" Richmond stretched out his hand to investigate.

"Don't touch it, Terry," Mike said, too late.

The wet, broken wood fell to pieces the moment his fingers came into contact with it and a shower of dry white bones tumbled down on to Richmond's head.

"We're under the graveyard," Mike said, stating the obvious.

Richmond dusted himself down, spitting repeatedly, an expression of disgust on his face. Carefully, he flicked the yellowing skull and bones with his toe to the side of the tunnel. "I hope that was no one I knew."

They passed several other coffins in various states of decay, jutting out around them like shop signs on the High Street, until they were brought up sharply by an obstruction. The tunnel was partially blocked by a waist-high pile of bones, some of them old and shattered, others newer. On closer inspection, Mike saw flesh still clung to some.

"How did these get here?" Richmond asked. Mike did not want to consider the answer, but Richmond was persistent. "It looks like they've been dug out and brought here," he continued, probing the bottom of the pile with his shoe.

219

"Terry, will you get away from there? God knows what kind of diseases you're going to pick up."

"Hang on. There seems to be a smaller tunnel behind it. Look, you can just see it."

"Terry, come away!"

"Let me just move a few of these bones out of the way . . ." He pulled out a long, fractured thigh bone. "Listen, can you hear anything?"

"Terry . . ."

"It sounds like – "

Mike moved quickly and grabbed him by the forearm, dragging him past the pile into the tunnel beyond. A large, whiskery snout poked out near to where his foot had been.

"Did you see that?" Richmond hissed. "A rat. As big as a bloody terrier!"

Mike moved him along quickly before he had the chance to disturb the nest any more. He remembered queasily the wave of wriggling, furry bodies that had swarmed over him when he opened the kitchen door in the deserted cottage. He shuddered to think how he would cope with the experience there, in the confines of the tunnel.

"Do you think the rats dragged those bones there?" Richmond asked.

"Rats don't behave like that, Terry."

The reporter considered the comment briefly and decided to let the subject drop.

An hour later, Mike was beginning to feel tired. After the graveyard, the tunnel headed down so steeply they had to keep checking themselves to prevent their legs slipping out of control. Their uneventful progress only served to heighten their tension, turning the screw until Mike wanted to confront something, anything, just to ease the pressure.

The ceiling of the tunnel had progressively lowered and they were both having to stoop to avoid cracking their heads on protuberances. He thought that was a good sign, recalling what Charlie Robson had said about the lowest tunnels being the oldest. In the torchlight, the walls glistened black and on several occasions Mike could see streams of water running down them and across the floor.

"Do you think these tunnels ever flood?" He splashed through a growing puddle.

"I don't think so," Richmond replied. "This has been a successful mining area largely because the seams were all above the water table and they didn't have to keep pumping them out."

"But what happens if we've gone below the seams?"

"Do you think we have?"

"I don't know. It was just a thought. I suppose we can turn back if we come up against any water."

"Have you read *Journey To The Centre Of The Earth*? Jules Verne? The characters in it came across an underwater sea with dinosaurs."

"I don't think we'll find any dinosaurs down here, Terry," Mike said. "I'll settle for finding my son."

After another hour they were both thoroughly confused. The tunnel network had become much more complex and they had passed several junctions with passages branching off to either side. Mike had originally tried to choose their route logically, but after a while he had given up, selecting each turning at random. Strangely, he felt intermittent breezes rustling past him, although he could not guess the source of the airstreams.

Soon he had other things to concern him. Once he thought he heard his name whispered at his elbow, but when he spun around, there was no one behind him. Richmond stood a step away observing him as if he had suddenly gone insane. Mike wondered if the strain had begun to affect him. He was so tense and anxious that his neck muscles felt like cables and he occasionally started hyperventilating for no reason. It was a reassuring explanation.

But the whispers did not go away. In fact, they got worse. His name reached his ears several times in different voices, he was sure, and sometimes there was more, phrases or even whole sentences. Each time he glanced at Richmond, but the reporter gave no sign he heard anything out of the ordinary. The words were so faint that Mike himself could not tell if it was just the echo of their footsteps or a ringing in his ear. And once he had the chilling sensation – and he was sure of this – of

221

hot breath on his neck. He started suddenly, his heart pounding, but he did not attempt to turn around; he knew there would be nothing there. The experience did convince him of one thing: that they were getting closer.

Mike was sure he was not alone in his fears. He saw Richmond freeze, then shake his head; he refused to say what was wrong. It was reflected in his posture; his sure stance had become a halting stoop and his voice, both their voices, barely more than a whisper, as if to talk loudly would disturb something sleeping. Mike stifled his initial urge to shout out Jack's name to see if he would answer.

At another junction, when they had stopped to argue which way to go, Richmond grabbed Mike's arms and pointed down the tunnel to their left. In the gloomy distance, strange pinpricks of light like fireflies angrily buzzed in the air.

"Do you see that?" he said beneath his breath.

"I think so," Mike replied. He squinted to see if it was his eyes merely reacting to the contrast between the darkness and the bright torchlight. For a second, a face formed in the centre of the lights, an angry, twisting face; but it faded quickly.

"Shall we check it out?" Mike asked. His uneasiness was growing.

"Let's not." Richmond's down-to-earth disbelief in the supernatural seemed to have abandoned him. "Let's keep going down, find your son and get out of here."

Mike glanced back down the tunnel and got the strangest feeling that the darkness was packed with people standing and watching; he could feel eyes, scores of eyes, upon him. But he could see nothing.

The doctor carried the electric fire into the bedroom and placed it as close to the bed as he could safely do. Whistling through his teeth, he rubbed his hands together near to the glowing bars then made a point of breathing heavily to one side; his breath clouded instantly.

"I can't understand why it's so cold in here," he said to the nurse who was bending over the still form of Hannah Leary. It was an understatement. It was colder in the bedroom than in the bitter wind and icy rain that had started to lash the side of the bungalow.

"Well, it's certainly not affecting this young lady here," the nurse replied. She had pulled on a thick coat and had borrowed Mike's scarf to muffle her neck. "She's burning up. Have you felt her forehead?"

The doctor did not reply. He opened his bag and placed it on the small coffee table which he had carried near to the bed. "Shall we prepare her?" he said.

The nurse pulled back the bed clothes and then eased up Hannah's nightdress. Instantly she clapped her hand over her mouth, a scream stifled in her throat.

"What in heaven's name is it?" The doctor rushed to her side. Hannah's belly was moving and stretching like elastic, as if something inside was trying to get out. The skin had a strange glow that made it almost translucent and when he looked closely the doctor thought he could glimpse a dark shape through it. A shape with two hands that were pushing and clawing and rending.

Before he could react, the movement stopped. Hannah's stomach returned to normal and the glow faded. "What was it?" The nurse felt her stomach turn and flip.

The doctor shook his head and sat down on the small wooden chair. The nurse asked him again, but the only response she could get was a baffled stare. "I'm afraid," she said, putting into words what she thought he could not say. "What's happening to her?"

He walked over to the window, looking thoughtfully out over the windswept fields. "We shall see," he said.

Mike guessed they were deeper than he had ever been before. There had been intermittent bouts of whispering and once he had received a faint tap on the shoulder which could, he lied to himself, have been a muscle spasm. He was also troubled by the water which dripped continually from the ceiling of the tunnel. His clothes were drenched and the iciness of it had chilled him so badly that he was finding it difficult to move his fingers. Richmond's thinning hair was plastered to his head and he had to remove his glasses every few paces to wipe away the droplets of water. "At what point do we turn back?" he had asked twice. Mike told them they would know when it was time to give up.

"My wife would have a fit if she knew I was down here," Richmond continued. "Poor old dear. She doesn't even like me working late at night. She's afraid I'll get mugged or something."

"Just think what a hero you'll be when you get out!"

"A hero? Well . . . I suppose so. The more likely result is that I'll end up confined to the house for six months. I hope she doesn't give me too hard a time." He was thoughtful for a moment then said, "Can I ask you something?"

"Sure."

"Do you really believe all that ghosties and ghoulies stuff? All that about the Tunnellers?"

"Of course I believe it. We've seen it with our own eyes."

"I just can't come to terms with it at all. I've spent a lot of time thinking about it and, you know, all the things you mentioned, they could all have a logical, rational explanation." He sounded unconvinced by his own argument.

Mike thought he heard a noise somewhere ahead of them.

"I've been trying very hard today to see some sign. Sometimes I think I hear things, but it's just my imagination. There are so many echoes down here, aren't there?"

"To be honest, I don't care if there are things down here or not." He too had heard a noise, but it was muffled and difficult to distinguish. "I've had my fill of being altruistic. There's too much to lose. I just want to find my son. I want my wife to get better. And I want to put Colthorpe far behind me. Some of the locals should do something – why should it be me that risks everything?"

Richmond muttered in agreement. "I wonder if the police have started looking for your son yet. Wouldn't it be funny if we bumped into them down here?"

"Very amusing." He held out his arm and stopped Richmond in his tracks. They were at another junction. Another tunnel, much smaller and in a comparatively poor state with rough-hewn walls, stretched off to their right. In the distance, Mike again heard the noise. A laugh – a short peal of jollity and high spirits. "That's Jack!" He spun around and grabbed Richmond's sleeve. "It's Jack! He's here!"

"Let's not go rushing off," Richmond cautioned. "We don't want an accident. If he's down there, he'll wait for us."

224

Mike was unable to contain himself. The pressures and emotions which he had corked up inside him burst out in a resounding cry. "Jack!" he yelled. "We're coming!"

The moment his excited voice echoed along the tunnel, it happened. It started as a vague buzz, distant but growing closer. Then the volume increased and in seconds Mike's ears were aching, the pain like needles in his head. He looked over his shoulder for the source of the din and saw it coming towards them like an express train. It was black, darker even than the surrounding darkness of the tunnel, and it was roiling and twisting like a cloud. Within it Mike could see jaws opening and closing, eyes staring with hatred and then disappearing, and something like a fan of knives which opened and shut with a metallic glint in the torchlight.

"Run!" he yelled. He scrambled into the tunnel, stooping to avoid the low ceiling then pulled himself rapidly along the walls. He could hear Richmond puffing and wheezing behind him. The tunnel had a slight incline and Mike began to pick up speed, buoyed along by another burst of childish laughter ahead of him and the fear of the unknown behind.

Then two things happened simultaneously. The ground disappeared suddenly beneath his feet and he fell. It was not a long drop, only about six feet, but he landed up to his waist in freezing water. Before the echoes of the splash had died away, with a yell materializing from Richmond's lips, there was a strange sound, like a cry of anger, and a deep, resounding rumble as the roof of the tunnel came down behind them. Richmond pitched forward, squealing like a pig. He plummetted into the water next to Mike, smashing his head against the wall. The noise of the collapse was as painful as if they had been standing next to a jet as it switched on its engine. It was followed by a billowing cloud of dust and a shower of rock.

It was not until the sound and tremors had subsided that Mike realized Richmond was unconscious. He was sprawled in the black water with just his head above the surface. Mike immediately checked his pulse. He was still breathing, but in the light of the torch, which had miraculously escaped damage, he could see a trickle of blood running down his face from a deep gash on his forehead.

"Shit," he said out loud. His legs had already gone numb. "What the hell are we going to do now?"

He played the torch beam over the walls, but could see no way out. The tunnel ended directly ahead of him and behind the way was completely blocked by the fall. Mike stared blankly around, trying to come to terms with the fact that he was trapped far underground with no hope of rescue. He considered digging at the newly-fallen rocks, scrabbling until his hands were bloody and raw. Then he noticed one other thing that terrified him. The water around his waist was rising, slowly, very slowly, but at the rate that it was streaming from the ceiling it would not be long before it would be over their heads. He grabbed Richmond and shook him madly, but he showed no sign of recovering. Mike flung him back into the water angrily and then covered his face in frustration. There was nothing he could do.

Hannah's body was burning with pain. Her head ached, her limbs were leaden and there was a network of fire throughout her being, eating away at her. She felt it through a narcotic haze, vaguely aware that it was wracking her, but unable to pinpoint its source. Her dark tomb, which at first had seemed secure and comforting, was now constricting, closing in all around her so that she had difficulty in breathing. Through it all, only one thing kept her from escaping into oblivion; the face of her husband, which rose repeatedly from the depths of her mind.

"Mike," she called out dreamily, "where are you?" She raised her hands to the cold stone above her face and pushed, the pain jabbing at her muscles. The rock moved slightly. It would be so much easier to give up, to lie back and drift away into the darkness where it was calm and soothing, but each time she tried, Mike's face convinced her to carry on. She strained again and the rock moved some more. "This is wrong," she said through gritted teeth. "What am I doing here? I've got to get out."

She pushed and pushed and the rock moved further away from her face so that she could move her head easily. A sudden burst of panic rippled through her. She felt that if she lay there any longer she would be lost. She pushed harder and harder, heaving with her shoulders until she thought her back would break. Then, as the rock gradually ground upwards, she heard muffled sounds coming from somewhere above. Voices. Worried voices.

In the bedroom, the doctor shivered and rubbed his hands together, shifting from foot to foot to keep warm. "She's close. She's very close."

"The poor dear." The nurse stroked her forehead gently and then looked at the doctor with a troubled expression. "I don't like this. There's something dreadfully wrong."

"Fuck off!" The nurse snatched back her hand in shock as the words barked from Hannah's mouth. But it was not her voice. It was a man's, an old man's. "Fuck off, you fucking cow!"

"Doctor, what's happening!" The nurse stepped away from the bed nervously. Hannah's lips rolled back in a snarl of animal hatred, but her eyes remained shut.

"This is beyond me," the doctor finally admitted. "I've never seen anything like it."

"Fuck off," Hannah growled again.

"What's causing it?" the nurse asked again. "It's frightening me."

"An extreme hormone imbalance, perhaps," the doctor said unconvincingly. "I think we'd better be ready. It's going to come soon. Can you get the forceps to hand?" The nurse saw him stare at Hannah's stomach as if he were trying to see into her through her skin. "We'd better be ready," he repeated.

Mike often wondered how he would react if he was faced with death. Would he cry? Would he be sick with fear? He was surprised to discover only a remarkable lucidity of thought, a great calmness. He pulled Richmond's large frame up and propped him against the wall, holding his head out of the water. The bleeding had stopped, but he was still out cold. The water was midway up his stomach, creeping dangerously over his chest muscles to his neck. He wondered obliquely if the air would run out before they drowned. Which was the worst way to go?

"Go forward."

He started in shock at the voice which carried dully through the debris. It took five seconds before he had collected himself sufficiently to reply. "Hello! We're in here. We're trapped!"

"You must go forward." The voice, though muffled by the thick wall of rock, seemed familiar, but he could not place it.

"You don't understand," he said a little more hesitantly. "We're trapped here." He realized, without really comprehending, that the voice did not belong to any living person.

"You must go forward. There is a way." The voice seemed to be straining somehow, as if the words were difficult to form.

"I can't see anything." He shone the torch frantically all over the walls and ceiling of their tiny prison once again, but no exit was revealed.

"Search harder. It's there." The words trailed off into nothing and though Mike called out several times there was no reply.

He turned to Richmond and shook him once more, and this time a weak, spluttering groan eased out from between his lips. "Come on, Terry. Wake up!" He shook him again and again until the reporter was staring around in a daze, fending Mike off with his forearm.

"What happened?"

"The tunnel collapsed. Now come on, we haven't got much time. We've got to find a way out of here before we drown."

"My glasses . . ."

"Forget your fucking glasses! Can't you hear what I'm saying?"

Richmond stared at him blankly until a flicker of recognition passed across his face. "I remember. The tunnel!"

"Well done. Now . . ."

"Someone pushed me!"

"What?"

"When the tunnel came down! Someone pushed me! I felt the hands on my back. That's why I landed on top of you."

Mike looked into his eyes as awareness slowly dawned on him. The voice. The familiar voice. It had been Charlie

228

Robson. "Come on, Terry," he said, focusing his mind. "If you love your life, and your wife, you'll help me look for a way out of here."

"A way out?" Richmond looked around and saw the extent of their prison for the first time. "Jesus Christ."

Mike put a steadying hand on his shoulder as the first signs of panic flickered across his face. "There's a way out, Terry. I know there is."

"How do you know?"

"A little bird told me." Mike handed Richmond the torch and waded through the steadily rising water towards the wall which formed a barrier across the tunnel. As he got closer he found himself suddenly dropping deeper and deeper into the inky pool. "Of course," he mused, "the tunnel goes down here."

"But that's no use, is it?" Richmond said, his voice bordering on hysteria.

"It depends if it rises up again soon. Perhaps it just drops for a few feet and then comes up above the water level. We could swim under."

"What gives you any idea that it might do that? It might just go down and down. We could find we've gone too far and drown."

"What's the alternative, Terry? Stay here and drown?" Though Mike was speaking in a measured tone to keep Richmond calm, his mind was racing. What if the voice was lying? It would be a horrible death. Choking and drowning agonizingly in the dark. And even if there were a chance of getting through, the risks were enough to make it a foolish chance; the water so black he would not be able to see his way, so cold he risked hypothermia.

"You know, Terry, I've never been the type of person to have faith in anything, especially myself. But I've got to have faith here." He looked him in the eye and asked, "Do you believe that if a person's good, that goodness survives after the grave?" Incomprehension showed on Richmond's face. "I do. I believe. I'm going to give it a shot and if I make it through I'll swim back so you'll know."

"And if you don't?"

"If I don't, you're on your own."

The panic that had been bubbling beneath the surface suddenly flared up. Richmond waded forward and grabbed Mike by the shoulders. "Don't leave me!"

"Terry, if I don't do this, we're going to die. It's as simple as that."

"Don't leave me!" His face was contorted in fear. Mike pushed him back firmly. Before he had time to renew his efforts, Mike took a deep breath and slid under the surface. The last thing he heard was Richmond's pleading wail, like the cry of a dying animal.

The shock of the cold water gave him a sudden crystal awareness, but he knew it would not be long before it made him sluggish and unable to swim. He kicked off quickly, using the roof of the tunnel to guide him in his sudden descent. The downward progress seemed to be never-ending and he was horrified to discover the tunnel was getting narrower and narrower. Eventually it was no wider than the rathole he had crawled through with Charlie Robson. Then there was no turning back. If he tried, he would flounder and die. His only hope was to press on and hope it would start to rise up quickly. His limbs were becoming heavier and his breath was like acid in his lungs.

Just as hope was about to leave him, the tunnel levelled and then started rising quickly, widening out as it progressed. With renewed hope, he struck out, reaching the surface within seconds.

His first breath was a huge gulp of life, filling his lungs. The darkness around him was complete, but he fumbled around and eventually managed to crawl out and lie shivering and exhausted on the cold rock. He knew he would not have long to recover. If he did not return soon, Richmond would start to panic. Mike feared the task of getting the reporter safely through the water as much as he feared making the trip twice more himself. By that time the cold and the strain would have taken a terrible toll on him. Would he survive? With a surprising inner strength, he did not even consider the question; he just knew it had to be done.

When he resurfaced on the other side of the water channel, shaking with the effort, Richmond squealed with delight. He was disturbed when he saw in the torchlight a

230

strange, unbalanced gleam in the reporter's eye; his smile was a little too wide. The water was up to his neck and it was difficult to stand upright. Between gasps, he explained the situation to Richmond, stressing that he should not give up hope; that even when his lungs were close to bursting, he should keep going because it was not too far. He hoped that was enough.

They kicked off together, with Mike ahead. He drew some sustenance from the knowledge that it was the last time. But at the bottom of the descent, when Mike thought he could go no further, he felt a thrashing in the water behind him and he knew Richmond was panicking. For one terrifying moment, he felt fingers brush his legs and close around his ankle. He was convinced Richmond was going to drag him back and that they would both die together. But he kicked free and propelled himself upwards, his relief providing him with the last drop of strength he needed.

Seconds after he had crawled out on to the rock, Richmond followed him. Mike could hear the sobs wracking his body, interspersed with the sound of mouthfuls of water spewing out. He put a hand on his back, but it did little to comfort him.

"Why did I come here?" Richmond said. "I don't want to die."

"We've made it through the worst, Terry. It's easy-going all the way now." It was another lie.

Though they had both survived the harrowing swim, the torch had not. Mike cursed as he flicked it on and off without effect and resigned himself to continuing the rest of the journey in darkness. It seemed like a small hurdle compared to what they had already been through.

They rested for a few moments, letting their breathing subside. As they lay side by side, Mike realized there was a soft glow deep in the water. It grew stronger and stronger until, with a sudden belch of air bubbles, something bobbed to the surface. It took him a second to comprehend what it was. A body. A small body, hanging face down in the water, unmoving. Jack's body.

A pathetic cry escaped from between his lips and he scrambled across the rock and launched himself half into the water to grab hold of the sodden coat. Summoning up his fading strength, he heaved the body towards him, fighting back the tears that burned his eyes. The calm, innocent face was white and bloated from its time in the water.

"No!" he roared, with a passion that brought tremendous, pounding echoes. "No!"

But Jack was dead, he could tell that as he pulled the body towards him. He was definitely . . . Then Jack's eyes sprang open, fiery and hateful, a hideous grin leaping across his face.

"Bastard," he croaked in a crackling, phlegm-edged voice. He swung his tiny fist with such force that it knocked Mike to one side. As he pitched face down into the water, he could feel Jack's steely fingers grip his arms and start to pull him under. He kicked, trying to find something to grab, swallowing a mouthful of water in the process.

Then, when he thought it was all too late, he felt Richmond's strong hands on his ankles, anchoring him. For one brief moment, he was at the centre of a bizarre tug-of-war, back and forth, his breath hissing out of his mouth. Slowly, Jack's grip loosened, his fingers clawing at Mike's face one final time before he slipped back beneath the water.

Richmond heaved Mike back on to the rock, putting an arm around his shoulders to comfort him. "It wasn't your son," he mumbled. "It was them. It was *them*." His voice broke and trailed off.

Mike allowed himself the luxury of a brief sob, trying to scour the churning emotions within him. He was at once terrified, sickened and relieved. Relieved that his son could still be alive.

Aware of the dangers of exposure in their sodden clothes, he took only a minute to recover before forcing Richmond to his feet to restart the trek. Though it was dark, the tunnel was level and the going was not too difficult. Apart from an occasional muffled whimper, Richmond remained silent. Every now and then he would grab hold of Mike's arm, drawing comfort from the contact.

They had travelled for almost twenty minutes, making agonizingly slow progress, when Mike noticed it was growing lighter. Five minutes later he could see his hand in front of his face. It was not the warm light of the sun or a fire or even a torch; it was something colder, unnatural. He could not identify the source. Eventually the tunnels became gloomy, like an autumn twilight. There was a strange smell, one he had experienced before in the deserted cottage: the smell of rotting, the stench of decomposition.

"Where is the light coming from?" Richmond muttered.

Dazed, the reporter stared blankly ahead, his feet plodding forward unconsciously like a machine. Mike wondered if he would be able to cope with what lay ahead. "I don't know," he replied. "Maybe it's something in the rock."

Richmond grunted in reply, not really caring.

Soon the still tranquility of the tunnels disappeared. There was a faint electric ringing in the air, like the distant humming of pylons, and the whispering returned once more, fading in and out of his hearing like an out-of-tune radio broadcast.

"They're coming. They're coming." The words hummed and whistled, the wind spoke.

Then, cutting through it all, laughter. Jack's laughter.

Mike quickened his pace, afraid to run headlong towards the sound in case it was another lure. But he could not dampen the sudden rush of hope that put fire back into his frozen limbs.

"They do exist, don't they?" Richmond said suddenly. "They do. I know they do."

They rounded a slight bend and suddenly they were out into a wider area. At first sight, Mike could not tell if it was a natural, low-roofed cavern or man-made. The movement of air over his head and the way his footsteps echoed loudly told him the roof was far above. He took a few tentative steps into it until, through the thick gloom, he could make out the tiny figure of Jack sitting cross-legged on the floor. He was playing with something.

Mike wanted to call out his name, but the word came out as a croak, dying on his lips. His legs would not move; he was afraid it was another illusion. Eventually, Richmond's fingers closed tightly around his forearm. "Get him," he whispered. "We've got to get him."

Richmond pushed him forward and they started to jog together. Mike speeded up as they got closer, his muscles protesting, but when he saw Jack look up and beam at him in

233

greeting, he found the strength to keep going. Jack giggled and laughed, waving as they ran.

His joy quickly turned to disgust. His son, his handsome, innocent son, had across his lap a severed arm; the skin was blue and mottled with decay, the fingernails black. Dried blood and tendons hung where it had been ripped from the shoulder. An arm. Charlie Robson's arm.

"Daddy," Jack said with a broad smile, "look what I've got."

Mike whisked Jack up in his arms and let the cold, dead limb roll across the dusty floor. Richmond's gaze followed its progress in disbelief. As Mike held Jack in front of his eyes, he could see a dark stain around his mouth.

"It tastes nice, daddy." Mike gagged. He had been eating it. "So nice. So fucking nice!" The voice dropped, becoming low and snarling, and Mike realized he had been duped once more. Before the thing in his arms had time to react, he threw the tiny figure away from him, closing his eyes so he could not see the face; it was spitting and snarling like an alley cat. Mike grabbed Richmond and dragged him away, running frantically before more horrors could be unleashed. Behind them, he could hear obscenities, shrieks and whoops – a foul mockery of a child at play. Mike fought back another sob, but the spasms were wracking his body.

They crossed the cavern quickly and then they were into another tunnel without a backward glance. Mike had to pause frequently to wipe the stinging tears from his eyes. He wondered how much longer he could carry on, how many more times he could pick up his son only to discover he was cradling instead something vile and twisted. With a massive effort, he discovered he could imprison his emotions deep within him. It was the only way he could continue. At his side, Richmond muttered to himself, occasionally touching the raw and bleeding gash on his head.

At the next fork, Mike took the left-hand path. They had not travelled far when he became aware of movement in the gloom ahead. Cautioning Richmond with a hand, he crept forward until they were close enough to see what was happening.

It was a terrible, fearful sight. Mike knew, if he survived, he would never forget it.

234

Another, larger, tunnel passed directly across the one along which they were travelling. Moving along it, in a continuous grim procession of death, were the Tunnellers: the trapped, hating spirits of the underworld.

There were miners, some horrifically injured, their limbs or eyes missing, their helmets dusty, their clothes rotting, bones protruding, yellowy-white. And there were others, wild-eyed, with swarthy skin and manes of matted hair. Other things were among them, frightening, nauseating things; pale, vaguely-human creatures with blind eyes and others, more monstrous, that defied description. They were slowly wending their way towards the surface.

As he watched the grim march of the dead towards the world of light and life, Richmond began to shake, whimpering under his breath.

"Come on, Terry, back the way we came," Mike hissed.

A low cackle stopped them in their tracks. Sitting against the wall behind them was a pale figure dressed in tatters. It was smiling, but it was a smile of mockery and hatred beneath cold eyes full of torment and despair. Mike recognized the bald pate and the pinched, mean expression. He had seen the face before – in an old book in Professor Williams' study.

"*Praise the Lord*!" The Reverend Arnold Collett's voice hissed like steam escaping from a pipe. Here was the explanation for his disappearance from Colthorpe's church.

"Stay back," Richmond said fearfully.

Collett slithered up the wall like a snake, and only then did Mike see what was behind him. Clutching on to his skeletal hand, was Jack. He looked dazed, almost drugged.

"You have been lax in your duties." Collett did not blink. "I have been forced to preach to the boy myself. He was unaware of God's will."

"Let him go," Mike said, confident that this really was his son.

"He listens. He learns." Fingernails caked with clay ran through Jack's hair. Collett's mottled grey tongue flicked out over his dry lips. "Your wife is dying. We will have your new child too." There was a glimmer of hungry anticipation in his eyes.

"Let him go," Mike said again. He felt impotent,

frightened and angry at the same time. He watched each stroke of his son's head in horror.

"You did well to get this far." There was a croak in his throat which could have been a laugh. "To get this far alive. Most of us had to die."

Mike took a step forward and Collett's fingernails instantly dug into Jack's throat. His snarl was not human. "We have waited so long. This world is dark and cold and painful. But now we are taking it with us into the light. Your world."

"Who are you?" Mike asked. He thought of Hannah and his unborn child and he prayed.

"Who are we? The dead. Only the dead. Generations who have passed on near to this cursed place. Every man who worked here was tainted, blackened by the foul presence. There was no escape from the moment we set foot here."

Mike launched himself forward suddenly. He snatched hold of Jack, but before he could escape, Collett's fingers closed on his thigh. He screamed in agony as the nails started ripping into the muscle. Richmond ran past them in the confusion, but Mike's eyes were on Collett who was spitting and snarling like a wild animal, his face melting and twisting. He was becoming something else – a formless shape, embodying hatred and evil. Mike yanked his leg from his grasp, feeling the flesh rip open. The pain almost made him faint, but Richmond was at his side, supporting him with one arm and Jack with the other, and leading them back towards the junction.

The thing that had been Collett spat and crackled with electricity, howling with a thousand different voices, but it did not pursue them.

"It's not following. It knows we can't harm them," Richmond whined. "We can't stop them. Why should it care now? They're going up." He sobbed. "*They're going up.*"

Mike closed his eyes and hugged Jack as tightly as he could. He felt a wave of love so powerful he thought he would cry. The daze slipped from his son's eyes briefly. "I don't like it down here, Daddy," he whispered. "I want to go home."

Mike kissed him and picked him up; his arms were weak and shaking. "Come on, Terry. We'll find a way out of here."

236

"There's no point," Richmond replied pathetically. "We can't do anything."

"We're getting out of here," Mike said. "Don't give up now." He convinced Richmond to move and they walked slowly back to the junction and turned left into the downward sloping tunnel. Mike was close to collapse. He could barely walk on his injured leg, the torn cloth of his trousers sticking to the flowing blood. The relief he felt at having Jack back in his arms was enough to keep him going for the moment, but he knew if they did not escape the tunnels soon he would collapse. One glance at Richmond told him he could not count on the reporter to get Jack to safety. Thankfully, Mike noticed, the exhausted young boy had gone to sleep in his arms.

The tunnel wound down deeper and deeper. Mike wondered how much further down they could go, but even before they had reached the bottom he began to sense what was to come. It started with a dull rumble at the base of his skull, a noise that was not noise, that seemed only to exist inside his head. As they moved on it became more intense, grinding upwards until he felt it would send him mad. There were other sensations, odd smells, strange flashes of light, and a prickling on his skin like he was standing in the centre of a dust storm. Oddly, he felt he was no longer a resident in his own body, that he was floating above it, watching but still aware. His mind occasionally drifted back to Hannah and he knew, somehow, that she was close to giving birth. He could sense her pain and her belief that she was producing something unnatural, a monster.

Finally, they reached the lowest point.

It was the darkness, the thing that was beyond and behind the Tunnellers, and it was calling to him.

Before him was a large, circular cavern with tunnel entrances randomly placed around the walls. A tiny ledge ran around the edge, but beyond that, only four paces in front of Mike, was a precipitous drop more than fifty feet across, a dark, yawning hole which seemed to go down forever. The darkness within it was churning, swirling around and around in a whirlpool with brief explosions of light appearing like distant fireworks within its depths. The stench that rose from

237

it was so overpoweringly nauseous that Mike clapped a hand to his mouth to prevent him choking.

The Black Well.

He knew, instinctively, that this was the cause of it all, the deep pit of malice that had been reactivated by the prayers and fears of the miners. It was alive now, he knew that: alive and sentient, bubbling with corruption from some nether region that wanted to rise up and flood out across the land. It provided life for the Tunnellers. It provided their motivation. Their hatred.

Mike felt faint. He could hear voices all around him, tiny, wheedling voices telling him to abandon everything, to leap blindly into the abyss and float away on the darkness. He knew Richmond could hear them too. Dropping to his knees, he peered into the darkness and was suddenly gifted with a blazing insight; whatever it was, it was communicating with him. He knew it was as old as the earth, a pure essence of darkness, of negativity, of evil, that would corrupt everything it came into contact with. He knew it was like a thick spider's web that held the spirits of those who died nearby, moulding them, polluting them with its touch. He knew that it hated with a purity that was terrifying. And more, much more, he knew that it wanted to get out. That it wanted to spread out across the land in a black wave, drowning everything in its path. Destroying it all.

There were souls within it; he could see them like bright butterflies of light, and he could see faces too, screaming in agony. For one moment he saw Packard's face rise to the surface, its mouth open in a howl of dread, before it slipped back into the depths.

With a tremendous effort, Mike broke the trance, feeling the probing tendrils of the well retract from his mind. It wanted him too, but he would not give in yet.

"Terry," he said hoarsely, "if we creep around the ledge we can get into one of those other tunnels. They must lead upwards."

For the first time in a long while, Richmond seemed to hear him clearly. "I'm not going," he replied.

"You must. What else are you going to do?"

"I'm going to stay here."

"Terry," Mike pleaded, "you'll die if you stay here."

Richmond's reply was in his eyes. There was horror there, a crushing belief that his own world did not really exist as he had thought, that there were more terrible, frightening things than he'd ever imagined. His sanity was slipping away like the water that was streaming from the roof of the tunnel. "I'm not going," he said with finality, slumping on to the floor.

Mike tried to grab him and pull him to his feet, but Richmond resisted. "I can't leave you here, Terry. I can't." Richmond ignored him, staring into the well as if he were hypnotised. Mike looked from him to Jack and then back again before saying quietly, "I'm sorry, Terry, I've got to get my son out of here. I've got to get to my wife."

Richmond looked up, suddenly lucid, and nodded. "Take him," he croaked. "I can't go on."

Mike could wait no longer. He placed his hand firmly on Richmond's shoulder in parting and then he set off cautiously around the ledge, not daring to look into the chasm, ignoring its insistent pleas. He knew they had lost, that when the Tunnellers got to the surface it would all be over. The power of the Black Well was too great. His only hope was to be at Hannah's side when it happened, reunited as a family. At the tunnel entrance, he allowed himself one final glance at Richmond's broken, dejected body, then he stepped into the darkness on his journey back to the surface.

Hannah screamed and cried. The pain! The terrible, crippling pain. She heaved at the weight above her and it shifted slightly. Whatever happened, whatever the agony, she would not give up. She wanted to see Mike again. She wanted to hold Jack. Her panic had subsided, to be replaced by a deep strength of spirit that gave her the hope to fight on. She knew that if she could move that crushingly heavy rock she would be free to be with her family again.

The doctor was afraid and his concern showed in his eyes. "It's coming," he whispered. "Any moment now." Hannah's stomach was twisting and shaking. Claw marks appeared in frenzied strokes on her skin, the red lines moving slowly down towards her groin.

239

Richmond stared into the swirling darkness for almost an hour. His mind wandered in and out of reality and only towards the end of his time did he gain some comprehension of what had happened. The Tunnellers were real. The evil was real – and he had lost everything. The Black Well called to him, but he ignored it; he had other things on his mind. He was drifting in the gloom of the cavern, looking back over his life, remembering his childhood, his parents, remembering his wife. Their wedding day came to him as clear as if it had been yesterday. She had looked so beautiful in her dress. He had wanted to cry when he turned around and saw her at the end of the aisle. He remembered the kiss, soft yet passionate, romantic yet sexy. He wished she was with him then. And there was more; as a boy on his bicycle, riding through the lanes to his grandmother's house on a hot, sticky summer day. He could smell the fields, the lush scent of nature. Inside he felt warm and content; his world had been happy.

Through the golden haze of his mind, he was disturbed to hear a voice. He could not tell if it was in a dream, a dim echo of some long-forgotten time deep in his head, or if there was someone nearby, just out of sight. He could hear the words ringing as clear as a bell.

"It's time."

"Time for what?" he asked weakly. His head rocked gently from side to side.

The voice came back, insistent, but weaker, fading slightly with each word. "You have the power now. The elements. Use the elements to end it all."

The elements? Richmond thought as he drifted along. A name flashed into his head and disappeared just as quickly. *Charlie*. He felt strangely sad. What were the elements? In the darkness, lights twinkled like cold stars. A drop of water fell from the roof and splashed on the back of his hand.

Water. His fingers rubbed on the rock beneath him. Earth. His breath went in, and then out again. Air.

And fire.

His hand slipped absent-mindedly into his pocket and closed around his lighter. It was there. Comforting. So comforting. He fumbled with it briefly, then drew it out, thinking of his last summer holiday, the floating sensation

240

that he loved when he lay back on the beach with his eyes closed. And the sun, beating down. Like fire.

It would not work, he thought. All the water, all the water. He flicked it once.

Mike would never guess what happened, would never know of the power of the foul, underground gases rising from the pit. But he felt the blast as he emerged, crying gently with relief, into the light. The ground shook violently, flinging the two of them face down into the mud of a field near the house. Behind them, a pillar of fire that radiated no heat rose up to touch the clouds, blazing with an unnatural light, and it was followed by a howling gale that carried with it bright flashes of light. Mike thought he heard voices one final time, jubilant, joyous, and then there was silence. High over the mine, a thick, sulphurous cloud of smoke and dust rose to blacken the storm-tossed sky.

As he lifted up his mud-streaked face into the rain, he laughed out loud; all the pressures and anxieties, all the fears of recent times rushed out of him, leaving him drained and weak. Jack was at his elbow, crying at the shock of crashing onto the wet grass and dirt. Mike put his arm round him and hugged him, limping through the mild drizzle across the sodden fields to the house.

When he ran into the bedroom, the baby was there, lying peacefully in its mother's arms. Fear gripped him once more and he searched long and hard for some sign in the child's face of the taint of the Black Well, but there was nothing – not even a passing flicker of darkness. It was a healthy, beautiful girl.

The look of relief on the nurse's face was even stronger than Mike's. "It's amazing," the doctor said, beaming. "I was so worried. I didn't know what was . . ." He paused and then continued. "There was that dreadful explosion and your wife cried out and then her eyes opened and she was awake. Right at the end – just before the baby emerged – she was fine. We expected the worst and it ended up right as rain." He looked out of the window at the grey skies and laughed.

Mike kissed Hannah and felt the joy only known by those who had been to the edge and returned safely. He nuzzled up

241

close to her and said, quietly, "It's over." Strangely, he knew that it was. He had no idea what had happened after he had scrambled up the long winding tunnels, but he knew, as sure as he knew that a new day would dawn tomorrow, that the darkness would never reach the surface. He could feel it had gone. It was as if a weight of rock had been lifted from his shoulders.

Hannah looked at him, not really understanding the extent of the horror that had surrounded them, and smiled.

"I had this dream that I was digging my way out of a deep hole," she said weakly.

Mike squeezed her hand. "I know how you feel."

Through the window, he could see the heavy cloud of dust and smoke dispersing in the wind. The final tremors of the explosion rippled in the ground beneath them and faded away.

Chapter Twenty-Nine

In the days and weeks that followed, a veneer of normality returned to Colthorpe. Pints of beer were consumed in the Colthorpe Arms, farmers tilled their ragged fields, tongues wagged and gossips gossiped. To the superficial eye, all was as it had been.

Beneath the surface of the residents' lives, in that world which no one could see and none would discuss, the scars were still raw. What had happened touched everyone, altered their existence irrevocably, although none could say whether for better or worse. No one realized how close they had come to a cataclysmic collision with the secret world beneath their feet.

The explosion had devastated the mine's tunnels, saving British Coal a protracted industrial dispute and the men a soul-destroying, futile fight. Those that had been picketing outside the main gate that day would never forget what they saw; a fireball as big as a double-decker bus surging up the main shaft and blowing the winching machinery one hundred feet into the air. The violent earth tremors were felt throughout the Midlands and had been measured on sensitive seismic equipment at universities around the country. No one knew what had happened. Experts talked, and there were articles written in the national papers and learned journals, but eventually it was forgotten, filed away as an interesting but inexplicable piece of trivia.

British Coal paid off all the mine's employees handsomely. Many of them were sated by their bloated bank balances, investing the windfall wisely to keep them content into their old age. Most of the younger ones moved out of the area, to Birmingham, Leicester or Nottingham, in search of jobs. Only a few mourned the death of their heritage and the grim sentence that had been placed on Colthorpe itself; a slow but progressive illness that would see the village dwindle and die without the life blood of local work.

Other interesting things which happened at the time included an anonymous note sent to the wife of a missing local newspaper reporter, Terry Richmond. It said he had died a hero, trapped underground during the blast while investigating the biggest story of his career. The police were called in to check out the veracity of the statement, but they never discovered whether it was truth or fraud, or, indeed, who had sent it.

The strange plague of dreams which had affected Colthorpe ended suddenly and it disappeared as a conversation point in the Colthorpe Arms shortly afterwards.

On the day after the explosion, Mike Leary wrapped himself in his scarf and thickest coat and walked from his bungalow to Tom Bulmer's house on the outskirts of the village. There were a few patches of blue amongst the grey clouds and it had stopped raining, although it was cold with a surprising flurry of snow in the air. In front of Bulmer's blazing fire, however, Mike felt secure and happy and he was surprised how quickly he relaxed, the first time he had felt at ease in days. Bulmer presented him with a glass of port before taking his chair next to the hearth.

"Off the hard stuff, then?" Mike asked, raising his glass.

"Don't drink that until the sun goes down, lad." Bulmer grinned broadly. "Bit of port won't hurt, though. On a day like this it'll warm the blood."

After Mike had sipped his drink, he looked Bulmer in the eye and said, "So . . . things sorted themselves out."

Bulmer nodded.

"I don't know what caused the explosion, but it seems to have done the job. I doubt there'll be any more trouble. I was down there, you know . . . just before."

"I thought you might have been. Bloody interfering Southerner." Mike was warmed to hear Bulmer's faint humour.

244

"At least we got off lightly. It could have been worse, I suppose. Much worse?"

"Some of us had a closer call than you think."

There was a strange gleam in Bulmer's eye that Mike could not fathom. "What do you mean?"

"Nothing. Let's just say I put the past behind me."

Bulmer refused to be drawn. He made a few more enigmatic comments about old times, but then the conversation moved on to other, more cheerful subjects. When it was time to leave, Mike felt strangely sad. There was an unusual bond between him and the bluff pit boss, but Mike knew it was unlikely they would ever meet again. When they eventually said goodbye on the doorstep, Bulmer shook his hand forcefully and wished him well.

Mike suffered from nightmares about his experiences underground for many days afterwards. He would often wake from a dream of tunnels and a darkness that descended to hell, feeling cold and lonely. At those times not even an embrace from Hannah would reconcile him. He hoped the dreams would fade soon, but he guessed he would carry them with him for the rest of his life.

One week later, after Mike and Hannah had packed their things ready for their return to London, they decided to go for one last walk in the countryside. Jack accompanied them, but their new daughter, whom they had decided to call Therese, stayed at the house with a babysitter from the village who had been looking after her while they made their final preparations.

The afternoon sun was warm on their faces but their breath quickly turned to vapour as Mike led them up to an abandoned railway line which had been converted into a nature walk. From the line's raised embankment they had a panoramic view of Colthorpe and the surrounding area: a tranquil land of greens and browns and golds and reds. Hannah squeezed Mike's hand tightly as they walked, while Jack ran off to explore.

"Hannah, there's something I want to ask you," he said. They stood side-by-side watching a farmer at work in one of the fields.

"Well, you can't be asking me to marry you. You've already done that."

245

"Would you mind if I quit my job?"

Mind? Hannah thought. *I'll throw a party for everyone we know.* "Of course not! I think it's the right decision."

"It just seems that the time is right." He squinted, scanning the distant, purple horizon. "Things have been put into a better perspective over the last few weeks. I don't need it any more. It was screwing me up . . . eating away inside me. The moment I decided I was going to put it behind me – get it out of my system – I felt an incredible sense of relief."

Hannah hugged him. "I'm glad, Mike. It was coming between us."

He put his arm tightly around her shoulders, at once serious and gentle. "Things are going to be tough for us, Hannah. Without my income . . . now we've got two kids to look after. And if Therese has got the same appetite as Jack . . ."

"Don't worry. You'll find a new job. Just take your time. Look for something you really want to do."

A middle-aged couple walked by while Mike and Hannah were hugging. The man, tall and tanned with stately, grey hair, threw a stick for two spaniels which romped and rolled wildly around his feet. His wife, her black hair framing a beaming, happy face, nodded in greeting.

"Enjoying the fresh air?" the woman asked.

"It's very refreshing," Mike replied.

She nodded at her husband. "Gordon always says you can really breathe out here."

Gordon dug his hands deep into the pockets of his outdoor jacket. "There's nothing like fresh air. Bit chilly though, dear."

"Oh, oh, that means, 'Hurry along, Mavis, I want a cup of coffee'!" She smiled. "Nice to meet you."

"They looked like they were at ease with life," Mike said after they had passed.

"You never know," Hannah replied, "it might be catching."

Jack ran up to them breathlessly, pulling at Mike's trousers for attention. His eyes sparkled with joy and life. Mike had dreaded looking into them for a while, fearing that he would see a vertiginous blackness that went straight down to Jack's soul. He had wondered, in the long dark of the night, if there would be a worm burrowing into his heart, the legacy of dead hands holding his son's fingers, dead hands on his son's head. He thought of all the things Jack had seen, all the words that had been whispered, and he hoped and prayed that they would soon be forgotten. But Jack seemed unmarked by his experience, with all the resilience of youth and of a mind not yet rigid through adult thinking. He had truly escaped.

They walked back to the bungalow hand-in-hand. As they entered, Mike took one last lingering look at the dark buildings of the colliery starkly outlined against the pale autumn sky and wondered, fleetingly, if there were still things walking what remained of the long, lonely tunnels beneath his feet. Would it all come back, rising to the surface, up from the earth's core?

Would it?

If there were worms in the earth and worms in the heart, it did not really matter. As long as they weren't fed until they were bloated, ready to crawl up. And out.

Into the light.

You have been reading a novel published by Piatkus Books. We hope you have enjoyed it and that you would like to read more of our titles. Please ask for them in your local library or bookshop.

If you would like to be put on our mailing list to receive details of new publications, please send a large stamped addressed envelope (UK only) to:

Piatkus Books: 5 Windmill Street
London W1P 1HF

PIATKUS